ALL THE GOOD THINGS

Clare Fisher

ALL THE GOOD THINGS

Europa
editions

Europa Editions
214 West 29th Street
New York, N.Y. 10001
www.europaeditions.com
info@europaeditions.com

Library of Congress Cataloging in Publication Data is available
ISBN 978-1-60945-517-0

Fisher, Clare
All the Good Things

Book design by Emanuele Ragnisco
www.mekkanografici.com

Cover photo: Skitterphoto/Pixabay

Prepress by Grafica Punto Print – Rome

Printed in the USA

ALL THE GOOD THINGS

1.

SMELLING A BABY'S HEAD RIGHT INTO YOUR HEART

O f all the good things that have ever been in me, the first
and the best is you. Every single part of you, from your
strokeable earlobes to the hope curled up in your toes.
Remember that. Remember it when the dickheads say you're a
bad or a so-what thing. Remember it when you're convinced the
good things are jammed behind other people's smiles.
Remember it the hardest when you feel like nothing at all.

Writing a list of good things may seem pretty retarded—at
least, that's what I said when Erika brought it up. I didn't
know Erika before they put me in here but now we have to put
up with each other for a whole hour every week. She has these
geekster glasses that make her eyes look bigger than any person's should; when I said the word "retarded," they grew so
big, it was like she knew everything about me and about the
universe and about whatever lay outside the universe, and that
made me feel small, and so I jumped up, gripped the back of
my chair and said, "I'm *not* a retard."

I waited for Erika to shout. Or press whatever button she
had to press to bring the screws running. Instead, she sighed
like I was some telly programme she wished would change into
a better one. I let go of the chair and sat back down.

"Now," she said, laying her hands flat on the table between
us. They were red raw and peeling, like she'd forgotten to wear
washing-up gloves. "Why don't you explain why you used that
word—*retard*."

"I don't know, do I? I open my mouth, the words come out. End of story."

"That's one way of looking at it," said Erika. "But there are others. For example, I, like you, know what it is to be a mum. I've got three kids." The way her face moved, even a blind man could've clocked how much she loved them. Would a blind man have clocked how much I loved you? Would anyone?

"One's mad on football," she went on, "the other on Harry Potter, the third on spiders and spaceships. One hates loud noises, the other hates to eat anything round. It just so happens that one of them is autistic. But they're all as real as each other." She paused and wiggled her eyebrows—eyebrows which, FYI, hadn't been threaded or even plucked. "Do you see?"

The grown-up reply would have been *sorry*. And maybe: *Thanks for talking to me like I'm just another mum. Like we're just two human beings.* But even though I'm twenty-one and have done 100% ™ certified grown-up things like wash up my own plates in my own flat, rubber gloves and all; even though I've had a job and a boyfriend and a baby, grown-up isn't always the way I am on the inside. I slumped down in my chair and mumbled, "Whatever."

"There are lots of ways to look at every person, and words like 'retard' are dangerous because they make us believe there's just one story."

I opened my mouth but no words fell out, not even an almost-word, like "Oh."

"I bet," she said, patting her grey-streaked boy-cut hair, "you know a thing or two about those kinds of words?"

Suddenly, Erika and her glasses and the custard yellow walls disappeared. I was back in that courtroom, not knowing where to look because whether I looked at the judge and his wig or the clerk and her computer or the lawyers and their ring-binders or even the fake-wood walls, all I saw was the bad things I'd done. The things that stopped the other prisoners looking at me unless it was to give me the evils.

"Bethany?"

Erika's voice shoved this memory to the part of my mind that's a bit like the patch of carpet under the sofa: it's close, dirty and dark, and although you mean to sort it out, you never do, because the only parts of you that ever see it are your ankles.

Back in the room, Erika was staring straight at me but for the first time in my life, I didn't mind; there was no way of knowing what a person was or wasn't thinking about me, and this was an O.K. or maybe even a good thing.

I opened my mouth and out came these words I'd no idea were there: "One of my foster mums, the fourth or like maybe the fifth, she was obsessed with cats."

"Oh?"

"She *loved* them. If I said I felt ill, she'd tell me to stop making a fuss. But if the cat sneezed, she'd shove it into this dark plastic box and rush it to the vet. Before she put it in the box, it'd be O.K.—a bit dribbly or moody or whatever but basically O.K. As soon as it clocked it was trapped, it went *mental*. Scratching and howling and yowling and shitting itself. Eventually, it'd go all saggy and depressed. Anyway, that's how they make you feel—those kinds of words."

Erika smiled like I'd done some better-than-good thing. I waited for her to tell me what it was; instead, she handed me this exercise book. "So you'll have a go at the list?"

"Haven't seen a book like this since school. I'll warn you now: I'm gonna get shit grades."

"I won't give you a grade," she laughed. "I won't even look at what you've written, not unless you want me to."

I made my best *whatever* face, but my hands were all over it, stroking its rough recycled pages, because it was a long time since anyone had given anything to them or me, and the ending of this time felt good. "What's the point then?"

"The point is for *you*."

"Write down the good things about my life?"

"Exactly."

"But what if . . . I can't think of any?"

If you've never seen a sad smile, you should've seen hers just then. "You will."

"Oh well. At least it's something to do."

I tucked it into my waistband and stalked out. It jiggled against my pants, and the only way to stop it falling down the left leg was to walk weird, but I didn't care, because every time I bent my leg I was reminded of you.

I was alone again at dinner that night but I didn't care. For the first time since arriving here three weeks ago, the shaking in my hands stopped. I even managed to stuff in a few mouthfuls of the brown stuff that was meant to be chicken curry. The noise of other girls talking and eating and laughing was just as loud, but it didn't poke holes in my heart. When I was locked back in my cell, I didn't mind the silence, or the blank space where the handle should be on the door. I was remembering your eyelashes; how they were thick and black from the moment you were born, *a heartbreaker*, said the nurses. Or the way you'd murmur in your sleep, as if you were already dreaming the best dreams. If it was a really good one, you'd blow a spit bubble. The way you'd curl and stretch your toes when I changed your nappy. Best of all was the ridiculously delicious smell of your head; pressing my nose to your fluffy hair and breathing in deep was better than any drink or drug or new phone or any other thing people buy to feel good; I'd breathe it right down into my heart. Making you into a shape on the paper would be the next best thing to the thing I'd already done, i.e. making the actual you.

Who knows? Maybe, despite everything, this list will find

its way to the *you* that I imagine growing up with some other mum, somewhere far from here. I hope this list, whatever it turns out to be, will show you that whatever bad or non stories you might hear about me and about the way your life began, they aren't the only ones. You might think I'm retarded for hoping such a thing in the light, or rather the *dark*, of everything that's happened. But you know what? I think it's good. I think it's a good thing to find hope where any other person would agree there was none.

2.
RUNNING UNTIL YOUR BODY IS A GOOD PLACE TO BE

The first time I got locked in my cell, I was bricking it. I ran my hands up and down the door until they were red raw; even then, they wouldn't quite accept there was no handle. I was bricking it when I first walked down the corridors, painted the same colour as the inside of someone's mouth—some skanky person who didn't brush their teeth or eat any vegetables. Obviously I was bricking it when I saw a woman get dragged out of her cell, blood all over her jeans and her tracksuit from where she'd cut up. When I got my first negative for leaving an IT lesson without a toilet pass, I didn't just brick it; I stared at the laminated poster of three women laughing and holding hands—each woman was a different race but they all wore polo-necks and had obviously never been to prison—with a speech bubble coming out of the blonde one's mouth saying, "Let's Be Friends With Everyone!" and I wanted to run. Of course, I couldn't run. Couldn't scream or even stamp my foot; the only thing I could do, in the three or so seconds between me opening the door and the teacher and the other girls seeing my face, was let a tear drop out of my eye. But what made me brick it harder than any of these things was finishing the sentence before this one. What if you weren't just the first good thing about me but the last?

When I sat down in the Progress Room, Erika smiled. "Hello, Beth, how have you got on this week? I've been thinking of you and your list." She smiled with her mouth and her cheeks and her eyes—as if me being in the room was better than me not being in it. I smiled back.

"Not bad," I said. "Actually, I just thought of the second good thing. It's running."

Her eyebrows jumped all over her forehead. "Running?"

My legs started jiggling as soon as they heard the word. I had to remind them—again—that there was nowhere to run, not in here. "It's the only time I feel good. When I went running after I did the bad thing, the one that got me locked in here—even then I felt good."

"Go on." Somehow, as if she'd pulled a plug inside of her, the expression drained out of her face. "Take me back." With her there but not there, the past felt like a good place to go.

There are days when I wake with a spring in my chest; maybe I'll run round the park with you in the pushchair; maybe I'll sing to you all up and down every aisle in Tesco; then I see the toilet bowl and the sink in kicking distance from my bed. The bars on the window. Then I remember. I remember the bad thing. It's as if someone is whacking me round the head with a sockful of gravel; it pushes me back down to the bed. Take a few deep breaths. Then I force myself back up because you have to get up when they tell you to get up, in here.

The days after I did it were the springiest of days; all I knew was I needed to get away. As fast and as far as possible, as soon as possible. What better place to go than a running festival?

Running for Fun was its name. I'd first noticed the poster months back, when you were this lovely warm weight inside of me, and I was waiting for my appointment at the Health Centre. Every human on the poster wore a happy red face: they were Running for Fun and Raising Money for Children with Cancer at the same time! They were also rich enough to afford £100, which apparently was a "fantastic deal" for two days of "inspiring talks from world fitness experts" plus socials, buffets and organized races. Worst of all, it was in Leicester. Getting to Tesco was a trek with a nearly-ready-for-the-world baby in my belly, never mind some weird town far from London. But the poster popped up everywhere—in the library, at the doctor's, at bus stops—and each time I saw it I felt angrier and angrier that I couldn't go.

In the days after I did the bad thing, I wasn't me. I wasn't anyone. I could do anything. I could go to Leicester. I could take out yet another payday loan and spend it on a Toni & Guy haircut. On new Nike leggings that stretched the whole Milky Way around my thighs. Go to a specialist running shop where they shove you on to a treadmill that works out what's weird about your feet.

"Every person," said the girl in the shop, her ponytail swinging though the rest of her was still, "puts their weight on a different part of their foot. You, you put too much weight at the front. I'm surprised you don't trip up! I'd recommend the Asol Gel Elite. They're actually marked down to £120."

Before this, I'd run in my last foster mum's old Reeboks, Primark leggings and my Somerset High School cross country team T-shirt, which was still two sizes too big. I was only in that club for a year before they chucked me out, but I was the best, the coach said so, *talent*, was the word she used, *the others can run, but you need to, I can tell, you've got something special.*

The coach looked like an old mum or a young grandma. She never ran; she just shouted and blew her whistle a lot. I made the rest of the team laugh by doing impressions of her waddling walk and the desperate way she flapped her arms when she thought we weren't running fast enough. Most of the time, I made sure to do it when she wasn't looking, but sometimes I slipped. Like that time in the changing room when I stuffed my T-shirt to make it look like I had a belly, the others were cracking up when, just as I was certain this was the start of them liking me, they stopped. Behind me I heard a sad screech, like the ones cats make when you step on their tails. It was the coach. She'd seen me. I couldn't tell if she was going to cry or tell me off. Instead, she shook her head, and said, *Honestly Bethany, I thought you were better than that.* Then she walked out of the changing room and the other girls turned away from me, and my stomach jangled about like I'd swallowed a fistful of forks. I wanted to run out to the coach and tell her I was sorry and that my favourite way of falling asleep was to replay all the good things she'd said to me, but I'd never said anything like that to anyone, and I didn't know how to start.

The coach was right though: I *was* good. Even though the other girls had longer legs and better trainers than me, even though I'd never done cross country because I'd been in London and there was no country to run across, only red tarmac tracks to run round and round, I ran faster than they did. I didn't get grossed out by puddles or cowpats. I'd run down the steepest slopes, leaping from stone to stone, sloshing through bogs. Sometimes, I'd be so far ahead, I'd run to the top of the hill and stop. Looking down on the Levels, which are these low, flat fields around Yeovil, often they were so misty, they looked like they were under water, I'd feel like I'd broken into a world that was new and special and 100% mine.

Ah, I'd forgotten how good it was, in the cross country club!

The problem with being an adult is there aren't clubs. If there are, no one invites you. Or you've got to pay a ton of money or do a certain job or go to a certain place at a certain time to join in. I'd run all over London but only when I was by myself, and usually when I was supposed to be doing something else, like getting a good night's sleep or sorting out a payment plan or going to the Job Centre. Then you got too big for me to run and then you were out of me and then I did what I did and so really, the Running for Fun conference was my last chance to be part of a good thing.

The Running for Fun hotel was right opposite Leicester train station. I expected to see Lycra-legged people all over reception, but there was no one. Had I come to the wrong place? My heart shuddered and I was about to bolt, when the woman on reception smiled as if she'd been waiting for me all morning.

"Welcome!" Her name badge said Amanda Here 2 Help. She smiled at the stars on my legs. "I'm guessing you're a Runner for Funner?"

A Runner for Funner! I nodded.

"I thought so. Name please?"

"Katherine Chapworth," I said, because Katherine Chapworth sounded like a person who ate five fruit and veg a day and turned her light out at ten o'clock.

"Hmmm . . . "

There was a massive bowl of mints on the counter and while Amanda Here 2 Help frowned at her screen, I stuffed a handful into my bag.

"You don't appear to be on the list, but we do have some last-minute cancellations which will mean you'll have to pay the on-the-day fee if you're O.K. with that?"

The loan I'd taken out to pay off the other loans (which I'd taken to pay off the fines for going over my overdraft) would not be O.K. with that. But that was for later. And later was never going to turn into now, not if I kept running. What mattered was that I had notes to slide across the counter right now.

"That's brilliant," she said. "You can pay the rest when you leave. Here's the key and your welcome pack." She handed me a red folder covered with people running wearing silly red wigs. Some parts of some of their faces were cut out by big white letters saying *Running for Fun: Welcome to Our World.*

"Any issues with your room, or if you need anything else, anything at all, give me a call."

"Thanks, Amanda," I said, and I even meant it; no one had said so many nice things to me for a long time.

As I walked towards the lift, I saw two short, solid legs and a head of grey curls. It was the coach! It was definitely the coach. It was another sign that I was in the right place, that if I just—

Except it wasn't the coach.

It was another woman.

She was wearing a bright red "Running for Fun" T-shirt, the "Fun" stretched by her boobs, which were so bouncy that despite telling myself not to stare at them because that's exactly what pervy guys do, I could only stare at them. When I pulled my eyes away, I saw she was smiling at me. We stood side by side in the lift and then we got out at the same floor and walked in the same direction down the hall. I didn't turn around to look at her when I reached my room, but I could still feel her smile; it was a good feeling, and I breathed it as deep as I could.

My hotel room was clean and white. The sheets were tucked into the mattress, the ironing board folded up against the wall, so there was no way of knowing who'd stayed here before. Lying on the bed, it was easy to fool myself I was back at the hospital, about to get my twenty-week scan, my heart yammering right up into my mouth as I waited for them to tell me you were a girl. Maybe your dad was about to walk in with a hot takeaway pizza. Or a hot water bottle. Maybe I'd finally found the button that said *reset*.

This maybe-I'm-not-so-bad feeling was shattered, a few moments later, by a knock at the door.

The knock I'd been waiting for my whole life, even before I did the bad thing.

But it wasn't the police; it was Mrs. Bounce.

"I hope I didn't disturb you? I couldn't help noticing you in the lift, so lovely and fresh and in those starry leggings, and I thought we might squeeze in a run before the reception what do you think don't you think it will be *fun*? Fun, you know like . . . " She pointed to the cracked-up word across her boobs, then laughed like this was the world's No. 1 joke.

I could tell she was a good and normal person but I could also tell that if we spent much time together, she'd piss me off, and then she'd know that underneath my leggings I wasn't lovely or fresh or any other good thing. I didn't belong in this club. But better to be in the club for a while, than not at all, so I said yes, what a great idea.

"Brilliant!"

When we were outside the hotel, she bounced on the spot while waving her phone in my face. "I've already mapped a route. Ten miles—up the canal, around a meadow and back. Is that O.K. with you? Which running app do you use?"

"I don't use an app. I just run."

For a second, she stopped bouncing. "That's incredible."

Have you ever been to Leicester? Perhaps you have. I imagine you with your new mum and your new dad living somewhere like this. Somewhere which is halfway between crowded and empty, between posh and skanky. A nice, normal place. A place where people looked at me and saw a lovely, fresh runner, not a woman who'd done a 100% ™ certified bad thing. Mrs. Bounce kept smiling back at me, chatting and pointing out a sign to the remains of Richard III—"They found him under a car park, can you believe that!"

"Whoa!" As we reached a big road, Mrs. Bounce stuck her arm out just in time to stop a Greggs lorry slicing off my nose.

"Didn't you see it?"

I rubbed my eyes. "Nope."

"Need to catch up on some sleep?"

"Umm . . . " It was then, watching her bounce while we

waited for the Green Man, that I realized the time between doing the bad thing and buying new clothes and a new haircut in that Milton Keynes shopping centre was a blank.

"I can't remember when I last slept through the night."

"Poor thing. Got a lot on your mind?"

Finally, the Green Man beeped and we ran across the road and down some olden days wonky steps to the canal towpath, and I don't know if it was because the sky was scattered in the water or because water always calms me, or because my ears were still ringing with the Green Man's beep, fooling me that now was a safe time, but I told her about you.

"I had a baby a few months ago. A little girl. She doesn't really *get* sleep."

"A few *months*?" Mrs. Bounce stared at my belly, whose you-shaped bump had long since been gobbled up by the rest of me, because, for reasons I won't go into just now, I'd had a bit of a bust-up with food.

"You must have one of those amazing metabolisms. Lucky for some. Or did you start running soon after the birth?"

If she'd asked me this when we were standing still, I'd have freaked out. But when you run, you reach a point where even your toes know that your body is a good place to be. The real *you* rises up, and your thoughts are as blurred as the ducks on the canal and the half-built luxury apartments and the windowless old factories, or whatever else it is you're running past; you're free.

"After the birth, I just wanted to lie in bed and hold her, you know? Sniff her head for hours on end."

"I know! That smell! Gemma, she's my first, they got her out by caesarean and I could barely get out of bed for *weeks*. She wouldn't forgive me for bringing her into this world—what a cryer!"

"Mine's a cryer, too."

"Don't worry—she'll grow up to be a right character. Just

like Gemma! You know, it was my mum that got me through it; she set up camp in the spare room. I was dead set against it, but in retrospect, I'm grateful; it's a stressful, scary time, having a new baby, especially the first baby, and between you and me, I doubt our marriage would have continued without her . . . "

In what her running app told us was 10.23 miles, I learned that she had two girls, one husband; one mother (alive), one father (dead) and two brothers (also dead); two cats, three dogs (one alive, two dead), five rabbits (one alive, four dead) and an uncertain number of stick insects. Her youngest girl was on a mission to make the cat love the dog, and the rabbits were forever spitting carrots at each other. She wanted to run a marathon on every continent before she turned fifty. Her husband told her she was bonkers before massaging her feet every night.

All I did was smile and nod and say "no way" and "wow" and "cool" when she paused for breath. I put one foot in front of the other, and the ground disappeared, and I breathed right down to the place where I can't usually be arsed to breathe, and I tried my best not to breathe out all the things she was telling me. I guess I must've started to believe her life was somehow mine, because when we were back at the start of the canal, stretching out, and she said, "So, where's your little one now? Bonding with her daddy?" I snapped.

Sweat was sticking my clothes to my skin, making me shiver. Mrs. Bounce's words rolled round and round my head. All the good things and the so-what things and even the bad things drained out of me. I imagined pushing her in the canal, her splashing around like some supersize fluorescent fish. That couldn't happen.

"I've got to go. Sorry."

I set off but *empty* spread right through me until I couldn't see and I couldn't breathe; after a few steps, I had to stop and bend over.

"Are you O.K.? Dizzy? Sit down." Gently, she pushed me on to the ground. I plunged my head between my legs and, pebble by pebble by kicked-in cider can, the towpath returned.

"Sorry. I blacked out."

"No need to apologize." She frowned. Then her face twisted with worry, which reminded me of Chantelle, who was the last person to look worried about me, and also one of the last ones I wanted to think about just then. "When was the last time you ate something?"

"Ummm . . . " But I was too empty to make anything else up. "I don't remember."

"Oh dear." She pulled a protein flapjack out of her bum bag and pressed it into my hands. "Eat this. I was sceptical of them at first, but the company kept sending me free samples, and I have to say, they got me hooked."

The flapjack was squished. It was big and heavy and it scared me.

"Go on."

I nibbled it. It tasted a bit like blood. Like metal.

The voice, the bad one, that comes and goes whenever it wants, it whispered: *You don't need this. You don't need food. All you need is to keep moving.*

But Mrs. Bounce and her smile and the worry-wrinkles in her forehead, they helped me to ignore it. I nibbled some more. And some more. A bit more. Until it was gone.

"Better?"

"Yes." But I didn't feel better, not exactly. I felt complicated. *Complicated* was an especially scary thing to feel right then.

"I've got a spare ticket for the VIP area," she said, when we were almost back at the hotel. "My husband was meant to join me but things between us haven't exactly been easy, and anyway, I've really enjoyed getting to know you. Would you like to join me?"

I nodded.

"Wonderful! I'll knock for you after we're rested and show-ered up."

I love showers; I love how the water scalds you all over like a too-tight hug. But Mrs. Bounce's flapjack was filling me up, and not just with energy—with memories from down under the sofa. Getting to know her would only make both of our lives worse. I picked up my bag and, before there was any chance of another knock at the door, I walked out of the hotel without knowing where I was going or why. As soon as recep-tion was out of sight, I broke into a run.

3.

When two people love each other enough to share silence

Writing about the good things is hard, because sooner or later you get to the edge, and if you're not careful, you fall off.

"Then look over," said Erika. "Hold on tight, so you don't fall. Take a good look. Write down what you see."

"What's the point?"

She said the point was to "integrate" the good with everything else. "Not being rude," I said, "but WTF does that mean?"

She pushed her glasses up her nose and said, "It means absorbing one's flaws into the hole."

I asked which kind of hole, the kind with the *w* or the kind without, because if she was talking about the *w* kind, like *whole*-meal bread from Waitrose, she was having a laugh because that kind of whole was never going to have a thing to do with me. As for the other kind . . . "Why is this making you angry?" she said.

"I'm not angry," I said. "I'm just . . . " But tears clogged my throat and I couldn't say it. I couldn't say that as well as being angry, I was sad.

Erika just sat there, like a stone, which only pushed me further over the edge of good, because what I'm used to are normal human beings, i.e. ones who shout back or—if they had been sitting where Erika was sitting—throw their titchy plastic cup of water over my head. I don't know why she didn't do any of these things, but she didn't, and eventually, I opened my mouth and there were no words, no scream, no bad things left.

Still, she said nothing.

I said nothing.

She scratched one dry hand with the other. I recrossed my legs. She licked her lips. We shared some more nothing.

I don't know how long it lasted, this silence, but I'll tell you now: it was good. It was so good that when I stood up to leave, I finally asked the one thing I'd been wanting to ask since we met: "Erika, why don't you just get some rubber gloves?"

She laughed. "Excuse me?"

"Your hands. They're kind of mank." She said nothing, so I added: "No offence."

"You know, my husband says the same thing. But I never get around to it. There's always something else to do."

"That's bad, Erika. One of the first things I did when I moved into my own place was buy some washing-up gloves."

She smiled at me with one eye, glanced at her watch with the other. I wanted her to tell me more about her husband. Her sink. Her life. Instead she said, "You'll have to tell me all about it next week."

The first person to breathe the same silence as me was Paul. Paul was Foster Dad No. 1. He was Foster Dad No. 1 in that he was the first one I had, but also the best one. He picked me up from school every single day. "You won't forget?" I'd ask him. He'd laugh and tell me he'd made a promise and he was going to keep it. Sure enough he was always at the school gates when the bell rang, a smile spreading out from under his grey mop of hair.

On our way home, he'd ask about my day, and even though he'd most probably had a call from some teacher listing my latest bad deeds, when I spun him some BS about winning a prize for my proper realistic drawing of a rabbit, or getting the highest mark in a spelling test, he'd just smile and nod and say, "Is that so?"

Then he'd point at a poster of a missing cat that wasn't there the day before, or if it was we hadn't noticed, and why was that, he wanted to know. What happened to the cat? And, he'd add, pointing to a real cat sunning its fat ginger belly on the paving stones, what was it like to be the cat who wasn't missing? And I'd say maybe the cat sunning its belly had eaten the missing cat, its belly was pretty big after all, or maybe the missing cat had just stopped loving its owners and found some better ones, e.g. ones who lived in a mansion with a swimming pool and an ice cream machine, somewhere fun and sunny, like Spain? Because why else would people leave other people? How could they?

When I said things like that, Paul's eyes got big and sad, but then he'd grab my hand and say why didn't we pop into Happy Shopper and he'd buy me a treat, anything I wanted, and I'd go into the shop, but it didn't make me happy, there were too many flavours of crisps and chocolate and sweets, and then there were other weird things like Mini Cheddars, and eventually he would say, hurry up now, just hurry up and choose, and I could see that he was getting angry, and I knew that when people got angry they didn't want to be near other people, and so I'd grab whatever was nearest, even if I didn't like it.

When we got home, Paul would do a few more hours of work and I'd sit at a mini desk at the other side of his office and, with the coloured paper and felt tips and fine liners and pencils and crayons he was forever buying me, I'd transform whatever we had or hadn't talked about on our walk home into a story. I'd try to make it like the books at school; neat smiling people and neat smiling words. Except the words always came out jumbled and the colours spilled over the edges of the things or the people they were meant to be. When I showed them to Paul, he'd say they were brilliant. Then he'd get me to sound out the words I'd tried to write down, but I never would; it was more fun to tell him what the shapes on the page meant to me, e.g. they were everything paving stones were thinking while people walked over them or the dreams of the lost cat. My ideas always made him laugh. You've got a real imagination, you! A true original. I tried to breathe his words and the smiles that went with them deep inside of me, so they'd never leave.

What I loved most was the silence; the stillness; there were things I didn't know, like where my mum was or why she'd left me, and there were things I'd never have, like real parents in the way that everyone else had real parents, but as long as I was sat there, scribbling into my silence, with Paul a few metres away, typing and hunching and hmmming into his, it wasn't a make-up-BS-stories-to-escape-from kind of a thing, it was good and it was special and it made me feel like I was, too.

So why don't you tell us why you punched that boy today?
Why did you cheat in that test?
Why did you swear at the teaching assistant?
Why Why Why are you so
bad
bad
BAD?

These are the kinds of things Susie would say when she got home. Well, some she'd say, some I'd feel, but her words and my feelings got so mixed up, I wouldn't be able to eat my dinner. When we'd fought until we couldn't fight any more, they'd send me to bed. But they never checked if I stayed there and so I'd creep out and sit at the top of the stairs and listen to them fight about the bad thing in their lives, i.e. me.

"Go easy on her," Paul said. "She's been through a lot. Give her time."

"That's not what the child psychologist said," said Susie. "She said that what Beth needs is reality, and God knows, letting her string you along in her little fantasies is only going to make her worse."

"But she's making progress."

"Progress? I don't know if weekly calls from school count as progress."

"Give her a chance. I mean, considering . . . "

"It's hardly surprising, is it?"

"What's that supposed to mean?"

"It means this isn't as easy as we thought . . . "

These conversations got louder and longer and more regular; even if I stayed in bed, their voices would rumble through the air and the ceiling and the floorboards and the carpet and the mattress, to my ears. The only way to block them out was to make my own. I did this by bouncing on the bed. Susie would tell him to tell me to stop but he'd refuse, so she'd march up to my room and in this squashed-in voice that hurt ten times more than a big, honest shout, say, "Beth, you simply can't do that. Now *please*, settle down."

At school, I got in trouble for bouncing, too. I'd bounce my leg under the table and some other kid would tell me to stop it and I wouldn't and they'd groan or say that I must have the "crazy dog disease," and so I'd kick them and before you knew it, we were fighting. I'd get out of my seat without asking and instead of walking to assembly, I'd run. When teachers asked whether I understood the rules, I got angry because I didn't know how to say that there was so much noise inside of me that sometimes I couldn't hear anything or anyone else; moving was the only way to turn it down.

Eventually, the teacher used the word "hyperactive"; that's when Paul started taking me to the park. As soon as Susie was home and defrosting chicken breasts for dinner, we'd change into shorts and T-shirts and run to the park. At first, I was annoyed, because I thought he was tricking me into an extra P.E. lesson. But running round the park wasn't P.E. It wasn't teams and rules and waiting for ages and ages in the cold. It was moving however you wanted. Moving as fast as your body needed. Moving until the noise in your head turned into a tune. Sometimes it even felt like my real mum was the one singing the tune, and knowing this didn't make me feel sad or angry or strange; it made me feel tingly and good. Paul never tried to talk to me while we were running round the park, but the way he smiled, I knew that he was inside his own tune, and he could see that I was in mine, and he was glad.

Whether they kept on arguing after we started running round the park, I don't know: as soon as my head hit the pillow, I fell asleep.

What poked a hole in the silence was my mum. There was going to be a visit. The visit would be in a Special Place. Paul and Susie would drive me to this Special Place. Paul, Susie, my mum and me would spend some time together; then just me and my mum; then Paul and Susie would drive me back to their house. It was going to happen in two weeks, next week, this week. Wasn't I excited?

Almost every day Paul would ask me this. He'd put on a Special Smile when he asked; it stretched right across his face. It must've hurt.

"Yes, I'm excited," I'd say, because these were the only words to make the fake smile go away.

"Good," he'd say. "Good. *Good.*"

I couldn't tell him I was nervous plus something else. Some strange feeling whose name was stuck deep in the silence and which I couldn't reach, not even if I ran until I had no more breath to run with. I couldn't tell him that every time I heard the word "Mum," I felt nothing. Saw nothing. It was a scary kind of nothing—the kind which, when you reached out to touch it, would tangle you up in its cobwebs. In the days before the visit, it followed me everywhere I went, even to my desk with all my colouring books and pencils. "What, no stories this week?" Paul said.

I said I was tired. I didn't know how to say that when I looked at a book, the words and the pictures felt far away—as if that mum-shaped nothing was dangling its cobwebs between me and them.

"I've got a great idea," he said. "Why don't we take some of your stories to show your mum?"

I said I didn't want to. But he said she'd love them. He laid them out all over the floor.

"See, aren't they beautiful?"

I tiptoed into a blank patch of floor between them. All around me was colour, texture, strange swirls, jagged lines, wobbling animals and scribbled words.

"They make me feel strange," I said. "But shy."

"Exactly," he said. "That's because they're beautiful. Now which do you think your mum will like?"

I didn't know the answer to this because I didn't remember anything about her. Instead I said: "I'll only show them to her, if I can bring them back."

"Oh, silly!" He half-hugged, half-tickled me. "Of course you can."

So I agreed.

The Special Place was a square red-brick building, surrounded by a car park and beds of waxy green plants which looked fake but were real. "What's so special?" I asked, as we got out of the car. But Paul and Susie were a few steps ahead of me, talking in tiny voices. Paul was holding my stories, but just before we got inside, Susie grabbed them and stuffed them into her handbag. She'd never been very interested in my stories before, and thinking of them alone, in the dark, with her tissues and her hand cream and her red leather Filofax, was a sad thought.

Inside, it was like a doctor's surgery but bigger. Everyone was waiting; their faces flickered between "worried" and "bored."

"Would you like a lollipop?" asked the receptionist, when she saw me.

The lollipops were red and shiny, exactly as lollipops should be, but I shook my head no because I couldn't imagine eating one because my throat was clogged with cobwebs.

"She'd love one, thanks," said Susie. Then she squatted down and handed me it and said, "It's O.K. to be scared, sweetheart."

Susie never called me sweetheart. She'd never told me it was O.K. to be anything other than good. I chucked the lollipop at the other bored/worried people and yelled that I wasn't scared.

The room went quiet then, in a bad way.

"Don't worry," Paul said, wiggling his eyebrows at Susie, who'd gone bright red. "Your mum will be here soon."

We sat down on some orange plastic chairs. I swung my legs back and forth but they didn't tell me to stop. They kept sharing looks. Susie kept glancing at her watch and opening her mouth but Paul pressed his finger to his lips the way teachers did to make kids shut up, and so Susie would gulp her words back down but narrow her eyes as if she was no way going to forgive him for this.

Other kids and grown-ups came and went from the seats around me. But we were still there. Still waiting.

"She's not here," I said.

Paul looked at Susie; Susie looked at the magazine rack.

"She's not coming," I said. "Don't be silly," said Paul. "Of course she's coming."

"Paul . . . " Susie shook her head. "I'll ask." She marched up to the reception counter. Her voice rose from a patter to a screech to actual words, like "unacceptable," and "forty-five minutes." And finally: "*Unbelievable!* We've known about this visit for weeks. There's really nothing you can do? No way to contact her?"

My head was all noise, the rest of me cobwebs. Swinging my legs didn't turn it down one bit. My fingers twitched and then my eyes fixed on Susie's handbag, which she'd left by her chair. The next thing I knew, I was jumping on it. Kicking it about. Hand cream, lipstick and tissues, some clean, others dirty, flew all over the place. The air was thick with other people's bad thoughts about me but I didn't care because I wasn't in Paul's silence any more, I wasn't in Susie's, I was breaking away from the cobwebs and the noise and everything else; this was so much better than being good. I reached for the Filofax but found my stories first. They were already creased from the way she'd stuffed them into her bag; the paint was flaking and cracked. I ripped and ripped, then chucked the pieces in the air. They floated down on to the orange chairs, like snow too ugly to paint on any postcard.

"Bethany!" Paul grabbed my wrist and pulled me towards the door. "I'm sorry your mum hasn't shown. But this has got to stop. And this," he waved the ripped-up story in my face. "You must never take it out on this. On this . . . " He gulped, and for a minute I thought he was going to cry. I'd never seen a man cry before and I wanted to see if it was possible. But then he looked up at the too-bright lights on the ceiling and his eyes dried right up. He went on: "Breaking things is never going to make you feel better, especially not when they're your own things."

"It's just a dumb story," I said. "The pictures are ugly and the writing's not even good. I can't spell or do joined up."

"Bethany." He squatted down so that his head was the same height as mine. "That stuff's not important. What makes this story important is that it's from the inside of you. That's the most important thing of all, do you understand?"

I did.

On the car ride home, Susie kept saying things like "unforgivable" and "unbelievable" and "what a woman" but I didn't care because Paul's words were still inside me, keeping me warm.

I'd just snuggled back into that after-school silence, with big ideas for a grown-up book with more words than pictures—which Paul had promised to help me with—when I stopped being able to use the bathroom in the morning because Susie was always in there, throwing up. It seemed like she was dying, except I knew she couldn't be, because by the time she shuffled out in her dressing-gown, she'd be smiling. Paul kept smiling, too. And when I asked him how to spell a word or to read a bit of my story, he'd say, "What?" as if he'd been somewhere far away, like Cornwall or Spain. It got difficult to sleep again, even though they weren't shouting, they were just talking. I'd crouch at the top of the stairs and listen.

Paul: "I'm sure she could handle it. She's getting better. No doubt she's probably sensed something already."

Susie said: "I know. But she seems . . . fragile. Like she might explode at any moment. I can never relax, you know?"

"Well, maybe," said Paul, "she's wondering about her future."

"She's seven!" said Susie. "Seven-year-olds don't wonder about their future."

"They want to know they're safe," said Paul. "That they're loved for good."

Susie said nothing.

Paul said, "Maybe, we should adopt her. Make a commitment."

Commitment. I remember hearing this word. I remember sounding it out and imagining what it would be like to write it down. All those looping *m*s and jagged *t*s. No wonder no one wanted anything to do with it.

"I can't do it," said Susie. Her words were joined up by tears. "I thought I could but I can't. I—I'm not strong enough."

"Ssshh," said Paul. "Don't cry now. It'll work out. We'll adopt her, she'll settle down. She'll be a lovely big sister! If you just spent some time with her, Susie, I think you'd see . . . "

"I'm sorry," said Susie. "I know myself. And. I've tried. I have. But I can't. I just can't. That's it."

It wasn't long before I was climbing into a white van that would drive me to another family in another part of London. All I took with me were two small bags.

"You travel light, don't you?" joked the social worker, who was supposed to make me feel like this was one big adventure, or something.

When I didn't reply, she said, "Don't worry, you've got a nice new foster family who's just dying to meet you."

But I wasn't worried, not really. I'd lost Paul, but the silence we'd shared and the stories we'd made in it, they were still inside me. No one could see them. No one could take them away. That's why, despite the years that stretch between now and then, despite all the things, good and bad, that have happened in them, I'm sitting on my bed in my cell and I'm smiling because I'm sharing them with you.

4.
FRIENDS YOU CAN BE WEIRD WITH

A good thing happened today. It wasn't even to do with Erika. I was shovelling down the tiny puddle of spaghetti-hoop-topped slop that, unless you're mates with the servers, passes as dinner around here, when a long speckled arm swooped the plate from under me.

I looked up to see the Lee. I don't know why she's called "the Lee" and not just Lee; she just is. She's been here longer than anyone else; no one bothers her. She shook her round face at me.

The first weeks I was here, I was too scared to talk to the other girls. Whenever one of them tried to talk to me, my heart beat so fast I couldn't breathe or think or see or feel anything other than bad. I just shut my eyes or turned my head or looked up at the ceiling to stop the tears. So when the Lee came over, I thought, this is it. This is the bad thing I've been waiting for. The one I deserve.

Except she didn't do any bad thing. She pushed my plate into the middle of the table. Then, to everyone and no one in particular, she said, "Look at this girl's plate! That's not a dinner, not even for a kid. Now, she's new and she's scared as fuck. If *I* can remember what that's like—how shitty it is before you give in and accept you're going to be stuck in here for a while—then we all can. Let's share." She scraped a bit of her spaghetti-hoop slop on to mine.

Laughter clattered around her table. Laughter plus a side order of grumbles. I tried to keep my eyes on my plate, as usual, but when you can feel other people's eyes on you, it's hard not to look back, and so, for the very first time, I did. I looked the other girls in the eye. It wasn't as bad as I'd imagined. It wasn't bad at all. Their faces weren't hammered up with hate; they were floppy and loose, sad and confused, tired, curious, and every possible feeling in between.

The Lee's crew each scraped a little brown slop on to my plate.

"Don't like the goulash anyway."

"Is that goulash? I thought it was curry. Don't know how you can tell. They cover it all with those stupid hoops."

"You'll get a proper portion tomorrow night, don't worry," said the Lee, as she handed the plate back to me.

The lump in my throat was so big that by the time the words "thank you" wobbled out of my mouth, she was gone.

I ate every drop of probably-goulash. It didn't taste good but it did taste a lot better than the nothing I'd have been stuck with otherwise. The Lee didn't say anything else to me that night; neither did anyone else. But I didn't mind. Just eating food that someone had given me, food that should've gone in their bellies rather than mine, it was enough. Enough to stop me feeling like an alien from a 100% bad planet; enough to remind me that I'm human and humans are connected to other humans whether we like it or not.

Being human doesn't just mean connecting to other humans; it means connecting the human you are now with the ones you used to be. Before tonight, I didn't believe in now-Beth; how could good things happen when she was locked up? But the Lee's action filled my head with other Beths. Other times when what started off looking like a small or bad or silly change ended up making a big difference. A good difference.

The person I'm thinking of most is Cal. Cal was the next person I really learned to be alive with, after Paul. We learned to be alive at the age of thirteen, although if you'd said that to us when we first met, we'd have laughed: we were enemies. Or so we thought.

Whenever I started a new school, I'd be good to begin with. At least, *good* was the word the teachers used, but if I had to pick any word, it would be *invisible*. I'd concentrate so hard on what other people were doing—was this a school where rolling up your blazer sleeves was cool or neeky? Would you get a detention for *not* standing up when a teacher walked into the classroom or for standing up without asking for permission?— I'd forget myself. Every school, every area, every foster family had its own set of rules for how to be alive. The moment I learned them was a dangerous moment, because no one can stay invisible forever; it's too boring. The only way I knew to make people see me was to do something bad.

A few weeks after I arrived at Cal's school, our English teacher, Miss Hanley, made us write an Alien's Guide to Stockwell. The whole class groaned, the way they did almost every time a teacher asked them to do something. Cal stuck her hand in the air and, without waiting for the teacher to say she could speak, blurted: "But aren't we supposed to be doing travel journalism? That sounds like something we did in Year 7. We are in the top set, after all."

If anyone else had done that, they'd have got in trouble. But not Cal, with her shiny brown ponytail, her huge pencil case, her brain that always knew the answers and got the highest marks. The teacher just smiled at Cal as if *she* were the joke. "We worked on that poetry essay all last month. It will do you all good to flex your imaginative muscles. And who's to say an Alien's Guide to Stockwell isn't journalism?"

"Right," said Cal, and violently flicked the page of her exercise book.

If I'd behaved like that, I'd have got sent out. But there was something about Cal that stopped anyone, even teachers, disagreeing with her. Whatever it was, I didn't have it, and it made me hate her.

As soon as I started writing, I forgot Cal and how much I hated her. I forgot how hard it was to fit in. I even forgot my new foster mum, Brenda, and how she only asked boring old-person questions—*What lessons did you have today? What did you have for lunch?*—and how, whenever I dared to bring up something strange or funny or interesting, like how one girl had got a detention for writing all over her friend's hand in glittery gel pen, she'd shuffle out of her seat. "Toast?" she'd shout, flapping her speckled old hands in front of my face. "Would you like some toast?" She would speak right over whatever I was trying to say. "Here's some toast. Why won't you touch your toast?" She'd never keep quiet long enough for me to tell her that I didn't need toast; what I needed was for someone to listen.

Writing an Alien's Guide to Stockwell was so much easier than writing about olden days poems or Japanese volcanoes; it was easy because the things I needed to write it weren't in some textbook or worksheet, they were inside me. Reaching for it made my insides whirl until I ended up at the same still place as when I ran.

I knew exactly what to say to that alien. How to turn their fear and their confusion into a fresh and funny thing. *Don't worry what the locals think of you*, I wrote. *They won't pay you half as much attention as you pay them.* I thought of my walk from Brenda's to school; of the tall, white houses whose polished, curtain-less windows begged to be stared through, and how Brenda warned me to behave myself on those streets, those people were too rich and too fussy, in her opinion—"Not that anyone ever asks my opinion, mind you"—but how the only people I ever saw coming out of these houses were Filipino maids who, struggling with huge pushchairs, piles of dry-cleaning, or tiny yapping dogs, never noticed me. I thought of the estate—"It used to be all right but not now. You've got all sorts there, now. You've got to watch out"—and how much life there was on its grass: guys on benches, staring at their future, or at their pasts, playing music out of their phones, smoking, sighing, chatting. There were mums who, surrounded by Lidl bags and screaming toddlers, had only stopped to say hello yet were still here, saying other things, an hour later. There were big boys on small BMXs and small boys in big trousers. There were mean dogs and dozy dogs. Words in every language you could think of and a lot of languages you couldn't. As soon as you got out the other side of the estate, there were Polish shops, Portuguese shops, Turkish shops, Ethiopian shops. Ten minutes, and you'd nibbled versions of life from all over the world.

The locals think they know about this place because they've lived here a long time, I wrote. *But that doesn't mean they're right. In fact, they're probably wrong. Look at the locals when they reckon no one's looking at them and you'll see they're no different from you; some days, they're not sure what they're doing here, other days, here feels like a strange and scary place. But they still find a way to belong and you will, too.*

Before this, teachers had said I had potential, especially where words were concerned. *Her reading age is unusually high, given her circumstances. She has a vivid imagination. Her academic progress is hampered by her disruptive behaviour and short concentration span. She also reacts very badly to criticism and is reluctant to engage with her learning targets.* But when a teacher marked a piece of work, all I saw were the question marks, the red lines. I didn't see the comments in green, and I didn't see the red pen as a way to get better. I handed in my Guide to Stockwell without hope of anything different.

Miss Hanley began the next lesson with a big grin on her face. "8b, I've got something very exciting to read to you. Not only is it the best Guide to Stockwell in the whole class, it's one of the best pieces of student creative writing I've read for a long, long time. Now, sit back, listen and enjoy."

A few words in, and everyone stopped talking and looking around to see if they could guess who'd written the best story. They stared at Miss Hanley's mouth as if the words tumbling out of it were important. It wasn't until they burst out laughing at a description of an old man trying to explain to his dog why rolling in a puddle of Red Stripe was a bad idea, that I realized the words were mine.

Mine.

Yes, I'd written them. They'd started life in my body but now, as they zinged around the classroom, making people laugh, they had their own power. Their own character. Kind of like you.

"Can anyone guess who wrote that?" the teacher asked, when she'd finished.

Silence. Several girls were still chewing on their gel pens, staring at something outside the room, maybe their own personal aliens.

"No. No one?" Her eyes fixed on me. "It was Bethany."

"Who?" said one of the gel pen girls. The popular girls.

Everyone laughed. I wished I'd die. Annoyingly, I didn't.

"Bethany's that new girl!" someone shouted.

Necks stretched and shoulders twisted as everyone tried to get a good look at the strange new girl, i.e. me. Of all the faces, it was Cal's I noticed: it was plastered with anger. Real anger. The sort of anger that bubbled away inside of me, all the time. I'd never have guessed it lurked in her, too.

"It didn't even have any long words," she said loudly, as I passed her table at the end of the lesson. "It was like a baby story."

"It was funny, though," said her friend.

"Yes, but we don't come to school to be funny. We come to learn. My dad says . . . "

I followed them without meaning to. I followed them all the

way to the canteen, the gap between us narrowing until some-one shoved me from behind and I toppled forward, on to Cal.

When she turned to see who'd pushed her, her lips pursed and her eyes narrowed, as if she couldn't decide whether this moment was exciting or dangerous.

"You got a problem with my story?" I said.

"What?" she said, her voice way smaller than the one she used in class.

"You heard me."

"*Cal.*" Her friend tried to tug her away by the shoulder of her blazer but Cal shrugged her off.

"You reckon it's a baby story?"

"I—"

"I heard you." I stepped towards her; she walked back-wards into a table. A few of the cool guys from the year above stopped munching their chicken burgers to watch. "What you said. And don't worry. I'm not gonna steal your place as teacher's pet or nothing. I can't help it if I wrote something better than you."

I started to walk away, towards the cool guys, imagining this to be my first step towards getting in with them.

But Cal shouted: "I'm not anyone's pet."

I wasn't going to let that slide, no way. I swaggered back. Waited a few beats, then shoved her into the ketchup stands. To my surprise, she shoved back. She shoved hard. There was a spark in her eyes like she wanted to hurt me, and I was glad. I yanked her ponytail until she screeched. Let go, let *go*, she yelled, but I gripped harder, until somehow, she flipped her whole body around and kicked me in the shin. I howled.

FIGHT! GIRL FIGHT! Someone shouted. There was a rustle of blazers and crisp packets as kids crowded in. They knew as well as we did that it was only a matter of minutes before some teacher came and ruined it. FIGHT FIGHT FIGHT! So we proper went for it, her as much as me, and even as she was biting and pulling and scratching, I had to admit: I was impressed.

When the teachers dragged us apart, I tried to catch her eye. I wanted her to admit she'd enjoyed it, too. But she looked the other way and even later, when we were friends, if I brought it up, she'd get fidgety and quiet before whisking the conversation into some more comfortable spot.

Our punishment was a whole week in the Head Teacher's Corridor. Students were only allowed there when they'd done something good, like winning a prize, or something bad, like making another student bleed. We sat on knobbly exam tables and answered questions from textbooks, or, in my case, pretended to. The point of the Head Teacher's Corridor wasn't work, though; it was for teachers to walk past and shake their heads, so there was no way we could forget we were 100% bad. Sometimes, they stopped by Cal's table (which was a few metres behind mine) and muttered Serious Words, such as "disappointing" and "grades" and "permanent record." When they saw me, they sped up and looked ahead. I didn't mind; I was used to adults acting like I was already somewhere else.

At the end of the second day, just as I was wondering whether I'd be dead from boredom by the end of the week, a small, hard thing hit the back of my head. I turned to see Cal smirking. She wiggled her eyebrows at a balled-up piece of paper by my foot. I opened it.

Mostly, the locals do stuff that's POINTLESS. As an alien, pointlessness is hard to bear.

This is still the best apology I've ever received. Not only did it not contain the word "sorry"; it made me laugh. There were no teachers about, so I quickly scribbled a reply on the back of the paper and threw it back to her.

It's a relief to find out you're not the only alien. Even if those aliens sometimes disguise themselves as humans who hate you . . . ;)

She took so long to reply that I answered a few more questions from the textbook to distract myself from imagining why she wasn't. As I was running seriously low on hope, a ball of thick purple paper landed on my desk. This wasn't any paper; it was a page from the pretty notebook I'd seen her sneak out of her backpack at the end of lessons.

Yeah, the locals get jealous when the aliens say it better than they do. Don't worry, they get over it though. Because everyone's an alien underneath.

It was a strange feeling to know that Cal, with her grades and her friends and her pretty notebook, was jealous of me. Me with my words. Anyway, it wasn't like I'd written anything clever; I'd just written what was obvious.

When the Head Teacher gave us his little end-of-day pep talk—"Well, girls, how are you doing? Have you had a chance to reflect on your actions?"—I found it ridiculously hard not to laugh. All I could do was suck my lips together and nod.

"Oh yes," said Cal. "Lots of reflection, yes. I can't wait to get back into lessons."

The Head Teacher looked from her to me and back to her again. "Good. I'm sure we won't see this sort of behaviour from either of you again."

We left his office together, walked down the corridor together, and as soon as we were out in the playground, we were stumbling about in the electric hysterics you get when you've been holding them in for way too long.

"I don't know how you stayed so serious," I said, when I was able to speak again.

"*Dying.* I was thinking about dying. Most of the time, at school, I have to think about dying, I want to laugh so much."

"But the teachers love you."

"Only because I get good grades. And because of the dying."

We stopped for the main road that sliced between the school and the estate. I thought she was going to say goodbye; instead, she linked her arm into mine and pulled me across the road, saying, "Let's play a game! Let's look at people and guess which ones are aliens."

I'd never been friends with anyone who'd suggest something like this. The friends I'd had were the sort you had to impress or they'd stop being friends with you. The friends I'd had before weren't proper friends, but I hadn't realized it until then.

We walked across the grass between the estate towers, nodding and whispering and pointing and giggling. *Alien. Not an alien. Not an alien but wants to be. Is an alien but wants to not be.* It was like we shared the same head. It was fun.

When we were halfway down one of the posh, quiet streets, she stopped.

"This where you live?"

She wriggled her arm out of my elbow. "Yeah."

The bricks of her house were so white it hurt. Like all the other houses on the street, hers had no net curtains, and through the windows I saw a canvas painting with weird shapes on, a piano, and lots and lots of bookshelves. Was this a house, a library or a museum?

"Wow. It's massive."

"It's not that big," she said. "On the inside."

What would she think if she saw Brenda's house? It was only around the corner but it was half the size of hers, and you couldn't see its inside from the outside; it had tiny windows and two layers of curtains. I hadn't asked Brenda whether I could have friends round; I didn't want to.

"Right."

The air between us went stiff.

I opened my mouth, intending to say bye, but instead I said, "My feet are frozen." My eyes wandered back to those bookshelves. I hadn't seen that many books for ages. Not since Paul's.

"Would . . . would you like to come in?"

"Oh." Ever since she'd written that first note, I'd been hoping she'd ask this. But now that she did, my belly wriggled with embarrassment. And fear. "You're probably too busy . . . "

"No," she said, stepping towards me. "I'm not."

"O.K. Thanks."

Cal showed me into her front room, then left me there while she leaped upstairs to the toilet. The room was terrifyingly tidy. Even the tissue box—which was an ordinary pack of Kleenex: I checked—was hidden inside a pretty woven box-glove thing. When Cal came back, she laughed. "Don't look so scared! Go on, sit down."

The room was about twice the size of Brenda's, but it felt about four times as big, given how neat it was and the size of Brenda's porcelain dog collection, which spilled on to every flat surface.

"Where?"

There was a small wicker chair and two sofas with the cushions laid out symmetrically. At Brenda's, there was a chair and a foot pouf that I was no way allowed to sit on because it was the only thing she'd inherited from her mum. The only place I could sit was the sofa, which was so saggy that when you sat on it, you had to rock back and forth if you wanted to get up.

"It's like a museum."

"A *museum*?"

My stomach clenched. Maybe I'd gone too far. Maybe she was already sick of me.

She laughed. "I can just about imagine what you mean. But

that's only because Celia comes on Tuesdays. Come on a Friday and we'll have messed it up."

"Who's Celia?" I asked, as I followed her down a sanded corridor and into the kind of kitchen that until then, I'd only seen on TV.

"Oh," said Cal, standing in the too-bright light of a huge silver-doored fridge, "she's our cleaner. She's actually trained as an engineer but she's got to work as a cleaner because she's from the Congo. She's really good. Look! We've got Ben & Jerry's. Want some?"

"Yes!"

We were in an advert kitchen eating advert food in an opposite-of-an-advert way, i.e. standing up, digging into the tub with our spoons, licking them, digging them in again. It was brilliant.

"Hello."

A woman was throwing a briefcase on to the kitchen table. She wore glasses, a stiff grey dress hugged to her waist by a thick leather belt and the same *I'm-watching-you* eyes as Cal.

Cal, who'd stuffed the Ben & Jerry's in the fridge the moment we heard her mum, grabbed my ice-creamy spoon out of my hand and chucked it in the sink. "Mum," she said, "this is Beth."

"*Beth?*" Her mum raised one eyebrow. "As in . . . "

"Yes."

Her lips quivered with the possibility of a smile. "You've certainly made up quick. Now tell me," she leaned across the tiles and laid her hand on my arm, "did my daughter apologize?"

"Mu-*um!*"

"Don't say 'Mu-*um*' like that, it's very irritating," she snapped. Then she turned to me. "Now tell me, did she?"

"Well . . . Yes. Yes, she did."

"You deserve all the Ben & Jerry's in the world, in that case."

Cal was hunched by the spice rack, her face hardened into the same angry mask I'd seen in the canteen.

"God knows her father and I have been trying to get her to apologize for *years*. But she just won't. She thinks everything she does is right."

Cal's chest heaved in and out, in and out, and she was sucking in her lips, which is exactly what I did when I was trying not to explode. I shot her a look to say, *it's all right*. She looked back like, *thanks*.

"Of course," Cal's mum picked up a wooden spoon, "*most* of what she does *is* right." She poked Cal with the spoon.

"*No.*"

"But not *everything*." She poked Cal again, this time in the side. Cal sprang out of her corner. She yelped and grabbed another spoon and poked her mum back. Pretty soon they were laughing.

"Oh, you're a maker of miracles," said Cal's mum, pulling away from her daughter and putting the spoon back in the pot with all the other spoons, as if she'd suddenly remembered me. "Wait until Geoff hears about this."

I wanted to tell her that the miracle wasn't me; the miracle was the love that could chase away anger with one wooden spoon. But then Cal's mum said it had been lovely to have me but I'd have to go, Cal would soon have to get ready for her tap dancing lesson.

"You do tap dancing?" I asked Cal, on the way out.

"Don't tell anyone."

"Don't worry," I said. "I won't."

I glanced in at the living room on my way to the door but it no longer looked like a museum; it looked like a home. Or maybe the difference was that after only an hour, it was starting to feel like one.

I went to Cal's the next night, and the night after that. We did normal things, like laugh and do impressions of teachers and watch TV, but we also did other things, things you'd never admit to at school, like brainstorming ideas for a magazine on this amazingly thick wavy paper, which still smelt like trees. The magazine would be called *What's Down?* Instead of *What's Up?* It would include articles on whether being a bitch made you more likely to buy gel pens or whether drawing all over your hands with gel pens poisoned you with bitchiness. (We both hated the gel pen girls.) A study of the brain to show that the older you got, the more your brain came to resemble a stone; "Which is why adults never change their minds," said Cal, "and also why they get so obsessed with houses." I suggested something about why you can feel when someone is looking at you from behind. "You worry they're going to attack you or take something from you, but usually they're just nosy, or they want you to move out of their way, or they can't find any other thing to look at." It was the best thing ever, just being able to scoop out the weirdest stuff from the bottom of your mind, and know that it wouldn't make the person you were with hate or turn away from you; it would make them love you more.

We'd share our ideas in Cal's room, which was stuffed with cushions, bean bags, mobiles, posters, books, boxes, clothes, and other random things, like a wonky pencil pot she'd made at a pottery party (whatever that was). "I'm sorry it's such a mess," she said. "Celia won't even come in here." I didn't mind.

What I didn't tell her was that even though my room at Brenda's was bigger than at my previous foster mum's, even though it was clean and warm, it wasn't *mine*. I wasn't allowed to put things on the wall or leave my bed unmade or leave stuff on the floor. Aside from my clothes, which I had to fold neatly in drawers, the only things I had were books. There was one from Paul and one from each foster family after that. A lot of them were little kid books and some were boring grown-up ones, like a *Reader's Digest*, that I'd nicked. I kept them in a pile, in my holdall, in the bottom of the wardrobe in my room. Most nights, before bed, I'd unzip the holdall and stare at them. I'd stare until I could see back to the me I'd been when I read them and through those old *me*s to the world on the other side of those pages that was still there, still waiting. I hadn't found any good books at Brenda's and I told her this. "You've got so many books," I said. "And even more downstairs. My foster mum doesn't even read maga*zines*."

Cal always went stiff and quiet when I mentioned my foster mum.

"She says it's because of her eyes," I said. "I think it's because she's old. She listens to all these audio books from the library, they're romantic ones, always some dumb story about a rich doctor falling in love with a poor maid when she swoons into the swimming pool and he has to dive in and rescue her. There's always a swimming pool and there's always swooning. Other things there are, are trembling bosoms and . . . quivering members."

She laughed, and just like that, the awkwardness was gone.

On the third night, Cal's mum said those magic words: "Would you like to stay for dinner?"

Brenda was expecting me back by six, but I didn't care; I didn't even stop the happiness leaking all over my face as I nodded yes to that question.

"Lovely." Cal's mum handed me a courgette. "An extra pair of hands."

"Mu-*um*," said Cal. "Beth wants to *eat* dinner, not make it."

Cal's mum raised an eyebrow. "Dice it, please, Beth, if you don't mind." She handed me a sharp knife. Then she began rushing around, somehow taking things out of the fridge and opening tins and boiling the kettle at the same time. Soon, the kitchen was all bubbles, steam, and carrot peelings. I stared at my courgette, which was still whole. What did it mean, to *dice* it? How did you do it? All I could think of were board games and how I never won.

"Everything O.K.?" Cal's mum asked.

"Erm . . ."

"Here." Cal's mum smiled as she took the knife. "I'll show you." She showed me how to hold the knife—"Make sure the sharp side is facing away from you!"—and how to slice. Then she watched while I did it, moving my hand this way and that until I had it just right. "Great work!" she said, when my courgette was a pile of tiny green cubes. I could hardly speak, it felt so good, to have someone give you what you need without you having to ask.

As the oven beeped to tell us dinner was ready, Cal's dad walked in carrying a crate of books. "Yes, yes, don't tell me. I'm late. I'm sorry. I know. But look! I come bearing bounty."

He heaved the crate down on to a chair.

Cal laughed. "Dad, you're going to be in big trouble."

"Don't tell me," shouted Cal's mum, without turning round from the counter, where she was busy spooning dinner on to four matching plates she'd heated in the oven. "He's gifted us with more unloved books?"

"Dad works in libraries," said Cal, in a tone that suggested this was something to be sorry for, even though I thought it was pretty cool.

Cal's dad wiped the sweat from his forehead with a tea towel. "I wouldn't say works in. It's more akin to life support. I manage libraries around the borough, you see, and many are on their last legs. They're always chucking books out and I just can't bear to see them wasted. I'll give most of them to charity, of course."

"No you won't." Cal's mum laid the plates on the table. "You'll leave them in that box until Celia comes next week, then she'll ask me what to do with them, and I'll say to leave them by the door, where they'll stay until they annoy me so much, *I'll* bloody take them to the charity shop."

Cal's dad sat down. "I don't like to rush," he said. "You wouldn't want to miss a gem." The steam from the plate had risen up and clouded his glasses; we all laughed.

"Yes, I'm hilarious, aren't I?" he said.

"Only when you don't mean to be."

I never felt so warm as at that dinner table, and it wasn't just because Cal's mum had warmed the plates in the oven, or because I'd helped to cook what turned out to be an ugly but surprisingly tasty thing called a veg crumble, but because of their words, which knocked into each other any which way, with no one caring if they came out wrong or right.

"I notice you've got your eye on the orphans," said Cal's dad.

I was about to ask what he meant when Cal rolled her eyes and said, "He means the *books*. He thinks he's being funny."

"Are you a book worm?" he asked.

As usual whenever anyone asked me a question, my insides tensed. But as I replayed his words, I realized it wasn't like any question I'd been asked before. It wasn't about the bad things I'd done or the bad things that had happened in the past. It made me feel good.

"More of a book *mouse*," I said.

They laughed.

"I like how books let you into another world, but how it's secret. Like, when you read, the world you see is different from the one someone else sees when they read the same words. It's just yours."

All three of them stared at me. I was beginning to wonder whether I'd said something wrong, when Cal's mum put down her fork and said, "Wow. That says more about what it is to read than most of the ridiculous papers I've had to mark today."

"Are your parents big readers?" Cal's dad asked.

Silence, which only grew stiffer as Cal and her mum shot him a *shut-up-now* look.

No one had ever asked me this, either. Normally, I did whatever I could to get away from the blank space where my mum was meant to be. But with a bellyful of warm food and warmer words, it felt O.K. Somehow, even though I couldn't see any specific memories, I knew the answer was *yes*.

"My mum," I said, "she used to read to me. We used to make up stories together, and stuff."

I didn't know whether this was true or not, but the thought that it might be and the tugging in my gut which told me it *was*—that was enough.

Cal's mum smiled sadly. "That's lovely. Are you . . . in contact with your mum?"

My head filled with the times my mum had failed to turn up. The time with Paul and Susie. The time after that, and the one after. Then the time when she saw me, burst into tears and said, "I can't do it, I can't do it," until the social worker hurried me out of the room. Then that visit from the social worker with the lopsided haircut who told me, in a voice almost too quiet to hear, as if the quieter she said it, the less true it would be, "Your mum isn't very well at the moment. She's not well enough to see you. We think it would be better for the both of you if we stopped contact for now. Do you understand?" My mum didn't want me. Yes, I understood.

"We don't see each other, no."

For a moment, no one knew what to say. Then Cal's dad opened his eyes really wide and asked if I'd like to rescue any books. He pointed to the crate by his feet. "Go on, have a look. Take any you want."

"Are you sure?"

"I'm . . . If it's possible to be more sure than sure, I'm *that*."

I picked up a book. It smelt of earwax and dust, and it was about political systems, which didn't sound interesting. I put it back.

"Ooh, *Catcher in the Rye*. I loved that. Have you read it?"

Cal pressed a skinny little book into my hand. Its spine was taped at both ends. It smelt of dust but no earwax. When I read the first sentence, I felt a hole opening up. I read another sentence and then another. It was as if someone had broken into my head and pulled out the things even I didn't know were there. "I'll take this one, if you don't mind."

"Great choice!" Cal's dad squatted beside me. "How about this, too?"

"Oh no, not that," Cal's mum cut in. "What about this?"

That night, I went back to Brenda's with a stack of books. Some of them opened up the most brilliant holes. Trying to read others was like bashing your head against a concrete wall. But I kept every single one. There were more of them than all the books from the other parts of my life put together.

When we were back in normal lessons, no one could believe me and Cal were friends.

"That new girl's clever, you know."

"I heard she was a psycho?"

"Nah, she's just weird."

If someone had said something like this about me in any of my other schools, I'd have kicked off. Kicked them, kicked the walls, kicked over a pile of Geographical Formations text-books. But with Cal's arm snuggled into my elbow, they just made me laugh.

Looking back, I spent way more time without Cal than with her; the only lessons we had together were English and History. She had rehearsals for her dance show most nights of the week, and she was always doing something for the whole weekend, like an orchestral residential or visiting her grand-parents in Shropshire. There were times when she'd say she couldn't hang out at lunchtime, she had an extra piano lesson, and then I'd spy her eating with the friends she'd had before me, on the steps round the back of the music block. Or when I'd run to find her after school, and a look would cross her face—only for a second—like she wished I wasn't there. Then she'd go red and mumble something about a last-minute rehearsal.

I didn't see any of this at the time; I couldn't. The only way to make things good was to imagine we were together all the time. When Brenda was telling me off for getting home late, when she was telling me some boring story about the man who was supposed to fix the drip under the kitchen sink but cleaned the windows instead, I was at Cal's. Most weekends, I'd eat up whole days with my face in a book, my head in the world of the book, and then, when it was finished, or I needed the toilet or a drink or something to eat so bad that I had no choice but to put it down, I'd imagine telling Cal's family about it. I'd say funny things, clever things, and they'd laugh. Sometimes I'd change everyone's names and write stories about it in the back of my Maths and Science exercise books; if I got a detention for not doing my work, I didn't care, because every time the whole of me went to Cal's house, every nice thing her parents said to me, every mouthful of food I'd helped to cook—I'd get more than enough reality to keep me dreaming for weeks.

What plopped between me and my dream was the social worker. I don't remember his name, only that he had brown hair and a ginger goatee, and he wouldn't make eye contact with me or even Brenda; he liked to stare at things that wouldn't move, like her porcelain dogs.

"I've got some good news," he said. "Your mum's now well enough to see you."

This wasn't good. Not even 1%. "I don't want to see her," I said. "She won't come, anyway."

He shifted his gaze from the dogs to Brenda's special foot pouf. "She was very sick, your mum. But she's a lot better. We think it would do you good to see her. Think on it."

But I'd already thought on and under and in and around it.

No way. As soon as Ginger Goat was gone, I stomped up to my room and opened the book I'd stayed up half the night reading. But the social worker's words were like a massive door slamming me on the outside of that soft bookish world; it made no sense. I chucked the book, wanting only to get it away from me, not for it to land on a mermaid-shaped porcelain lamp, which smashed.

For a few seconds after the pieces had settled, I felt calm. Then I heard Brenda plod up the stairs. She panted for a while on the landing before waddling into my room. She didn't knock, not like she'd promised she'd always do when I first moved in.

"Oh no," she said, shaking her head too fast, gasping. "Oh, no, no, no." Her face was very red. "I won that in a raffle in 1984. It was the only good thing in the raffle and I won it. Look," she put her hands on her hips, "I know you're upset about your mum, but this is no way to behave, really. You're going to get into a lot of trouble if you just go round breaking things when they don't go your way."

"I didn't—"

"You should know by now that I'm not one for excuses. Now go and get yourself a dustpan and brush while I go and lie down."

I went downstairs but I didn't get a dustpan and brush. I didn't want to sweep anything up. Through the ceiling, I heard the bed creak around her weight. A few minutes later, I heard snoring. It was a Thursday and Cal was at a dance rehearsal but I put on my shoes and my coat and I walked round to hers. As soon as I was out of Brenda's house, I felt better: the sun was out, there were two little boys chasing each other down the street, and my chest filled with hope that Cal's rehearsal had been cancelled. That she'd be at home, bored and alone, like me.

Except, she wasn't. No one was. I stood in her front garden and pressed my face up against the window. There was a pair of striped woolly socks, a book and a glasses case on the sofa.

A magazine on the floor. Some letters and a scrunched-up tissue on the coffee table. But no people, not one.

Maybe they were on their way home. Maybe they were just around the corner, carrying bags of food they were about to cook and eat. I sat down on their doorstep. I leaned my head against the wall and closed my eyes. They'd be back soon, I was sure of it.

"Beth, what are you doing?" Cal's mum was frowning into my face. My neck was curled stiff. My bum and one of my legs were totally numb.

"I don't know."

"Oh, come inside now. Let's get you warm."

"Where's Cal?"

"Geoff's taken her out for dinner. It's good for the two of them to spend some time alone."

She wrapped me in a blanket while she made tea, a hot water bottle, and cheese on toast. She looked so much smaller without Cal and her dad beside her. Older, too. And tired.

When I'd scoffed the cheese on toast, she said, "Is there anything you want to talk about?"

I shook my head. I was warm. I was full. Feelings flooded back into my legs and to the other place, the difficult place that wanted more than to be warm and full—it yelled to go home. Not back to Brenda's or anywhere else I'd ever been; to a place where it could stay, whatever.

"I know you've got a lot going on," she said, her too-quiet voice reminding me of too many social workers. "But you can't just . . . I'm not angry with you, please don't think I'm angry with you, but we really can't have you camping out on our doorstep. It's not fair on your foster mum, for one thing. Although I'm guessing that things aren't so great between you?"

All I heard of this was: *we don't want you.*

"I'll leave then." I threw off her blanket and marched into the hall.

"Beth."

I slammed the door behind me but a few moments later, she was by my side. She rested her hand on my arm. "I didn't mean for you to leave, but if you want to, I'll walk you home. Maybe I could pop in for a quick chat with your foster mum, if she's around."

I didn't like the thought of her talking to Brenda, stood in Brenda's house, which she would think was ugly and stupid. I decided to ignore the part about her coming in. "It's only round the corner. I've walked home by myself a hundred times before."

"I know. But I'd like to."

"Do you mean that?"

She squeezed my arm, then let go. "Yes. We enjoy having you as part of our life."

I didn't get to enjoy these words for very long, and I didn't have to worry about Cal's mum coming in; there was an ambulance outside Brenda's house.

"What's going on?"

"Ah, Bethany." Ginger Goat was back again. "I'm afraid there's some bad news. Brenda's not very well."

Not very well. The exact same words he'd used to describe my mum. "What do you mean? What the fuck do you mean? Why does no one ever tell me what's going on?"

I kicked a flowerpot. It hurt my foot but I kicked it again and I kept on kicking it until Cal's mum pulled me away. "That's enough, Beth," she said, quietly. Except it wasn't. Once whatever it was inside me that needed to break things woke up, nothing was ever enough.

The ambulance man slammed shut the ambulance doors. Then the sirens came on, the lights started to flash, and we stood aside while it drove off.

"Now Beth, don't worry, we've got you somewhere to stay tonight. Just run inside and get your things."

"What happened to her?"

"One of the big blood vessels in her head went pop. It's called a stroke."

"Is she going to die?" I asked. Without waiting for him to answer, I said: "I don't care if she is. I didn't like her, anyway."

"You'll be feeling very upset so I'm going to pretend I didn't hear that. Now go and get your things."

There was blood on the carpet outside my room, a trail of porcelain pieces and a dustpan and brush. I hadn't put the dustpan and brush there, which meant Brenda must've done it. Which meant she must've been doing it just before she had the stroke. Which meant the stroke was my fault, sort of.

My fault.

I grabbed my holdall but I emptied it of books. The only thing I could hear was the voice that said, *things can only get better if you make them worse.*

By the time I was able to hear other voices, kinder voices, it was too late. Brenda had died, I'd signed a form saying I didn't want contact with my mum, I'd messed things up with my next foster family so bad that they trialled me for the "Fresh Start" scheme, which meant I got shoved on a train to Somerset, where I'd be fostered by the Stanleys until I was sixteen. They were O.K., the Stanleys, but whether they could've loved me, I'll never know: I never let them in.

Cal and her parents wrote me letters, but I didn't reply; they only reminded me of what I'd lost. With the first letter, they sent a book. I stayed up all night reading it. It made me cry. It made me shake. It filled me with feelings too big and terrifying to fit in my new room. So I stopped reading. It was easier. It was what I deserved. Anyway, I was busy making myself into a new person, a person who didn't care about books or anything besides having fun. A person who didn't even care when the letters finally stopped.

5

CURLING UP IN A FLEECE BLANKET, IN YOUR OWN HOME

Erika didn't ask how I was this week; she didn't have to: I'd butchered my face from crying so hard. I opened my mouth. But the badness had wedged itself between the words and me and so I shut it and slid further down in my seat.

"It's O.K., Beth, take your time." I raised my eyebrow at this.

"What?" She slid her hands across the table. They were as raw as my face. Imagining her at home, rushing to do the washing up, it made me feel a bit better, like the distance between her kitchen and this room had shrunk.

"Just. Funny you should say that. You know, in *here*. And considering what they do to you if you're late for anything."

"Of course." She shook her head. "Sorry."

"No, it's fine. Funny's good. I'm reading a book that's sad but also funny. It's just, I can't feel the funny bits right now. All I can feel are the sad ones."

"Oh yes?"

I closed my eyes and tried to remember what reading felt like—and not just in my head, but in my body. Especially in my body. "It's like someone's got a massive torch and is waving it around inside of you, and sometimes it lights up a good bit that you'd forgotten was there, and other times . . . It shines on a bit that makes you sick. A bit that, once it knows it's being looked at, grows and swells and then it's tumbling out on top of you and you don't know how to get out from under it."

Erika nodded. "This is a safe space, Beth. You can talk about those things here. You can cry here, if you want."

I didn't want to talk about those things yet. No way was I going to cry in front of her, either.

"That's not why I've been crying, not really. I was crying because, well, I was just starting to feel O.K. here; I've got the library, I'm studying for my GCSEs, I've got this, and twice a week I get to go on the treadmill, which isn't as good as running outside, but it's still good. Then the other day, the Lee invited me to sit with her lot at dinner, who are basically a bunch of misfits, but I didn't care; people are people; I felt like I'd won the lottery or something."

I told her how I didn't properly get their jokes because they were all to do with shit that had happened way before I got here, like when that quiet woman, Moira, she went missing and so the whole prison was on lockdown for days and days, locked in their cells and no choice but to start hearing voices, it was too lonely, otherwise, and then it turned out she was in the garden, half-frozen to death, or was she in the laundry, or had she been there all along, was it just a rumour, it was started by the screws for their own amusement, or was it an accident? What the truth of the story was I had no idea because the woman telling it, she's called Jeannie, was stuffing bread into her mouth at the same time. The others kept looking to see if I was getting scared, but I wasn't; I was just glad not to be eating alone.

The trouble began when I ate dinner with them the next night.

"Six days until Family Day," said the Lee. "I can't wait. A whole day of people calling me Mum. Not *the Lee*."

"First thing I'm gonna do," said Jeannie, "is cane row my daughter's hair. My sister-in-law don't know nothing about Afro hair, she just lets it go mental. Last time, there was a pen lid buried in it. A pen lid!"

"I've gotta tell my son to respect his girlfriend. She's a good one, she is, and I'm not having him doing what his dad did to me."

"My son . . . " Lanky Linda mumbled something into her plate that no one heard. While the others talked over her, I felt her big, brown eyes and their big, purple rings all over me.

"My daughter's gonna love the cards I been making her in Craft."

"No she won't. They look like a dog's dinner. No offence."

"She loves dogs."

If the words from all my reading and writing hadn't been swirling round my head, concentrating on chopping my potatoes into smaller and smaller pieces would've been enough to push the real me deep down beneath the *me* everyone saw; whatever people said or did to me wouldn't matter because it was way too far away to feel.

But it's like these sessions, maybe the books too, they've ripped some skin off me. Things are so much closer. Bigger. Louder. I never used to cry before but now I can't stop. I even cried in the dining room. The Lee stared at me and said, "Come on, our chat's not that bad, is it?"

Thinking they'd had enough of me, I started to stand up, but Jeannie pushed me back down on the bench. "Don't be an idiot," she said. "Wipe your nose. Fuck's sake."

"Truth is," I said to Erika, her face all wobbly through the tears in my eyes, "I don't deserve anything. I don't deserve to be sitting here now. Talking to you about the good things."

Erika said lots of nice things after this, but I'm not sure what they were, I was crying so much. When the tears finally dried up, she was saying, "It's at times like this that it's most important to focus on the good. To prove to yourself that it's really there. Now, what's next on your list?"

"I haven't written it yet."

"But you have an idea?"

I nodded. "It's probably stupid."

She laughed. "That's just what my second son says whenever he wants to tell me an idea for a new Lego creation. But once I weasel it out of him, there comes a point where his eyes light up and he's talking without worrying about whether it's good or stupid—he's happy. The way you look when you get going—you remind me of him."

I didn't even try to hide how good this made me feel.

* * *

There was a time when nothing scared me. When, even though I didn't have all the things and the people around me that other people had, I belonged. Nineteen years old and I had a job, a flat, some friends, a life. I even started to believe this was how my life was going to be from now on. I never imagined it would only last a few months.

When I first moved back to London, I didn't believe I'd make any kind of life, let alone a good one. To get to my flat from the main road, you had to walk up a ramp, across a piece of grass, through a gang of huge metal bins, then up another ramp and six flights of stairs, by which point you'd be 100% knackered. The bathroom ceiling was black with mould, the furniture smelt of people giving in, giving up. The walls and the ceilings and the windows were so thin, there was always some chunk of some other life in my ear—a laugh, a shout, a bass line, an exploding can of Coke—and I was glad: silence was the worst. It was in the silence that I'd see the things and the people in Somerset I'd been so desperate to leave. The things that had come between me and my GCSEs, me and, as my last English teacher put it, my future. It was the silence where I saw the faces of my last foster parents when we said goodbye; they were sad and disappointed about the way things turned out, but they did care. They cared more than I let myself see at the time. Now, I was in London, but it had almost nothing to do with the place I remembered, the place where I'd met Paul and Cal. The place where my life had begun. When I finally made my way out of the disgusting flat, the city pushed and shoved and shouted until there was no kidding myself that it remembered me, either.

"O.K., so it's not exactly the kind of thing you'd see on *Location, Location, Location*. But it's yours and you'll be surprised how little it takes to make it nice." These were the words of Marcia, my Personal Adviser. I thought she was just going to tell me which forms to fill, which bus to get to the Job Centre, etc., etc., but she turned up for her second visit with a big box of cleaning stuff.

"I've already cleaned it," I said, which was true.

"You've made a good effort," she said. "But, and don't take this the wrong way, I'm not being funny or anything, but there's cleaning and there's *cleaning*. Let me show you."

She showed me how to cheat the mould with a "violent scrub," how to clean the inside of the fridge and the oven, how to unblock the drain in the bathroom and dust the windowsills. Then she told me to put on my coat because she was taking me to spend my moving-in allowance, which I hadn't even known about.

"But you filled in the form for it last time, remember?" I didn't. I didn't have a coat, either, just a hoodie, and when we were waiting at the bus stop, which was just a lamppost with numbers on it, not a shelter, and rain splatted all over our heads and our shoulders, she tutted. "Life's hard enough *with* a coat," she said. "Never mind without one. What sort of coats do you like?"

I shrugged. "Never had one that I liked."

"That's about to change," she said. "Don't you worry."

The problem was, I didn't know what I liked. When Marcia held up two different bath mats, two different rugs, two different sets of plates and cups, I couldn't choose, and the not-knowing scared me; it made me feel like I was less real than the people who marched in and grabbed the lamp in the shape of a pineapple because it somehow matched up with who they were.

"You must like one more than the other."

"I don't." I picked things at random: a tiger-print fleece blanket, a turquoise bath mat and soap dish and toothbrush cup, a set of plates and bowls edged with rainbow stripes. I was acting moody and I knew it but she acted as if she didn't know it, she just smiled and chatted and chatted and smiled, and by the time we were eating cream cheese bagels in some deli where everyone was Polish apart from us, I started to perk up.

"What do you like doing, Beth? What makes you happy?"

"I don't normally like eating that much but this bagel is really good," I said. "It's better than the ones we used to get from Sainsbury's."

"That's good—athletes need their food. Because you're an athlete, aren't you?"

"An *athlete*? Nah. I just like to run. And I was good at it. I . . . " And suddenly it hit me, how bad things had got in Somerset. How long it had been since I'd done anything for me—rather than for other people. Bad people. "It made me feel really good. Like God. Like magic."

"So do you think that's something you can do here?"

"Here?" I looked at the boxes of biscuits and dried sausages that dangled from the ceiling. The aisles of pickled pickles and olives and cabbage. "It's a bit cramped, in here."

Marcia laughed. "Not right here, silly. I mean in this area. You live right between two parks." Then she got out her phone and was showing me the best shortcuts. "Not that I run, mind you," she said, patting her belly. "Zumba's more my thing. You got some trainers?"

I did. They were in the bottom of my suitcase, still caked in Somerset mud. Thinking about them made my belly ache in a good way. My leg twitched under the table.

"And what else do you like doing?"

It was a simple question. The kind we had to write to imaginary pen pals in French in Year 8. But it was a question no one had asked me for a long time, or, if they had, they'd asked it in a rushed way that made it clear they wouldn't listen for a real answer.

As I told her about reading and writing and making things up, about watching people and doing impressions of them, about finding people you could laugh and be weird with as well as silent, the inside-me sat up. *Yes*, she said, *I'm going to do this. I'm going to make a fresh start.*

On the way back to the bus stop, I noticed a fur coat in a shop window. I stopped and stared at it.

"You like that?"

To my surprise, I did. "But it's in a charity shop. It's trampy, buying stuff from charity shops."

"Nonsense." She pushed me towards the door. "Try it on."

"Nah."

But I did. It smelt a bit like Brenda, but when I saw how it looked in the mirror, I didn't mind; it looked good.

"Stunning! Like a film star."

Looking at myself in that skinny charity shop mirror with Marcia's smiling face behind me, I didn't think "ugly" or "spotty" or "minger," not like usual; "film star" was a bit much, but I did look on the good side of all right.

"I'll get it."

Marcia was disappointed to find the fur was fake but I didn't mind; the main thing was that this coat was different from anything I'd worn before.

There was a huge bookcase by the till. Marcia caught me looking at it. "Anything take your fancy?"

It had been ages since I'd read properly. I didn't recognize any of the titles.

"How about this one? Oh, and this is really good. And this one, my sister's always going on about it. I'll get them for you. My treat."

"Thanks."

I wore the fur coat all the way home and even at home, until

I got too hot. I laid out the soap dish and the toothpaste cup and the plates and the blanket, and suddenly, it didn't matter whether or not I'd chosen them; what mattered was that they were here. When I looked at them, I didn't feel the people who'd lived here before me, or the *me* I'd been in Somerset; I saw Marcia's hands flying about as she told me some story about the state of her daughter's shared house at Uni and how I'd learnt how to look after myself a hell of a lot quicker than most people my age. I snuggled up close to my new fleecy blanket and I had to admit, it was really soft. The tiger print made me feel like maybe my life might become fun.

It was the same when I got an interview for a job at the Odeon: yeah, so it wasn't my dream job—I didn't have a dream job—but it was a job. After weeks of boring appointments at the Job Centre, it was the only interview I'd got. The woman at the Job Centre told me to talk about my key skills and qualities, but Marcia, who I'd rung as soon as I got the interview, said, "Rise above that claptrap. The key is to act like you can do anything. Even if they ask you if you can do something you've never done before, say you can."

"Basically," I said, "you mean I should chat like I'm the best person in the world?"

This made her laugh. "That's about it." She hung up before I had a chance to say thank you.

The Odeon was just down the road from the Polish deli. There were pigeons chilling on the massive "O" above the doors, kids chilling on the steps below. Inside, a big mixed-race girl and two short, round white girls were chilling behind the Snack Station. The air was sticky and sweet with popcorn. I already felt at home.

"Rah, are you Beth?" The big girl swaggered towards me and introduced herself as Chantell. She waved a Walkie Talkie in one hand, a bag of Maltesers in the other. "No offence, but, like, how old are you?"

"Nineteen."

"For real?"

"For pretend."

She screwed up her over-pencilled eyebrows and threw back her head. "You're weird."

My heart, my belly, everything sank. I'd already messed up. I could imagine Marcia watching me, shaking her head.

"But weird is O.K. as long as you're not a retard. Can you read good?"

Best person in the world. *Best person in the world.* I repeated it until it felt maybe 10% true.

"I can read a whole book in a night. Long words, short words, weird words; I can read them all."

She kissed her teeth and turned around to mouth something to the two short girls by the Snack Station, who immediately giggled.

"Well, you ain't gonna have to read no books in here. It's just we keep getting these retards who can't even read the title of the film. Or maybe they're too lazy to, I don't know. But it's long. And it makes the queue bare long, especially on Orange Wednesdays. You worked a till before?"

For my Year 10 work experience I'd worked at Yeovil Morrisons. I was only there four days, but in those four days I did spend two whole mornings sitting beside a woman on the checkout and pretending that I was watching carefully, rather than thinking about my boyfriend, and how I'd spend my lunch hour getting off with him in the park (which would eventually stretch to two and then three hours and so get me chucked off).

"Yeah, it's fun."

She kissed her teeth. "You won't be saying that on Orange Wednesday, trust. O.K., what about tickets? You ever done box office?"

I shook my head. "But I pick stuff up quick."

"What about cleaning? You know how to clean?"

"I know all the tricks." By now, the Marcia in my head was beaming.

Chantelle absent-mindedly dug the aerial of her Walkie Talkie into her cheek and stared me up and down, down and up. "You ain't no mouse, either. Even if you are, like, the size of a ten-year-old. I mean, no offence."

Normally, I went mental when people went on about how small I was. Or when they said anything about me, really. But there was some wild, warm thing in her voice that made me laugh. It made me want to hang around her until she liked me.

"If you want the job, you can start tomorrow."

"Great."

"Come get your T-shirt then."

I followed her over to the Snack Station, enjoying the few moments when no one was looking at me and I could smile as much as I wanted to; I'd got the job and I hadn't even had to answer any of the dumb questions the Job Centre lady said I'd have to answer, e.g. "Can you give me an example of a time you used team work to solve a problem?"

"Nicole, Lisa, this is Beth. Beth, you just heard who they are."

"Hi!" they said together.

"Don't just say *hi*, get her a T-shirt then."

They shuffled away. Chantelle shook her head at them. "Fuck's sake, it's not like they *both* need to go. They're retards, but you got to love them. They're good in here," she banged her boob. "Which is what counts."

"You mean, they've got good boobs?"

She scrunched her face at me again. Maybe this time I really had gone too far. Then she laughed. "Boobs, heart, what's the difference?"

Nicole and Lisa returned, holding a huge grubby T-shirt on stretched-out arms.

"It was Jake's."

"He ain't washed it."

"It stinks of skunk."

"And cum."

"And—"

"His breath stank of cum. I reckon he sucked his own—"

"That's not possible. Remember, I looked it up on that site and—"

"Maybe it was someone else's?"

"All *right*," said Chantelle. "I'm sure Beth don't mind cleaning the boy out of it, do you?" Then she shoved the T-shirt in my face and got out her phone, and while Liking a Facebook photo of someone's kid sitting in a box, she said to come back tomorrow at 7 A.M.

"Seven?"

She made a don't-mess-with-me face. "If you think you're just gonna swagger in here and get the best shifts straight away, you've got another think coming. You'll be here at seven. Darrell will open up and you'll clean up from tonight."

I got there at 6.35. It was freezing but I unbuttoned my fake fur coat and looked at my reflection in the Odeon door window. My T-shirt, which was soft and fresh against my skin, was too-bright blue, and baggy, so my legs dangled out from under it, like they weren't sure whether they belonged there or not. It clashed with the coat, but not in a bad way; it clashed in a way which made me feel being me was strange but O.K.

By the time Darrell whizzed up on his micro scooter—he wasn't even embarrassed to be riding a micro scooter—my feet were numb but I didn't mind; it was so good to know I was about to get into a place that needed me.

"You've gotta, like, vacuum and stuff?" said Darrell, as he showed me into a cupboard crammed with buckets, mops and cartons of bleach. "I've got to sort out the box office."

By sorting out the box office he meant sitting in the box

office and looking at his phone, but I didn't care; pushing the vacuum across the carpet of Screen One hours before any film would show on its screen, I felt sure I was in on some secret, even if I wasn't 100% sure what it was. The Odeon vacuum had an extension lead that went on for almost ever, plus all these special extensions so you could suck out stray popcorn and jelly babies from under the seats. I was hot and sweaty by the time I was done, but not in a bad way; it was satisfying to know that people would sit down in a clean cinema, and all because of me.

By the time I was done cleaning, Nicole and Lisa were at the Snack Station.

"What, you've done all that?" said Nicole, when I said how many screens I'd cleaned.

"You only have to do like one or two things. And you don't have to bother with the vacuum every day," said Lisa. "You just want to get rid of the big things that people notice, like Coke cups."

"But Chantelle said—"

"Nah," said Nicole. She pushed a clipboard under my nose. "If you've done the obvious stuff you can write your initials next to ladies' toilets, Screen One, etc."

They were both wearing their hair in a side ponytail. Every time I looked at them I wanted to laugh.

"If Chantelle's in a good mood, she'll let you initial it anyway," said Lisa.

"But you've got to be careful," said Nicole, her voice superserious, as if she was talking about nuclear war. "You can't predict what mood she's in."

When no one said anything for a while, I asked, "What should we do now?"

Nicole and Lisa looked at each other. Then they both shrugged.

"Wait."

"Yeah. Chantelle will tell us what to do."

So we sat and stared through the glass doors at the buses and the people and the occasional dog lurching up and down the High Road.

Chantelle stomped in at about midday. "Don't talk to me," she said so loudly that the two mums who were trying to pull their kids away from the Pick 'n' Mix turned and stared.

"Don't talk to her," said Nicole.

"Yeah," whispered Lisa. "Don't talk to her."

"Cardo is such a dick. Such a *dick*. He said he was gonna take Jayden out for his birthday, Jayden's been chatting about it for weeks, and I'm like, he's just your dad, and one of these days you'll grow up and you'll see him for what he is, but he's your dad, and you got a right to see him, but you know what he did? He fucking went and cancelled. Two days before and he cancelled. Sorry babes, I've got to take Lucy to Miami. Like fuck he's going to Miami! He's probably just round hers, getting high or whatever. Now Jayden's acting up and I'll bet you his school are gonna be on the phone by the end of the day, acting like it's all my fault, I mean they never say it, but they say it without saying it, you know what I mean, and I'm like, you don't know the full story, you ain't even had one bite of the story, so get your head out of your computer screen for two minutes and stop judging."

"Cardo is Jayden's dad," whispered Nicole to me.

"Jayden is Chantelle's son," whispered Lisa.

"I *said*, don't talk to me!"

"We weren't talking *to* you, we were talking *about* you," said Lisa.

Chantelle smacked her palm against the counter. "Jesus Christ, then what are you doing now? Seriously, I don't know why I don't fire you two. I could do that, you know. I am the deputy manager."

Nicole's face wobbled like she might cry. But Lisa opened

her eyes wide, as if she'd just had an amazing idea. "Chantelle, who's, like, the *manager* manager?"

"The *manager* manager?" For the first time since she'd walked in, she was silent. "It's. Like. It don't exist. It's just so they can pay me less. Dickheads. But like I said, don't talk to me."

The air around Chantelle was hot and sparky, like if you touched it, things might get either very exciting, or very dangerous. I risked it: "Not being rude, Nicole and Lisa, but I got to ask you something. This morning, did you, like, text each other to wear a ponytail on the same side of your head? Or did you *just* know?"

Chantelle stared at me. Then she hit my arm and burst out laughing.

Lisa and Nicole looked pissed off. "No, she SnapChatted me to see if it looked good and I already had it so—"

"No, I SnapChatted you first!"

"You know who you are?" I said, looking at Chantelle. "The Chuckle Sisters."

"The Chuckle Sisters." Chantelle slapped the counter again, but in a happy way. "Oh, you're *gooood*. Chuckle Sisters. That's what we'll call you from now on."

Chantelle looked at me as she said this and it felt good; it felt good to be part of her "we."

"Chuckle Sisters," said Nicole, like the words were foreign. "It's kind of original?"

"It's dumb," said Lisa.

"*Sisters*," said Chantelle, a smile spreading across her face. "Chill out. It's *funny*."

We all laughed.

Soon after I started at the Odeon, I got back into running. I'd run past the African men playing football on the grass outside my block, and I no longer hated them for laughing and joke-punching each other, i.e. having a good time. When I stopped to tie my shoelace and the goalie nodded at me, I nodded back. I smiled, then he smiled. Then he leapt for the ball and I ran away from the game and on down the high street, ducking and weaving between yawning young men in suits and mums trying to juggle a child and a scooter and a smartphone and a bag of shopping at once. I ran to the park, which was covered with groups of blonde women in red bibs who'd be doing whatever the real-life Action Man instructor told them to do, e.g. "110 press-ups and no chat! Chat means fat. *Chat*, ladies, means fat!" I ran past couples wriggling about on benches. Past big men walking small dogs, small women walking big dogs. I didn't hate these people the way I'd hated them when I'd first moved back to London; they were living their lives and I was going to keep on living mine.

Right now, I don't have a fleece blanket, a fur coat or a clean T-shirt. I don't have a soap dish and I have gross grey powder instead of proper soap. I'm not in the Visitors' Centre with the others, laughing and chatting and fighting and drinking Coke and eating Skittles with my family on Family Day. But I do have these words and the world, just behind them, where I can be with you.

6

READING OUT LOUD TO PEOPLE WHO LISTEN

D id you really have no one to see you on Family Day?" Lanky Linda's voice poked a hole in the snuggly silence of the library.

I could've slapped her. Instead I bit my lip and stared at the title of the book on the shelf in front of me: *Computer Programming for Dummies*. I read the title forwards then backwards. I breathed in and out for five breaths, like Erika had taught me to when breaking things felt like the only thing to do. Then I looked at Linda. You could see right through her skin to her veins, and her cheekbones stuck out, but not in a model-way, in a bad way; my heart softened; how could you be angry with someone who's hardly here?

"I wish it was a joke," I told her. "I wish I had really met up with my family in some other Visitors' Centre where none of you lot could see me. But I didn't. I don't. Spent most of the day in my cell."

Linda's eyeballs roved around their sockets. "Oh."

Finance for Dummies. Travel Writing for Dummies. Catering Management for Dummies. Why was everything for dummies?

"I didn't have a good time anyway," she said.

The librarian screeched her trolley to the end of our shelf. She gave me an eyebrow wiggle like, *is everything O.K.?* Which made my heart race. What if the Lee and Jeannie and Lanky Linda and all the other weirdos had been pretending to like me just so they could get me alone and do bad things to me? This was the first time I'd seen Linda in the library, after all. Or what if that was all bullshit? What if Linda just wanted to chat? For once, I chose to believe the better option. I forced my mouth into a smile and the librarian and her trolley screeched away.

"That's a shame," I said.

Linda jerked, like she couldn't believe I'd listened. "You read good, don't you?"

It felt strange to admit I did anything well. But I did; I nodded.

"Thought so. I seen you, coming here. Carrying your books. And you looked, well, I could tell you weren't just coming because you're in Education or whatever. You looked like you liked it." For a moment, she looked pleased with herself, but as her eyes skirted up and down the shelves beside us, her pleasure faded. "I don't read good. Never did. I tried. Just never seemed to get nowhere. Last week, my son, I was trying to tell him how he had to behave at school, how it seemed stupid now but if he settled down and got on with his work, he'd be able to do clever things later, he'd be glad he tried, but he was like, Mum, you don't understand, my teachers have got it in for me, my English teacher especially, she kept me in for a whole lunch just because I said the book we're studying is stupid . . . I was like, Brandon, she's a teacher, she's not gonna be stupid. I asked him what the book was. He didn't want to tell me but I pushed him and I pushed him because these are the things you miss, you know? Little things. Like knowing what book they're doing. Maybe finding it at the bottom of their school bag, under an empty bag of Doritos. Eventually he said: *Of Mice and Men*. I said that sounded fun. Animals were good. He laughed this mean laugh that reminded me of his dad, who isn't a man I like to be reminded of, and so I lost it then, a screw came over and said the visit was over and my son said, good. I don't want to talk to my dumb mum any more, he said. Then he was gone. That was it. Family Day. The End."

My throat was lumpy by the end of her story; lumpy with how little she thought of herself, how hard she tried anyway, and with missing you.

"*Of Mice and Men*," I said. "You want to see if we can find it?"

Linda smiled.

"Let's get away from all these Dummies books. Come on."

Of Mice and Men was squashed at the bottom edge of Modern Literature. Its pages were curled at both ends and there were greasy thumbprints all over the cover, which showed two men, a short white one and a tall black one, squinting into the sun, a thick forest behind them.

"I remember this!" I said. "We did it for GCSE."

"Oh, GCSEs! Bet you did well in them, didn't you, with all your reading?"

My English teacher had said the same thing. She was young and her name was Miss Watson and I bet she smiled even in her sleep. She'd keep me behind after lessons and, in this Quiet Yet Serious voice, she'd say things like, "Is there anything you want to tell me? You're capable of so much more than this, I can tell. When you try, you do great work. But most of the time you don't. Impressing the boys may seem like the most important thing now, but it won't always." Her hope was so bright, it hurt my eyes to look at it directly, the way it hurts your eyes to look at the sun directly. And so I didn't tell her what had happened with Cal, and how I'd decided, since then, that caring was too dangerous; people would just take the people and the places that you cared about away from you. I didn't tell her that the future felt as unreal as the diagrams of the solar system we had to draw in Science. I couldn't explain why I couldn't give up impressing boys and being bad just as I was getting good at it. I just said rude things to her and stormed out and then bunked her lessons until, eventually, she gave up.

"No. That's why I've got to do them all over again, in here."

"Oh."

We both stared at our feet.

Then she said: "But at least you can read now."

"Yeah." I liked the lessons, too. It was better than school. People actually stared at the teacher's mouth and they listened. I didn't worry what the others thought of me; I just tried to listen and read and write down as much as I could. Sometimes, if I didn't think about what was outside the classroom, about the walls and the locks and the cameras and the screws, I'd forget where I was; it would seem like I was just living my life, going to college like I'd planned to.

"Do you think . . . "

"What?"

She shuffled backwards. "Doesn't matter."

"No, go on."

"Well, do you think you could read me a bit of this?" she asked my feet.

"Yeah!"

"Don't tell anyone, though. It's so I can show him that I'm not, you know . . . stupid."

"Course you're not."

"I probably am."

"You're not. Look. Let's start."

We sat down in the study area and I whispered the story into the air between us.

As I read, I remembered reading to Chantelle's kids. How they'd yell that they weren't tired, not one bit, but how, as soon as I got them under their Frozen or Action Man duvet covers, as soon as I filled up their room with my reading voice, they'd go still. The world of the story would squash between us, like a huge pillow. By the time I reached The End, they'd be asleep. I'd look at them for a few minutes before I slipped out of their beds and tucked them in and turned the lights out. When Chantelle came back, full of vodka and orange, and stories of how her date tried to take liberties, she'd never believe I'd got them to look at books. "Normally they fall asleep in front of the telly and I carry them to their room. And let's be honest; those kids' books are bor*ing*." I didn't tell her that they interested me. They made me think of my own mum, and how she'd read to me; I couldn't see any proper memories, but I felt them. I felt her voice reading to me as my own voice read to her kids. All I said was that I'd be happy to babysit, any time. "You don't have to," she said. "Oh, I know," I said. "But I want to. They're good kids." She sobered up at these words. "For real?" "For real." Then I'd tell her how Jayden had said a prayer for each spaghetti hoop before he ate it. Or how Sharina sang me what she called an "X Factor" but was just a song, then pretended to be a judge, and gave herself 125 out of 10. Chantelle would stay quiet while I told these stories and for a few seconds afterwards, too. Then she'd squeeze my shoulder and say thank you.

We only got a page or two in before the bell went and Library Hour was over. The chairs were hard and the library was freezing but every part of me was warm.

"Next week?" I said.

Linda nodded. There was colour in her cheeks, too.

"Thank you," we said, at the exact same time.

FLIRTING ON ORANGE WEDNESDAY

Y ou're smiling," was the first thing Erika said to me this
week.

"No I'm not," I said, but my lips kept jumping away
from my chin.

"Any particular reason?"

I told her about reading to Linda. "Before then, I felt like I
was the problem. But now, well, it's reminded me how good it
feels to help people."

Erika smiled extra-wide and I saw all her teeth and also the
spinach trapped in the narrow space between them, and I told
her so.

"Thanks," she said, digging it out with her nail. "The number of times I've looked in the mirror at the end of the day,
seen a huge herb, and thought, *Jesus*, I've been walking around
like that all day and no one dared tell me!"

"Would your husband tell you?"

"He wouldn't notice."

"What about your son with . . . "

"Autism?"

I nodded.

"It's O.K. You can say it. With him, it depends on the day.
But let's bring things back to *you*. What do you want to talk
about?"

"I want to talk about what we're already talking about."

She raised her eyebrow. *Don't switch back to teenage
Bethany*, is what this meant, so I tried not to.

"O.K.," said Erika. "Let's put it another way. What *don't* you want to talk about?"

I knew. I knew exactly what it was. "Him. Her dad. I wanted to write about him all week but I couldn't. I couldn't remember why I'd seen him as a good thing. I was so *dumb*." My hands jerked, wanting to punch my thighs, but I sat on them instead.

Erika grinned. There was still a shred of spinach trapped in her teeth but I didn't say anything. "You've been writing then?"

Sucking in my lips so I didn't smile, I nodded.

"Have you been surprised by how many good things you *did* find?"

Another nod.

"In that light, I think your past self deserves a little more respect, don't you?"

I hate to say it but she was right.

When Chantelle wasn't in, the rest of the Odeon staff would bitch about her: "Why can't she buy clothes that fit? I don't want to see her arse on a morning!" "How come she never gets on the toilet rota?" and "You noticed how she just ticks off that she's cleaned shit when she's spent two hours jiggling about to shitty music on her phone?" "She never shuts up!" "It's her kids I feel sorry for."

"You shut up," I'd tell whoever it was who said this, "or I'll be telling her. And she'll be firing your hairy arse before you know it. She's, like, the manager."

I meant it, too, because Chantelle filled my life with jiggling and teeth-kissing and buzz. The air always buzzed wherever she was and no matter how long I hung around her, trying to breathe it in, I could never get enough.

There was always some boyfriend or ex-boyfriend or sister's ex-boyfriend swaggering up to the Snack Station, to see her.

"Chantelle about?" they'd ask, and I'd try not to laugh at how scared they sounded, despite their hard man bulging muscles. I'd Walkie Talkie the Chuckle Sisters, who'd tell Chantelle, who'd either appear a few moments later, squash the guy in a bear hug, or would be "somewhere else" and, once the guy had slouched off, would come out of the cleaning cupboard or wherever she'd been hiding, and then she'd tell some long, twisting story about how that guy used to be safe but then that thing happened with his friend and her cousin and he took liberties and no way was she gonna let that go, although if the rumour was true that he was buying up some place in Marbella and would let his mates stay there for free, she might.

When someone—and it wasn't always a guy; often it was a friend or a cousin or an aunt—walked in and she wanted to talk to them, she would. If she was midway through serving a customer, she'd yell at me to take over, and I'd step right on to the spot she'd been standing and I'd smile like I was the luckiest Odeon Customer Services Assistant (CASUAL) in the world.

Even the Chuckle Sisters would bitch about this: "It's like, not fair?"

"Yeah, because that time I stopped serving popcorn to answer the phone and she had a massive go at me?"

"I *know*! It's like, she can just do what she likes. Because . . . I don't know why."

"Because she's *Chantelle*, dumbo," I'd say. Say what you want about her but she knew what came first: not taking popcorn orders and answering questions about seats and running times, but people. She had so many people, they were always wanting to talk and laugh and eat Maltesers with her, and watching them walk in and out of the Odeon, it was hard to remember they weren't my people; that her life wasn't my life.

Often, I'd follow her round Lidl at the end of the shift. "Oh my days, they don't have none of those potato smileys Sharina likes. They only got these ones, and she won't eat them, says they look like clowns! Guess we'll have to eat potato-shaped potatoes. Tssh." I'd grab things from the bottom shelves and when her trolley got too full, I'd carry stuff for her, like bog roll. Sometimes, I'd follow her all the way home, and whatever she was making for dinner, I'd eat it too.

"Is Beth our aunty?" Sharina asked one evening, after I'd persuaded her to eat her clown potato smileys by making the clowns "talk."

"Shut up," said Chantelle, grinning at me. "Course she is."

Jayden, her son, who reminded me he was seven and *three-quarters* every time he saw me, sat up straight and banged his fork on the table. "Can you tell that to Miss Campbell? Because, we had to do this thing where we said how many uncles and aunties we had, and when I said, she said I'd done it wrong, because Aunty Shazz ain't my aunty by blood, and neither is Aunty Felicia or Uncle Paul or BJ or Ahmed. She didn't get how there are two types of aunties and uncles—the blood ones and the, the other ones—the ones you see because they're fun . . . Like Beth!"

I liked watching the Chantelle show, but what I liked best were the moments, like when the kids were in bed and we were drinking white wine on the sofa, and she'd wrinkle her nose and look me up and down, like I'd just arrived in the room, and ask me a question, like, "Hey, where did you say you lived before this?"

"Somerset." The blood rushed to my cheeks.

"Somerset? Is that, like, west London?"

"Nah. Country."

"Oh. Country." She said this word carefully, as if it were foreign. "What'd you do down there anyways?"

"Just. School. And stuff."

"Why'd you leave?"

"This is where I'm from, in'it?"

"Oh yeah." Her eyes flickered and she opened her mouth, and my stomach clenched because I could tell she wanted to say something like, so where's your family? Where are your other friends? Thankfully, she swallowed, and then she moved back to the familiar topic of, "You got a man then?"

"I already told you no. Not interested."

"You like girls?"

"I don't like anyone. Not like *that*. Not after . . . "

"What?"

"Nothing." I put my ear to the wall. "Is that Sharina? She crying?"

Chantelle punched me on the leg. "Don't try distracting me."

"I'm not."

"You *are*. I clocked you. You had a man down there, in'it?"

I gulped. My time in Somerset churned through my body, like a big dinner I still hadn't digested. "Yeah."

"Spill."

I didn't want to but I did. And I'm glad, because, as Erika says, it's the things you don't want to talk about that you really should. His name was Dale. He clung to the edge of the group of boys in the year above who, for reasons I never 100% understood, the girl group I clung to the edge of had decided was cool. I first noticed him one Friday night at the park; the whites of his eyes shone at me through the dark. I was squashed at the end of the girls' bench; he was squashed at the end of the boys'. When he saw me looking back, he smiled. He was looking at me like I was important—more important than the popular girls, more important than our jumbo bottles of White Lightning, more important, even, than the stars, which were so big and twinkly compared to the permanently purple sky in London.

We didn't get around to talking to each other until our groups pushed us behind the bins so I could give him a blow job. He was going to give me 50p in return. I didn't want to do it but all the other girls and boys had so I thought I had to. When the others were out of sight, he didn't pull his trousers down; he just stared.

"What's wrong," I said. "You gay or something?"

He shook his head, then grabbed my hand and said, "I want to. I wanted to since I first saw you, like. But not like this. I wanna chat to you first."

The person I'd pretended to be crumpled. "Whatever."

"We could . . . hang out, like, another time? Without them?"

I said nothing until he suggested a place—the fields beyond B&Q at the bottom of town—and even then I did the world's smallest nod.

"Great," he said. Then he stood up. "Will you do me a favour? Can you tell them it was massive? Like, you couldn't fit it in your mouth?"

"O.K." He pressed a 50p into my hand. "Thanks."

* * *

That first "date," we walked and talked through the fields until our mouths ran out of words and our feet ran out of steps and our lips moved towards one another and there was nothing we could do about it. We lay down on some splintery old door and looked up at the sky and then we rolled on top of each other and kissed until our lips bled. We'd both kissed people before but not like this. Not like we might kiss our way to some other world. It was only when the rain slopped down our necks and our backs and into our pants, and we had to slosh our way back to town through the grass, ready to face the respective adults in our lives, that we remembered we were still in this one.

And that was it; we were hooked. Obsessed. Horny. In love.

Whatever. He'd get up extra early just so he could meet me at the end of my street and walk me to school. He'd hold my hand so tight that I could see the outline of his fingers on mine for the whole of my first lesson. This meant that I didn't do much work in my first lesson, or any lesson; at last, I wasn't at the edge, but at the centre; I didn't need good grades, or anything else.

The only problem was where to hang out: we couldn't go to his house—his dad and both brothers were "alcoholics who tried to hump anything that moved," or so he put it—and my foster parents had a strictly no-boyfriends rule. But it was O.K. because cross country had taught me the best routes up into the hills from school. As we climbed, Dale would sigh and moan, but when I told him to shush, it would be worth it, he would, and when we got to the top of the hills, when we found a good rock to sit on, when he saw all the fields stretch blue-green and misty across the Levels below, when he'd gasped his breath back into his lungs, he'd squeeze me tight and say, "You were right. It is worth it. And so are you." And I'd tell him he was worth it. No, no, not as much as you, he'd say, nuzzling his words into my neck. Then I'd nuzzle his neck and so we'd go on, not caring if we were being gross or cheesy because we were a long way from other humans, and as for the grass and the sky and the irrigation ditches and the cows and even the stinging nettles, they don't judge.

I'd have been happy to hang with Dale and no one else, but he wouldn't let go of his boy group. Our first proper argument happened when it was raining; I wanted to hang out in this barn we'd found, but he said it was too cold, too damp, and anyway, a "thing" was happening at Tom's house. Tom was the most popular member of the boy group he was almost-but-not-quite part of.

"Why?" I said. "Tom and that lot don't even care about you. They use you and then they dump you. Let's go somewhere we can snuggle just us." I slipped my hand under his shirt but he threw me off.

"I'm going. You can come with or you can go somewhere else. It's up to you."

"Great. So you don't even care about me." I made a sad face and slouched off.

"Beth!" As I predicted, he came after me. He slipped his hand in mine. His face softened. "Course I care about you. But it's fucking freezing. And I miss hanging out with the guys. Besides," he gave my almost-boob an almost-squeeze, "Tom's house is massive and his parents are never in. There are, you know, rooms we could go."

So we went to Tom's house. It was big and cluttered and the walls were either dark brown or green or a puke-coloured yellow, and if you moved anything, a spider or a beetle would be guaranteed to scuttle out from underneath.

"This isn't no house for girls," he said, when he saw me, so I stuck my chest out and told him I wasn't a girl, I was a woman. He laughed. Then he handed me a spliff. Pretty soon, we were sitting on these saggy old beanbags, bodies buzzing with smoke, and I didn't have to worry whether Dale liked me a little less than before, I didn't have to worry what my foster parents would say when I got home, or where my mum was, or whether I'd see her again, or whether I'd win my next cross country race, or how difficult I now found even English, it had been so long since I paid attention; not one little worry could get through the buzz.

We hung at Tom's more and more after that. There'd always be smokes, often drink, and sometimes Tom would hand me baggies of weed and tell me to hand it to so-and-so at the end of the street. Other times, he'd get me weighing and bagging it up while the guys killed zombies on the PlayStation. At first, I was happy to be needed. Then, I started to get bored. Why was I always the one to do the bagging, not them? Was I their slave? Was I invisible? I'd pretend to be more fucked than I was and I'd stand up and start dancing around or say I was hot and unbutton my shirt. At last, their eyes would move from the PlayStation zombies to me. They'd laugh and cheer me on, and Dale's eyes would narrow, and he'd tell the others to stop perving on me, and then he'd take me upstairs.

Upstairs, we'd kiss and wriggle and rub against each other. We'd lie under the duvet and wrestle each other's clothes off. Then one day he said, do you want to do it, and even though I was happy just wriggling, I said yes. And so he pushed it into me. It hurt. It really, really hurt. Afterwards, I didn't feel like a new or bigger or more grown-up person; I just felt empty and sore. It wasn't so bad the second time. After that, there were times when it wasn't bad at all; the only problem was that often, just as I was feeling all tingly and good, he'd press his hand against my throat or jerk me into a new position, or he'd come. Other times, we'd be drunk, and we'd knock against each other and whether it was good or bad I never knew because my body felt fuzzy and far away. When it was over, we'd lie in a sweaty pile, and he'd kiss me and say he loved me. I love you, too, I'd whisper. For about two minutes, it would feel just like before. Like how you were meant to feel when you were in love. But when I went back downstairs and squeezed on to the sofa next to him and the other boys, I'd feel so invisible, that if there hadn't been a spliff going round, I'd have cried.

Those minutes after we fucked—they were enough for me to cling to when grown-ups started to worry. When social workers and teachers and my foster mum and dad were constantly wrinkling their foreheads at me and saying things like: *You're a bright girl, Beth. You've got real talent but you won't get to use it if you don't apply yourself. What are you even getting out of the way you spend your time now, anyway? Why don't you apologize to the P.E. coach and see if they'll have you back on the cross country team?* I tried and tried to find the

Beth who could nod and say yes, she was sorry. Yes, she'd made a mistake. Yes, she was upset. And she cared. I looked all over my school and Tom's house and Dale's body and my body and my foster family's house. I looked up the hills and down on the Levels. But that Beth was gone. Lost.

The few times I did try to do school work, the words jumped about on the page; I hadn't paid attention last week or the week before or for months before that, and the questions, the books, the answers, they were too difficult, too far away. Easier was to go to Tom's. To wait until Dale led me upstairs. When Tom said, could I do him a favour, he'd pay me for it, I said yes. Then he'd put some weed in my hand, tell me to stuff it down my bra, then he'd tell me which address to take it to. When I got back, I'd get a share of the money. It was usually a quid or two per trip but it was more than I'd had before, which was nothing. Plus, I liked walking. It wasn't as good as running, but it was good to move.

Tom's got raided about two months before I was due to take my GCSEs. When I got back from my walk, there were police vans in the front garden. Tom, Dale and the others got Community Service. I got a caution, which I didn't care about, because Dale ended it with me. He didn't even do it to my face; he did it in a text. I DON'T LOVE YOU. YOU ARE ANNOYING. DON'T COME NEAR ME AGAIN. I GOT TO SORT MY LIFE OUT AND YOU CAN'T BE IN IT. SORRY.

Looking back, I can see how hard my foster parents tried. Hear their soft-soft voices asking were there any other revision books I needed and would I like something special to eat while I was revising? I can see the hurt in their eyes as I pushed their snacks away, shrugged my shoulders and mumbled that I wanted nothing.

What I couldn't explain to my foster parents or my teachers, what I started to realize as I told this story to Chantelle and am realizing more right now, is that the inside of me was already messing up. My body was too heavy to move, my mind too jumpy to sleep. Food felt 100% wrong. When I opened a book, it was like I'd forgotten how to read; like my brain had forgotten how to do life. All I could do was sit or lie or shuffle here and there. They thought I was being moody and bad but I wasn't; I was depressed. That's what it was.

Chantelle was silent for an unusually long time when I finished this story. Then she kicked out her legs, balanced her feet on that huge cuddly duck Sharina won at some fair and said, "Shit, girl. That's tough."

That's tough. Those two little words made me feel a lot better. Like maybe it wasn't all my fault that I'd failed my GCSEs, then had to spend the time I could've been doing A-levels retaking them. That maybe, given everything that had happened in my life, I wasn't doing too bad.

"But don't let that dickhead ruin love for you," Chantelle said, as I finally put on my shoes and my coat to leave. "There are plenty of other dickheads in the world, but plenty more who aren't. There are some that are even safe. At least, I hope so, I've got to, otherwise, like, what's the point?"

We shared one last squeezy hug before I left.

Telling Chantelle about Dale had reminded me that the end wasn't the whole story; there was a beginning and a middle and a lot of it was good. Suddenly, there were couples everywhere. On the bus, on the street, at the bank, at the cashpoint, in the newsagent's. Orange Wednesday was the worst. They'd be feeding each other popcorn before they'd even paid. It was the worst. When Chantelle left me to do it by myself so she could go eat Nando's with some guy she'd met at her sister's birthday, it was hard for me to smile and nod like she expected me to.

"What's up with you?"

"Nothing."

"What's up? Come on. Tell me. Tell Aunty Chantelle."

"*Nothing!*"

"Whatever." She kissed her teeth at me. "You best not have that attitude when I get back, or just you watch."

Then she swaggered out to eat Nando's in her tightest newspaper print leggings. Loads of people were off sick and it was the first time I'd done the tills alone; the queue soon stretched right back to the doors, and the faster I tried to put in people's codes, the more I messed up. Almost every person who came to the till gave me the evils for making them wait so long. All I wanted was to get down on the Fanta-soaked floor and curl in a ball until everyone got that I couldn't handle Orange Wednesdays; I couldn't handle anything; I couldn't handle grown-up life. *Maybe Dale was the only one for you after all. Maybe the social worker and the police and your foster parents and even those bitches at school who came and tried to warn you in the toilets—maybe they were all wrong.*

Somehow, I kept punching tickets, and just when every couple and group of friends and couple of couples had disappeared into a screen, this guy glided up to the counter. I'd never seen anyone glide before, and I'd never seen anyone like him in the Odeon; wavy brown hair without an ounce of gel in sight, suit and waistcoat, and he made eye contact right away, smiling at me as if, already, we were in on some secret.

"I've got an Orange Wednesday," he said, flashing an iPhone with a picture of a woman and boy with matching round chocolate-smeared cheeks on its screensaver, "but there's not much point, is there, seeing as I'm by myself?" He laughed too loudly.

I didn't find what he'd said even 1% funny but he was the first person who'd said something other than "This is my code" or "You best not give me a bashed-up Magnum" all night, so I laughed too.

"Oh God," he said. "That was more tragic than comic, wasn't it?" He rubbed his eyes. "I always miss the mark. But thanks for laughing anyway."

I'd made him happy. And that made me feel like maybe I *could* do life, and Orange Wednesday, after all.

I leaned across the counter and whispered, "I can put it in for you half price."

I'd watched Chantelle give her friends and her friends "special promotions" enough times to know how.

"Oh, that's really nice, do you know that? Nice things like that never happen these days."

Again, with the too-loud laughter, but I didn't mind; it was like getting high; it blocked everything else out.

"*These days?* Who am I?" he said. "I sound ancient."

I liked how he was wrapped up in this constant battle with himself—just like me. The difference between us was, he wasn't scared to admit it. He could make it funny. Sexy, even.

"Yeah," I said. "That *was* kind of a granddaddy thing to say."

"Granddaddy! Jesus," he said. "I'm only twenty-nine."

I didn't know what to say to that, so I slid his tickets across the counter.

"Next."

A grumpy-faced couple bustled towards me and I tried to concentrate on them, I really did. Except my eye wandered over to Screen One, where the funny-not-funny man who'd turn out to be your dad was looking at me as if I was the most special thing he'd ever seen. Then he disappeared into the dark and I smiled into the couple's grumpy faces; at last, I dared hope that the next thing that happened to me would be good.

8.
FALLING ASLEEP WITH YOUR LEGS TANGLED UP
IN SOMEONE ELSE'S

W hen your dad turned up the following Wednesday,
it was impossible not to smile.

"So." He grinned. "I do have a code but, erm, I
thought you could put through that deal you did last week,
remember?"

He was earlier this time, and the women behind him were
shifting from foot to foot and sighing. Plus, this blabbermouth
spotty sixth-form student, Tom or Josh, he was on the next till,
and I could already feel his ears twitch in my direction. That
bad, bitchy voice, the one that told me there was no point, rose
up from wherever it had been hiding and hissed: *Don't start
thinking you'll get with someone like him. He's clearly used to
getting whatever he wants. Why not give him his first taste of
disappointment?*

"Sorry," I said, "I don't know what you're talking about. I
can give you an Orange Wednesday but that's it."

"But—"

"Orange Wednesday or not? It's the same price either way
but you better decide. People are waiting."

Tom or Josh's eyes were all over me—he'd tell Chantelle I'd
been rude—but I didn't care. When your dad mumbled he'd
go for a normal and then I gave it to him and he finally shuffled off, I felt, for the first time in ages, like things weren't just
happening to me; I was making them happen.

Orange Wednesday came and went and, at last, I was
rushing to the bus stop, stomach rumbling, already looking

forward to the beans on toast I'd microwave when I got home, when a voice called: "Hey, Miss Wednesday!"

There he was, slouching on the Holiday Inn steps, fag in hand, shirt sleeves rolled up to reveal two sturdy forearms. He kept twitching, like he couldn't get comfy inside the role of bad boy. The streetlights caught on his chin and his cheekbones in a way that made me want to stare and stare at them.

Just keep walking.

But I'm curious.

Think of your bed.

It's cold and boring.

Do you really want a repeat of Dale?

He's. Not. Dale.

And so I stopped.

"Hope I didn't get you in trouble," he said.

"Nah, don't worry about it. Good film?"

He frowned. "Yes. I mean no."

"I've seen the first half four times and it made me laugh but not in the way you're meant to laugh," I said. It wasn't until my words were mingling with the smoke between us that I realized how hungry I'd been to say them—and how many more words were trapped inside of me, hungry to be heard.

"God," he said, "that must be annoying. In my job, *I'm* the one I have to bore. The same presentation, over and over again. Most clients hide their boredom well but occasionally they'll let out a yawn, and it takes everything I've got not to join them."

"Maybe you should. Maybe you should just be like, fuck it."

"All right then," he said. "If you say so, Miss Wednesday. Fuck it!" Then he threw his butt on the pavement between us and squished it flat.

I tut-tutted and put on my best mean-policeman-or-parking-warden voice: "I'm afraid I'm going to have to give you a £50 fine for that, Mister. You can't just go around doing whatever you please, Mister. It's time the likes of you learned your lessons."

He laughed and laughed. "Jesus, you're spectacularly terrifying, Miss Wednesday."

We were closer now, our toes either side of the butt. He smelled of those Christmas-tree-shaped air-fresheners that always dangle in minicab windscreens.

He grinned. "What can I do to stop you dobbing me in?"

"Well . . . " *Don't say it don't say it don't say it. He can't possibly like you, a guy like this—not a boy like Dale, a real man.*

"Would a drink do?" He nodded towards the Holiday Inn lobby. "It's not the most *happening* bar in the world, but it's fairly well stocked."

I sighed dramatically. "I guess."

The Holiday Inn bar was empty apart from one or two Humpty-Dumpty-like businessmen hunched over a beer and an iPad.

"That," your dad whispered, as he led me into a fake-leather booth, "is how I'm determined *not* to end up."

"What," I said, "like Humpty Dumpty?"

He laughed. "Exactly. Now, what *tipples* your fancy, Miss Wednesday?"

"Nipple? Did you say nipple?"

He flushed. "Certainly not! What do you think I am?" He scanned the drinks menu. "How about Sauvignon?"

I didn't know what that was but I said, sure. A mini chandelier dangled over our booth, and although a few of its bulbs were blown, I liked it; it made me feel like I was somewhere far from Streatham and a lot more exciting, like New York or Tokyo.

His hand shook as he poured the wine. It was a nice hand; big but delicate, smooth-seeming skin. Shaking or not-shaking, it was beautiful.

"Cheers." We clinked our glasses.

"I hope it's not too dry."

The only thing I know about wine is that I hate it, but I swallowed half that glass in one. He took neat little sips but somehow managed to get through his just as quick.

"You haven't got Parkinson's, have you?" I blurted. I'd only eaten a slice of toast and half a pack of Maltesers all day; I was already pissed. "Not being rude or anything," I added. "It's just, you've got the shakes."

"Oh," he snuck his hands under the table, "that happens when I'm nervous."

"Does it?" I stretched my legs under the table until my toes hit his shins, which were radiator-hot. "And why would you be nervous now?"

He downed the last of his glass and poured himself another, topping up mine while he was at it. "To be honest, I've never done anything like this."

"What? Had a drink? You a Jehovah's Witness or something?"

He laughed. "You know what I mean . . . "

"Really," I said, kicking off my ballet pumps and wrapping my feet right around his calves. "I don't."

"You really want me to spell it out?"

I nodded. "Spelling's not my strong point."

The rest of his wine disappeared into his mouth. "Right. Here goes. I'm married with a kid. I'm only here three nights a week for work. But then I met you. I . . . " His fingers fluttered about in the air. "I couldn't stop thinking about you. And now, now . . . I really, really want to take you up to my room."

I downed my wine to stop me saying anything.

"Not the smoothest way of going about it, I know, but then, I was never smooth."

"Don't worry," I said, "I prefer crunchy."

"Excellent," he said. "Me, too."

Your dad's room at the Holiday Inn is one of the places I've felt the safest—not because he scattered pants and tissues and receipts and ties and other pieces of his life over its beige-and-brown-and-beige-again surfaces, but because we were in it and somewhere between us and its walls was love and lots of it. Not that this made things easy; love never makes things easy. What it makes them is shiny and if you're not careful, they shine so bright, you stop seeing the thing beneath the shine.

"This is the TV," he said, buzzing open the flap to reveal the TV. "And in here," he opened the wardrobe where three identical white shirts lurked on the locked-to-the-railing hangers, "is the kettle. You know, if you want a cup of something." He pointed to the bedside table and told me it was the bedside table. "And this," he said, his cheeks blushing as if, just beneath his skin, a bottle of ketchup was exploding, "is the bed."

"Yeah," I said, "I wondered what that big squishy thing was. And *that*," I pointed at the glimmering white toilet bowl, "I've been wondering what to call that all my life."

"Oh God." He combed his fingers through his hair. Then he laughed—just a few tuts at first, as if he didn't mean it, but pretty soon his whole body was shaking, there were tears spurting out of his eyes, he flopped on to the bed and I flopped down beside him and then I rolled into the dip where his still-shaking body was.

"Are you all right?"

He stopped shaking. "I'm not . . . dead." A bit more laughter, and then he rolled on to his side, propping his head up on his elbow, and said, "I'm sure of that. For the first time in a long time, I'm sure I'm alive."

"Do you ever have days," I said, reaching across the sheets and stroking his hair, which was soft, like a rabbit or a cat. "When you're not sure?"

"Oh yes." He stroked my hair in return. "You wake up feeling like there's a person—a heavy person, who you don't love or even know—lying on top of you."

I knew what he was talking about. I knew exactly. "And it makes you feel like, what's the point?"

"Yes."

"And, is this it?"

"Yes!" he said, then wrinkled his forehead and added: "But you're so young. Surely you can't feel like that already?"

I wanted to tell him. I wanted to tell him everything. Even the things I'd never told myself. But when I opened my mouth, the wrong words came out: "I'm not the one hiding away in a Holiday Inn."

He raised his eyebrows. "True."

"And you're too young for a mid-life crisis. Even if you have got a wife and shit."

He went red. "Maybe it's a quarter-life crisis. That's a *thing* now, apparently."

I stared at him. He stared at me. Then he grabbed me round the waist and climbed on top of me, but carefully, propping himself up on his forearms so he didn't squash me.

He kissed me on the lips. "You're so beautiful," he said, between kisses. "So tiny and cute."

I wasn't sure I wanted to be tiny and cute but I did want to be beautiful. And I liked the way he breathed all three words on to me like they were good things. What I loved was the way he didn't just kiss me on the lips, not like Dale; he kissed parts of me that had never been kissed before, like my neck and my shoulders and my thighs. He kissed parts of me I never usually thought about, like the strip of skin between my collarbones, and my knees. He let me kiss him everywhere, too; let me play with his hair, kiss the soft strip of skin behind his ears, rest my cheek against his bicep, the smooth, muscled slopes of his back, and what he referred to as his "four-pack."

When it was over, he didn't fall asleep or go straight to playing zombies, not like Dale. He smiled at my body. "You are unbelievably hot, do you know that?"

"I'm not." I was used to ignoring my body as much as possible. It seemed like a whiny, annoying thing. I'd never thought of it as beautiful. But the way your dad cupped my bum and my boobs, said it didn't matter that they weren't bigger, they were perfect just the way they were, it made me wonder whether my body could be a good thing, too.

"I'm peckish," he said. "How about you?"

"I don't know."

He laughed. "How can you not know?"

"When I get hungry, there's often not food around. So I just ignore it until it goes."

He shook his head. "Let's get some room service, then."

I started to shiver so he let me wear his jumper. It came down to my knees and I had to roll up the sleeves about ten times before I found my hands.

"Cute!" he said.

Room service turned out to be paninis, chips and onion rings on a plastic trolley. I crammed one chip in my mouth. Then another. And another. The chips were like a massive alarm clock going off in my stomach: WAKE UP, WAKE UP! Before I knew it, I'd scoffed most of the chips and a whole panini.

Your dad picked at an onion ring, watching. "That's quite a performance, for someone who's not hungry!"

"I guess I was," I said. "I just didn't realize it."

At Tom's there would often be takeaway but the boys would scoff most of it before I got a look-in.

"Well, you eat," he said, kissing my forehead. "You eat as much as you want."

I don't know why, but as I watched him watching me eat, I realized: I didn't know what his name was. He didn't know mine. I started to laugh.

"What? Let me in on the joke, Miss Wednesday."

"We . . . " I told him.

"Oh." Disappointment sucked some of the sparkle from his eyes, and I got why; it had been great, acting like we could be whatever kind of humans or animals we wanted.

"My name's Beth," I said. "Although you can keep calling me Miss Wednesday if you want."

He smiled. "Mine's Phil."

We fell asleep with our arms and legs tangled. We'd only been together for one night but I could feel our insides getting tangled, too.

9.
When you're so happy it hurts

S poke to my son yesterday." Lanky Linda smiled into her pie and mash. "Told him I was reading *Of Mice and Men*."

"Oh?"

She shoved her plate to one side and leaned towards me. "He didn't believe me. But when I started telling him all about it, how it was about two guys who you wouldn't expect to be friends but who were, and how they cared for each other even though they didn't have anything else, they were living in some barn on some farm in some woods, he got interested. At first, he was saying 'It's gay' and 'I hate it,' but then he admitted it was good to start off with but it ended shit because no one got what they wanted and good people did bad things."

The Lee and a few of the others looked our way. "What you two whispering about?"

"Nothing," I said.

"Don't look like nothing," said the Lee.

My stomach clenched and I remembered; I wasn't at home. Everywhere, there were rules. Rules for what to do and how and when. Rules that got shouted at you five times a day. Rules, like the "don't have private conversations at dinner" rule, that crouched in the silences, then, just as you were starting to feel relaxed, they pounced.

"She's telling me about her son," I said.

"She speaks!" someone yelled.

"Oh, her *son*." The Lee leant across the table and forked

some mash off Linda's plate and into her mouth. "Better you than me."

When they'd stopped staring, Linda whispered, "You do better to keep quiet. There was this woman last year and she got it bad because she kept going on about how it wasn't—"

"So what happened with your son?" I said.

Linda shrugged. "Oh, you know. I said the book was still good even if it ended bad, he said I was dumb, I hadn't even got to the end yet so how could I talk, blah blah, it was almost like we were at home, arguing on the settee, when that was it. Ten minutes up." She nibbled at her mash. "Even so, it was better than usual. Much better. So, thanks."

The next time we were in the library, she stopped me after a few pages.

"We've still got forty minutes," I said.

"But this is a good bit. They're dreaming about their farm and stuff. I know it ends sad, but it would be nice to spend this week imagining they'll have it."

I've been reading that book ever since. Reading it alone, in my cell, in my head, isn't so good as reading it out loud to Lanky Linda. But it's still good. I won't ruin the story for you in case you read it; I'll just say that it made me cry. A lot. I didn't just cry because I was sad, though; I cried because I was happy. Because the story wasn't about whether you get what you want or you don't. It was about caring for people even though they're not perfect. It was about daring to dream even when you're in a place where dreams aren't meant to reach—*especially* in those places.

Those first months with your dad made me so happy it hurt. We ate and fucked and laughed and talked and slept with tangled limbs two or three nights a week. We talked in silly voices. We talked in serious voices. I don't know what we talked about but we'd talk until the sun was nudging at the edges of the Holiday Inn curtains and we couldn't talk any more.

He'd text me once or twice a day. He'd text stuff like: I'M MEANT TO BE WATCHING A POWERPOINT BUT ALL I CAN SEE ARE YOUR TITS. Or: YOU ARE THE JAMMIEST GEM OF SOUTH LONDON. Or: DOES ODEON RUN A SEXIEST EMPLOYEE OF THE MONTH AWARD?? Or even: YOU MAKE ME FEEL LIKE I COULD DO ANYTHING.

In the hours between his texts, images of him would float through my head and a stupid grin would spread across my face. At first, Chantelle would hassle me for the details— "Which position did you do first?" "How long did he take to come?" "Did he ask you to do anything kinky?"—but after a few weeks, her eyes would glaze and she'd interrupt me by shoving her phone in my face and insisting I looked at her mate's Facebook post about her new Armani handbag, "Because she reckons she's all that but she ain't. I hate it when people act like they're all that when they ain't." Or if she saw me grinning for no reason, she'd say very loudly to the Chuckle Sisters: "Jesus, Beth's thinking about *him* again." She'd laugh, though, so I knew she didn't mind really; she thought it was funny.

I didn't even mind when she got rude. I didn't mind the Chuckle Sisters ambushing me in the toilets with dumb questions like: "But is it real love?" "How do you know it's real?" "Does he ever read you poetry?" Didn't mind when the bus was late because some dickhead was shouting at the driver about how his travel card from two weeks ago was really valid for today; I'd just stare out of the window at all the people walking, limping, running, cycling, slouching, skateboarding into their days, and think how amazing it was that each and every one of them had as many things going on under their skins as me. And when some old geezer with hairs busting out of his ears and his nostrils marched up to the Snack Station and went off on one about the online booking fee and how *extortionate* it was and how also, while he was at it, the pop-corn prices were a *disgrace*, I just smiled and said: "You're right."

I got why people had stayed away from me when things were bad; I didn't mind that, either. Humans have a sixth sense, and it's not for ghosts or any of that goth stuff, it's for happiness. When you're sad, bad, mad, etc., people feel it and it repels them. When you're happy, it's a different story. People's eyes linger on you a moment longer and you, because you feel good, you smile at them, and they open their eyes wide and then, if you're lucky, they smile back. They see you and they ask for directions. Ask you to help carry their bag. Ask if they can use your phone to make a call, they're terribly sorry but their battery has died and they hadn't noticed until now that there weren't working pay phones any more? They just sense that there's more love inside of you than you know what to do with.

"You're looking healthy!" Marcia said, when we met up for our next check-in.

"I am," I said. We were back in the Polish deli. Before, their bagel filled me up for the rest of the day. This time, however, I scoffed it so quickly that Marcia asked if I was still hungry. Yes, I said, I was. Did I want a cream cake as well? Yes, I did. Yes, yes, yes. I'd never said yes so many times in a row before. It felt good. I didn't even care that my clothes were getting tight; I had more energy, I was sleeping better, and when I looked in the mirror, I saw less bone, less shadow, more colour, more curves: a proper shape. "I feel happy. I never thought I'd have so much in my life."

But there was one more thing I wanted and she was the person who might help me to get it. Phil had told me a lot about his time at Uni; how he'd had time to think and to read and to party. How he'd organized marches and reviewed films and interviewed politicians for student newspapers. How, even if he was now doing a job he claimed to find "mind-numbingly" bor-ing—I was never sure exactly what it was; something to do with business and spreadsheets and numbers—at least he'd had three years of freedom and fun. How, when I told him how I'd messed up at school, he said it was a shame. "If you went back now," he said, "you'd appreciate it way more than most people."

I asked him to show me some of his Uni books, and he did; we stayed up all night reading and talking about them. They were about big and difficult questions like, What is Reality? And, What are the Proofs of Freedom? They made my head spin in a good way. "It's lovely," he said, "to discuss ideas again. These days, Jenny wouldn't know a good idea if it hit her over the head." When he was asleep, I picked up one of the books and turned to the front page. Jenny's name was written into the front cover. I picked up another book. Her name was in that one, too. Her name was in all the books. I put them straight back in your dad's suitcase and lay facing away from them but it was no use; the letters of her name whirled around my head, wedging themselves between me and sleep.

I was about to ask Marcia how to do it, how I could get to Uni, when she brushed some crumbs off the table and said, "Beth, there's something I need to tell you."

"What?"

"I'm retiring."

I waited.

I breathed.

I totted up all the good things in my life: Chantelle and her kids and her laughs and her too-tight hugs; the Chuckle Sisters, and how easy it was to impress them; scoffing popcorn when it was still hot from the machine; watching the sun set from the top of the hill in the park; Phil; Phil and the way he looked at me and the way he touched me and the way we could talk with our mouths and with our bodies without our brains having to do anything; the way I felt when I looked at his body;

and how a part of him stayed with me even when, from the outside, we were apart.

"It's bad timing," she said. "I'd have liked to continue building a relationship with you but the time's come. My mum's in Jamaica and she's not getting any younger—it's a miracle she's still here at all—and it's about time I spent some proper time with her. But don't worry, you'll be getting a new adviser. It will be someone nice, I promise."

"I don't mind. Have a nice time with your mum."

"You don't want to get in touch with yours? You could, you know," she said.

I didn't want to think about that part of my life; it didn't seem to matter any more.

"I'll be all right, thanks," I said. "But really, Marcia, I'm happy for you."

She frowned at me. "You're a funny thing, you are."

* * *

Marcia leaving did change things. Although I hadn't seen her often, knowing she was there, knowing that when I did see her, she'd be pleased to see me—I didn't know how much it mattered until she was gone.

"What's up with you?" your dad asked, the next time I was in his room.

"Nothing." He wouldn't get it about Marcia. "Hey, you got those Uni books again?"

"What?" he asked my boobs. "Nah. Didn't want to risk Jenny noticing they're gone."

I rolled over so my boobs were out of view. "I wanna go to Uni."

"Uni?" Now, he was talking to my bum.

"Yeah. I been thinking about it. The Odeon's fun for now but I don't wanna be there for ever. At first, it was satisfying to learn how to work the till and to work it good, but now it's just boring. It would be good to do something more clever and—"

I was trying to figure out how to tell him that earning £7 an hour was the opposite of fun. That having to smile all day at people, some of whom were rude, others of whom were nice, most of whom just looked through you as if you were a human-shaped machine, emptied the "you" out of you. That having £2 left over when you've paid your bills and bought your food and the odd drink in Wetherspoon's doesn't bring much relief, because what about next month? What if you get less shifts next month? What if you lose your Oyster Card? What if someone jacks your purse with your last £20? What if one of the soles of the shoes you've been walking around for months with holes in finally falls off? What then?

But he went off on one about how shit his job was: "You wouldn't believe the amount of bullshit you have to do in so-called 'clever' jobs. Take my job—everyone has a 2.1. We've got Philosophy, History, Medieval English, Physics grads, but do any of them use what they've learned? Oh no. It's just like you said with the Odeon: you learn what to do and then you do it and then it's piss-boring. That's why so many of us get into cars and coke and fancy holidays and stuff. Well, the ones who weren't stupid enough to have kids in their twenties, dear God, and of course, because Jenny's the female and a teacher, I'm the one paying most of the mortgage, and sometimes I want to stand up in the office and scream, knowing I'll be trapped there for twenty, thirty, forever years . . . "

I looked around the room. iPod, iPad, laptop, fancy head-phones, fancy leather shoes, fancy trainers, fancy shirt and suit jacket and coat. Then there was his wallet and the way he'd fling cards and notes out of it at any opportunity, as if it would magically fill itself up.

"Yeah, but you don't have to worry about money," I said, when he finally stopped talking.

"I wish. Like I said, with the mortgage, and now Hamish and the frankly ridiculous nursery fees . . . Oh God, has it come to that already? I'm moaning about nursery fees? Dear, dear, dear . . . " He nuzzled my back, which I usually loved, but not then. I wriggled to the edge of the bed and pulled the duvet between me and him.

"Oh, Beth, what's wrong?"

"I want to go to Uni. And you don't think I should. You don't think I'm . . . smart enough."

"Oh, don't be silly," he said. "Of course you are. It's just, I'd have no idea how you'd go about it, to be honest; I suppose you'd have to do some A-levels? Everyone I know went straight from school. Now," he rolled me over and grabbed my boobs, "let's see if we can cheer you up."

I moved in the way he expected me to move. Made the faces he expected me to make. But inside there was a little voice say-ing: *So he only likes ideas when they come after a fuck? Is that how it is? You've got to do things when he wants?*

"*So*," Chantelle said, one deader-than-dead Odeon after-noon, "when we gonna meet the famous Phil?"

"He's famous?" squealed Nicole. "You didn't say he was *famous*."

"What for?" said Lisa. "I bet he was on *The Apprentice*!"

"Retards," said Chantelle. "Go and clean Screen 4."

"But—"

"Go. Now. Before I put you on earlies for the rest of the week."

The Chuckle Sisters sulked off.

Chantelle said nothing. I noticed all the noises her voice usually blocked out, like the swoosh of the Slush Puppies and the buzz of the traffic outside. "So," I said, just to break it, "how're things going with . . . with . . . ' But so many things were going on in my life, I'd stopped remembering the details of hers. "That guy you went to Nando's with?"

"Oh, nothing."

More silence.

"You want me to clean the Coke machine?" I pointed at the layer of brown goo under the tap. "It's kind of mank."

"You a retard or what?" She waved her clipboard in my face. "I'm the deputy manager, remember? It's my job to check whether you've cleaned it or not, and"—she ticked a column on the paper that was clipped to the board—"it looks like you have."

I hoped she'd be revved back up to normal, but, after one more painful silence, she looked out of the window and said: "The kids miss you. Jayden's all like, when we gonna see Aunty Beth?"

For the first time since we'd met, she looked sad. "I told them Aunty Beth's got a new lover boy, didn't I? They laughed and then they said well why can't he be our uncle? Why can't he come for clown potato smileys, too? I didn't know how to tell them he weren't that kind of uncle."

There are no words for how bad I felt then. I wasn't just tangled up with your dad; I was tangled with Chantelle and her kids, only I'd forgotten, and now the strings that joined us were so stretched out, they were about to snap.

"He *might* come round."

"Hah! Where do you guys even hang, anyway?"

"Just . . . around." We always stayed at the Holiday Inn but I didn't want her to know that. "But you know what, I'll ask him. I'll ask him if he'll come."

She raised an eyebrow. "Whatever."

"We see each other Mondays and Tuesdays now."

She shook her head. "Can't go out on a Monday—it's, like, illegal. Monday their Aunt Tracie comes round. I don't like the woman but I can't stop her. Tuesday they're at their dad's."

"But . . . "

"So he only loves you on a Monday and Tuesday, this Phil?"

"No!"

"Beth," she shook her head. "You got to sort this shit out. I seen it happen enough times before and it's not good. Trust." I waited for her to say what it was that happened. And how. And how I could do it different. But she walked off.

The next time I saw your dad, his hotel room seemed stupidly small.

"Let's go out?" I suggested.

"Out?" He pinched my waist in the exact spot he knew would make me yelp. "What, outside, in that horrible world? A world I'll be forced to *share* you with?"

"Yeah," I said, wriggling away from him. "There's something I've been meaning to tell you for weeks."

"Oh God." He sat up. "What is it?"

I put on my best serious face. "I'm sick of these room service paninis."

He stared at the duvet for a minute. "Fair enough."

"Where shall we go then?"

"I don't really know Streatham."

"Let's just walk down the street and see what we find."

He didn't move.

"What?"

"Nothing."

But there was. There was something between us now, and it followed us to Julio's Trattoria and stopped me from feeling like I was in one of the couples I used to stare at when I walked past, wondering how they stayed that happy.

Want to come to dinner at my friend's house? Meet her kids? The words slipped between bites of garlic bread and olive oil and fresh, sloppy pizza, and wine. They wouldn't come out, though. Phil kept twitching and looking about, and when I asked what was the matter, he'd say it was nothing, or that he thought he'd seen someone he knew. By the time we'd finished a bottle of wine and were picking at some chocolatey dessert, the bad thing was gone; we were back to silly voices, playing footsie under the table, and so I swallowed the words back down to the place where I could forget them, and as he leaned across the table to kiss me on the nose, I thought: *this is enough.*

But it wasn't. It wasn't long before I stopped being able to pretend it was.

I didn't know how to continue this story for a long time after this.

"Basically," I said to Erika, "I got greedy. If I could've stayed satisfied with what we had, I'd still have it. Instead—" I stopped talking and started to punch myself.

"Beth." She raised her eyebrows. "Come on now. You've been doing so well."

"Have I?"

Her eyebrows relaxed. "You have indeed."

"Right. Thanks."

She smiled and I suddenly noticed that I'd stopped noticing her geekster glasses; I could see her whole face; it was almost beautiful.

"What was going through your mind when you punched yourself?"

"Nothing. That's the problem."

"What about just before?"

"I couldn't stop thinking, what if I'd stopped myself from wanting things? What if I'd just been satisfied? Then I wouldn't have lost it. I wouldn't have lost all that happiness."

"Oh, Beth." She sighed. "What did we say about *what ifs*?"

"They're bad."

"Yes, and don't you think you're being a bit hard on yourself?"

I looked right into her eyes. "I was an attention-seeking bitch."

"Look, there isn't a human in the world who doesn't want love, things, attention—a place to call home."

"But . . . " Already her words were reminding me of *Of Mice and Men*, and what it showed me about dreaming and how you had to do it even when you weren't supposed to.

"And you're human, aren't you?" She angled her head towards me and if there hadn't been a table between us, I'm pretty sure she'd have rubbed her head against mine, as if we were just two animals.

"I've always felt like I was something so much worse than everyone else, I had to act like I didn't want the things they wanted just so they'd think I was all right. But now . . . Now I think maybe it was O.K. Maybe it was O.K. to be happy for a while. Then to grow out of it."

"Oh Beth."

"Stop saying *Oh Beth*."

"Oh, sorry."

And we both laughed. Because that's how it is now, between me and Erika; we can laugh at each other.

10.
WHEN YOUR BODY FINALLY GROWS UP

Depending on how old you are when you read this, you'll have heard absolutely nothing or absolutely loads about periods. You'll have heard how gross and annoying and painful they are; how they turn reasonable women into moody clumps.

If you'd known me at fourteen, fifteen, sixteen, you'd have heard all this from me: I refused P.E. and homework; I demanded paracetamol and ibuprofen and can't you give me something that actually *works*? You wouldn't have been alone in telling me to shut up and get on with it, like everyone else.

But it was just an act to make me *appear* like everyone else. Because I'd never found so much as one drop of blood in my pants. Because no matter how much I ate and prayed and wished, my body refused to grow taller and hippier and boobier—to grow up.

"You need to eat more and eat better," said the only doctor I saw before the doctor who told me all about you. "You need to sleep more and sleep better. You need to look after yourself. This is your body's way of telling you that it can't support any extra life."

"So I don't need to bother with condoms?"

"STIs are still—"

"But I can't get pregnant?"

"Nothing's ever guaranteed in that department, but I wouldn't have thought so, no."

After that, I told any guy who asked that I was on the pill. I got so used to saying it, I forgot it wasn't true.

One evening, we were fighting over the last takeaway spring roll and my boobs started to ache. They ached and they ached and when your dad grabbed them, it wasn't tingly and good; it hurt. I told him to stop. Then we fucked, but I spent the whole time wishing it was over, so I could work out what was going on in my belly, i.e. why it felt like an army of mini-blokes dragging my organs down towards my hips.

The next morning, I went to the loo and there it was: a brown smear on my pants. Brown, not red—which is how those teen magazines said it began, I thought, suddenly remembering how I'd scour them for any article on the subject, hoping to unlock its secret.

"What are you so happy about?" your dad asked, when I came out of the bathroom.

"Oh," I said, "just being here with you."

He wouldn't get why, after nineteen years on this earth, my body had finally decided to grow up—and how happy this made me.

The happiness lasted until halfway through my shift the next afternoon when wetness dribbled down the inside of my thigh. "Fucking hell."

"What?" Chantelle looked at me like I was a mentalist.

"Didn't realize I said that out loud."

"What's up?"

No one else was around so I told her that my period had suddenly got heavy.

"And you don't have anything with you?"

"No." I stared down at my feet, suddenly feeling like a dumb kid. I'd been so excited about getting my period, and it had seemed so harmless—just a thin brown stain in my pants—I'd forgotten about the *stuff*.

"Honestly, you'd think it was your first one."

I tried to focus in on the dirty yellow swirls in the carpet, but it was no use; my cheeks were burning up.

"It's not, literally, your first one?"

My voice wobbled as I admitted that yes, it was.

"Shit!" she said. Then she hugged me. And it wasn't one of those *I'm only hugging you because I reckon I should* wimpy-ass hugs, it was a proper one that squeezes the wind right out of you. "It sucks, doesn't it?"

"Yeah," I said, laughing and crying at once. "You know, all this time, I've been desperate to know what everyone was on about, but now I've got it . . . I wish I didn't. I don't know how anyone puts up with this every single month."

"Aw, hun!" She squeezed me some more. Then she gave me this look like she proper loved me. Finally, she yelled at whichever spotty stoner was checking the tickets on Screen One, told him to man the Snack Station, and pulled me towards the toilets.

She gave me a pad and told me to stick it into my pants proper hard because you didn't want it "boogying about" down below. "It feels like you're wearing a massive nappy," she said, "but don't worry, you'll get used to it, and it will feel a lot better if you wear one of these, too." She chucked a few tampons under the cubicle door.

"Umm, how do you . . . ?"

"Ain't you ever fingered yourself before? It's like that. I mean, it's the same angle."

When I didn't reply, she added: "Try with your finger now."

I did as she said. It was wet and squishy. I kept poking the wrong bit and it hurt. A lot of wincing, poking, bloody tissue and four tampons later, I did it. I pulled up my pants and flushed the loo and opened the door and washed my hands.

"Thanks," I said. "Seriously, you saved my life."

Chantelle blushed and punched my arm and glanced at herself in the mirror. "I'm proud of you, my little weirdo." Then she pressed two pills into my palm. "These will make it better."

I dragged my feet, so as to stretch out what I already knew would be a moment too good to lose.

Your dad's face when I told him we couldn't fuck because it was my time of the month—you'd think I'd just slapped him with last week's panini. "But I thought you could choose when you got your, erm, times of the month because of the pill? You *are* on the pill?"

"Course I'm on the pill. It's just I went to the doctor and he said I should give it a break every couple of months, just for a week or so." I hadn't even thought about it and yet the lie slipped out, fully formed.

"Right," he sighed. "What shall we do then?"

"Same as always. Minus the fucking."

"Hmm . . . A takeaway?" He never wanted to leave the Holiday Inn if he could help it.

"I wanna go out. I want to do stuff that's, you know, normal."

"Beth . . . "

"Why not? You paranoid? You reckon Jenny's got some spies following you?"

He frowned. "I'm not crazy." But from the way his cheeks went red and he started fiddling about on his laptop, I knew I was on to something. I'd known it since that first and last time we went for pizza and he couldn't stop looking around. He was embarrassed to be seen with me, or worse: scared.

"Apparently you can get a good curry in Tooting. It's not far. That is, unless she has spies in Tooting . . . "

"Fine. Tooting it is then." He shoved the laptop towards me and loosened his belt. "Why don't you Google places to eat while I grab a shower?"

"Sure."

It took me about five seconds to find about three different lists of Top 10 Tooting Eats; the rest of the time, I browsed his

Facebook. He hadn't done any new posts since last week, but as for Jenny, she posted about four times a day. There'd be a blurry selfie of her smushing her lips against Hamish's cheek. Then a moany but jokey one: *OMG can anyone tell me how to mark Year 11 coursework AND cook the dinner AND entertain a two-year-old AND not eat my weight in Hobnobs?!* A bragging one: *So I come home to this!! Best. Husband. Ever—with Philip Hamilton.* Underneath this a photo of a note in the spidery handwriting I recognized saying he was sorry he had to work late tonight but here was a printout of a Groupon offer for tapas and a comedy night. Once or twice a week there was a moany but serious one: *OMG sometimes it's all too much people can't be trusted and to top it all off I've put on eleven pounds since I started Weight Watchers again. PM me if you want the details*: (Underneath would be ten or so comments saying, *Hope you're O.K. hun!* And, *I'm PMing you RIGHT NOW!* And, *You look gorgeous just the way you are!* Etc.) She wasn't particularly pretty. Or tall. Or happy. Or clever. So what was it? What did she have that I didn't? The answer, I hoped, lay in their Center Parcs photos—a 37-photo album which she'd uploaded and 19 people had liked, none of whom was him—but I was only on the first one when your dad came out of the shower and I had to flick back to the safe topic of Tooting curry.

"Find any good places?"

"Loads."

"Great. Let's get a taxi."

"It's only one bus," I said.

He wrinkled his nose. "I *hate* the bus."

There was no point arguing; he was the one paying.

When we were sat either side of a wobbly plastic table in a restaurant with too-bright lights and bright red walls whose window was Blu-tacked with 5 star reviews and awards, Phil said, "Thanks for pushing me to do this. Jenny's always having a go at me for not taking enough risks, and she's right—I don't."

"Jenny," I said. She wasn't just an idea any more; she was a face, a body, a ton of emojis and words. "She's got a lot to complain about," I said.

The waiter brought our poppadoms but he didn't even flinch. "What's that supposed to mean?"

"Nothing."

"Beth? What did you mean?"

I whacked his arm. "I was just joking, you div! You're the one who's always bringing her up."

He opened his mouth to argue but I pressed my finger against his lips. "And when you do bring her up, she's *always* moaning."

I laughed and he laughed with me, but in that weak way which came from about 12% of him, his eyes narrowed like the rest was thinking, *what have I got myself into?*

"I'm not moaning, am I?"

"You? Christ, no. That's one of the things I like about you."

"Then why not—"

I was about to ask why he still spent five nights with her, only two nights with me. Whether he could meet my friends, come round my flat, be joined up with all the other parts of my life. Except then the waiter wheeled over a trolley piled with enough food for ten hungry humans. Where our words would have been, we stuffed naan and chapati and rice and onion bhajis and chicken korma and chicken tikka and lamb something-or-other and vegetable something-else.

"Which is best, the tikka or the korma?" your dad asked.

"Can't choose. It's like, I'm in Tooting, but my mouth's in India. It's sick."

He laughed and slid his hand over mine but our skin was so greasy, it slipped off. "There's actually a nice pub just across the road. Fancy a drink when we're done, my funny little food critic?"

"Yes!"

The pub was crowded with other couples and a mash of different chairs, including a row of folding velvet cinema seats, a granddad armchair, and some sort of joke throne. There were random things on the wall, like a black-and-white family portrait in a bright pink blow-up frame. There were shelves of old books and of board games.

"Whoever decorated this pub," I said, "was like a car-boot sale junkie, or something."

Phil nodded. "It reminds me of my childhood. Which I suppose is the point. Especially," he pointed at a faded cardboard box with the word RISK written across the side, "that one. My brother and I used to play that for hours at a time. Heaven knows why; it's so boring."

There was Monopoly, Ludo, Cluedo, The Game of Life. "My first foster dad *loved* board games," I said, trying not to notice him flinch at the word *foster*. "But my second, he said it was a waste of time. When the third family tried to get me to play this game to learn how to tell the time, I was having none of it. That was the end of board games for me!"

He didn't laugh. He opened his mouth like he was about to say something but drank some more beer instead. I looked at the other couples; some of them were silent, too. Others looked like they might be arguing. Then there was this couple in the corner, her in the granddad chair, him on a kid's stool, and he was talking non-stop while she was looking around the room, her eyes like, *help!* When our eyes met, I gave her a look that said, *I hear you!* But she buried her face in her phone.

"We should probably get going," said Phil, as he watched them leave.

"I'll just go toilet." I wanted to stay away from the Holiday Inn as long as possible.

When a woman in the toilet asked if I had a spare tampon, I smiled and gave her two.

"One's fine."

But I refused to take it back.

I stayed in the cubicle long after I heard her flush and wash and dry her hands and leave. In that pub, I was just another woman in a happily unhappy couple. Me and my body were a proper grown-up team; we could handle anything.

11.
OWNING UP TO BAD THINGS YOU'VE DONE

L anky Linda didn't want me to read her books today; she wanted me to read a letter. "It's probably full of bad stuff. I used to just chuck them away, they made me mad, knowing I couldn't read them, but this is from my son, I recognize his handwriting, I'm not that dumb."

I wasn't used to hearing someone being as mean to themselves as I can sometimes be to me. It made me sad, but I wiped the sadness off my face with a smile and said, sure.

The letter was full of crossing-out and spelling mistakes and one big, silver-grey smudge where he must've leaned his hand while he was wondering what to write next. Once I'd read it in my head a few times, I understood it enough to read it out.

Dear Mum

I was out of order to you on the phone last week. Proper mean. I'm sorry. It's just that sometimes I don't know what to say to you. Don't know what to say about school or books or that Xbox Dad got us. Or anything. Not knowing what to say makes me want to break things.

Words fly all over Aunty Gina and Rob's place but they don't do no good. Rob's moods have got even worse, if you want to know. He puts the telly up proper loud. He watches it all day and all night and it even gets into your dreams (that's if you get to sleep). You can't tell him to turn it down or off or that he should get a fucking hearing aid; he goes proper mental. I DIDN'T FIGHT IN THAT WAR TO BE

TOLD I CAN'T WATCH TELLY IN MY OWN FUCK-ING HOUSE THANKYOUVERYMUCH. He went mental at me the night before I had that fight with the English teacher. Yeah, yeah, I can already hear you saying that's no excuse, and maybe it ain't, but still. Just saying.

You're probably also telling me not to disrespect Uncle Rob, he's been through hell, blah blah blah (that's if you're even reading this—CAN you read this? I knew it weren't your glasses that stopped you reading those letters from the Council and from the Electric and from School. Just saying). But the war DID make him deaf. And mental.

Sometimes I think about the way I'd feel when I got back to our house after school. Just the smell of our hallway. The way you'd smile at me when I got into the kitchen, it made me feel . . . I don't know. Like just by being me and doing normal stuff like coming home from school was interesting, special. Or how you'd sometimes, I'd be lying in bed, proper starving, but I couldn't be arsed to go downstairs and make myself something, and you'd bring me a slice of toast and butter, it was amazing, how you just knew.

I'm trying to do those kinds of things for Ella. I'm not as good at it as you are but I'm trying. Bought her new socks in Primark the other day and everything. Her old socks had holes in and I remembered how upset you'd get when you saw holes in any of her clothes, and so I got her a new pack, and she loves them so much, she's gone and bloody named them.

I didn't want to say sorry for those things I said because I thought I'd never feel anything else about my life or about you but I'm glad now that I did because I feel lots of other things. I can almost hear you laughing. When I finish this letter, I'm gonna tell Ella I spoke to you on the phone and that you send your love. It didn't happen but I know it's true. Brandon

Linda couldn't speak after I finished reading; neither could I. Her son's words knocked me into a place where I could see the things I didn't want to see. The hard things. Right now, I can see my hand and the paper and my pillow and the cell wall. I can also see that it isn't only the hard things that are the problem; it's the other things I did, the worse things, to stop from seeing them. It was time to look them in the eye.

There were a lot of things you couldn't ask Chantelle—how come she was eating a family pack of Doritos five minutes after saying she was on a new diet? Why did she let the guy in the tight red trousers who met her outside the Odeon stick his tongue down her throat when she was with another guy? Was there anyone she was scared of?—but there were lots of things you *could*.

"How do you know when a guy really cares about you?" I asked one night. I'd been wanting to ask ever since the hunger started to take over, but I had to wait for the right time and place: two drinks into a night off, on her squishiest sofa, the Chuckle Sisters out on a double date, her kids asleep (or pretending to sleep) in the next room.

"Hmmm . . . " Chantelle slopped some more vodka into her glass. "I used to think it's when he buys you stuff. But then I learned the hard way. IT'S NOT WHEN HE BUYS YOU STUFF. Actually," she slurped her drink, "that's probably a sign he's *stopped* caring."

"But people who're married. They're always buying stuff for each other." I thought of Jenny's recent Facebook post: a £100 voucher for ASOS and a box of Milk Tray from the *#besthusbandever*.

She raised her drawn-on eyebrows. "Exactly."

We sat back and slurped. There was a cry from next door, and she sat up, ears pricked, but it didn't turn into a child stomping towards us, so she sat back.

"I guess it's when he'll do things he doesn't want to do because it makes you happy. Or because you *need* him to do it. I only clocked this, right, because it's what Jayden's dad wouldn't do. Like, he'd only do things when *he* felt like it. If I wanted to do something just 'cause *I* felt like it, forget it." She slurped the last drops of vodka from her curly straw. "Dickhead."

I waited for her to ask about Phil. But then the crying started up again, and she stomped into their room and there was a lot of shouting, and then she came in with a small floppy boy over her shoulder, and she didn't have to tell me that our night had reached its end. Part of me was glad she'd not had time to ask, but the other part was disappointed.

Do you love me?
When will you leave Jenny for me?
Why do you stay with Jenny when you don't even like her?
If you don't want to stay with me, what are we doing right now?
Who the hell are you?

These were the questions I wanted to ask your dad but couldn't. The other thing I couldn't do was admit that not being able to ask was a sign things between us weren't 100% good. It could lead to admitting that sooner or later I'd have to live without your dad. Where would I be then? Who would I be? And what would Chantelle say when she found out I'd been lying? Easier than asking myself these questions was to block them out.

I didn't ask your dad to take me out to dinner again; instead, I'd say I was starving for Caribbean, and he'd say, but they don't deliver, and I'd make what I hoped was my cute face, and mumble that I'd been looking forward to it all day. And then he'd sigh and kiss my forehead and say, all right then, and as I watched him put on his shirt and trousers and coat and gloves, going out in the world just for me, I felt good. As soon as he was gone, the good was broken up by something else, some shaky, nasty thing, and the only way I could escape it was to go through his laptop. His bag. His briefcase. The more parts of his life I knew about, the harder it would be for him to leave.

I found, folded between his dorky white vests and his granddad diamond-print socks, a card with his son's handprint on. The hand was printed in bright red paint. On the back of the card, in scarily neat teacher—i.e. Jenny's—writing, it said: "Daddy, I really miss you when you go away for work. Don't forget to Skype me! xxx." I put my hand over Hamish's handprint. My hand was bigger than his but not that much. I could imagine him giggling as our palms touched. Out of nowhere, the tears came. Tears for that kid—stuck in the middle of he'd never know what.

I found a diary. I copied every entry out of the next few weeks: everything from "tiny tots football—pick Hamish up" and "LIGHTBULBS!" and "Mum and Dad—lunch?" to "Rachel's birthday bash—Bella's, Soho, Friday 26th" to "Amsterdam—stag do—pay deposit by 22nd." I also copied down his address, and Jenny's mobile number.

I found a bottle of mouthwash.

Also, a ring. His wedding ring.

The ring was thick and gold and way too big for me but I tried it on. I tried it on every finger. It fitted on my big toe. Then I zipped it back into the pocket I'd found it in and closed his suitcase and pretended to sleep. When he came back with spicy chicken and macaroni cheese and collard greens and mash, my heart would be beating so high up in my throat, I'd be full after a few mouthfuls.

"I thought you were starving?" he'd say, forking food out of my container.

Then I'd touch him where he'd be guaranteed to like it and wink. "Only for you."

Surprised, he'd push the food away, and I'd climb on top of

him, almost believing that I'd climbed back into the beginning of our relationship—almost.

"Does he, like, even exist?" Lisa said, the next time they were grilling me about Phil.

And that was it. That was the thing that pushed me over the edge: "Err, yeah? And you lot can meet him. He's invited us to this exclusive party in Soho. It's at Bella's."

"*Bella's?*" Chantelle squeezed my shoulder so hard, her fake nails dug into my skin. I didn't tell her to get off. "For real?"

I didn't know what Bella's was but it was obvious from her face that it was good. As in VIP good. "For real."

"Oh my days. Girls. We're going to Bella's. Oh my days!"

Lisa and Nicole exchanged a look that said: *WTF is Bella's?* Then: *Who cares? If Chantelle thinks it's good then it is.*

"When is it though?" asked Nicole.

"Umm." I closed my eyes and sure enough the diary page was there. It didn't even feel like someone else's; it felt like mine. "Two Fridays' time."

"Sick! I've got bare time to sort out a babysitter. *You,*" she hugged me close, "are a legend."

I smiled, even though my insides were one big frown.

How're things with Jenny? She doesn't mind you're still working away?

You know, we really hate my best mate's boyfriend. Do Jenny's mates hate you?

What you up to this weekend?

These were the questions I got good at asking your dad. The trick was to wait until we'd drunk and eaten and fucked and pissed—then, as he walked away from the bathroom looking 100% pleased with himself, I'd pounce.

"They're not great, if I'm honest. But they're not terrible. And they have been terrible. So I guess that's a positive." He'd say this as we lay side by side, naked. "Seeing a bit less of each other helps. Absence makes the heart grow fonder, and all that?"

If I wanted him to carry on—and if I wanted to carry on listening to him without screaming—I'd crack open whatever was left of the mini bar. Usually, it was whisky or vermouth or some other weird thing I didn't like, but I'd down whatever it was, closing my eyes and, as far as possible, my ears, until the edges of me and of the world were blurred—like when the papers fuzz out criminals' faces to stop you telling who they are.

"Her friends aren't exactly my number one fans; they don't try to hide the fact that they think I'm a bore who stops her going out. What pisses me off is this couldn't be further from the truth; she never *wants* to go out. Well, hardly ever. If there's a night *I* want to go out, you can bet *she* does. Get her any other night, however, and she'll start on about how she's socially anxious—never mind if she can happily boss around sixty misbehaving kids day after day—blah blah blah, she'd rather stay in with me and Hamish . . . Just us. She says it in this baby voice, as well: *just us!* It drives me mad."

I waited for him to ask about me. About my friends and their boyfriends. About the feelings I hid from everyone else. He never did.

"This weekend? Oh, Jenny's sister Rachel is having some birthday thing. It's her thirtieth but you'd think it was her *third*, the way she's going on about it. She's a party planner, or some such nonsense, so she's managed to get some swanky place in Soho, at least, she keeps *saying* it's swanky—apparently celebs have been papped there and so on—but we had our office Christmas do there last year and it was, just, you know, another bar." He drained his glass, and I thought, maybe this is it. This is the moment he asks about me. "Come to think of it, we were in the basement. Yes, not the proper venue; the basement."

I lurched to my feet. The room was spinning. I grabbed the bedpost until it stopped, then staggered across the carpet.

"Where are you going?"

"The bathroom. Fuck's sake. Am I not even allowed to go to the bathroom?" I stomped in and, for the first time, locked the door. I slammed down the loo seat and sat on it and pressed my face into my hands. I tried to cry. I couldn't, though. *Of course he still loves you. He loves you more than anyone else has ever loved you. Paranoid bitch.* I unlocked the door and flopped on to the bed and hugged him. "I'm sorry," I said. "I'm such a bitch sometimes. It's just . . . I love you."

I love you. Those three massive tiny words rolled out of my mouth. I waited for something to happen, e.g. for the lights to fade or for a happy soundtrack to start up. Instead, he hugged me to his armpit, kissed the top of my head and told me I was cute. *Cute.* Great. He got love. I got cute.

"Ouch!" He leaped out of my grip. "Fuck." He was rubbing his belly, where there were three deep red crescents imprinted on his skin; I must've been digging my nails into him, but the weird thing was, I didn't even feel it. "This better be gone by the time I get home. Fuck."

Then he stomped to the bathroom and locked the door. I heard the shower turn on.

He doesn't love me.

Yes he does.

No, he doesn't.

I could've lain there fighting with myself all night. Well, I didn't. I dived into his case and before there was time to ask any questions, like was this really a good idea or would it just make everything worse, his ring was in my palm and then it was stuffed in my bag.

"You mean," said Erika, when I told her this, "*you* put it in your bag. *You* stole it."

"Obviously, yeah."

"It's just the way you said it: *it was stuffed in my bag*. Like it happened by magic. Like it wasn't your responsibility."

Her words turned my face red. She was right. So I said it again: "O.K., *I* stole his wedding ring." There. I'd done it. And it wasn't as bad as I'd imagined; it was just one small part of me, and owning up had shrunk it. New space was opening inside of me—space for new and better things.

Erika nodded, but her eyes reminded me I'd have way bigger things to own up to before long.

A few nights after the night I stole the ring was the night of Rachel's party. The night Chantelle had got a special babysitter for. The night we'd been chatting about for weeks. Butterflies flip-flopped around my stomach every time she brought it up: "We ain't been out in Central in TIME and we ain't never been to no VIP place before."

"Is that the place where thingy and thing from *X Factor* got off?" said Nicole.

"Don't matter," said Chantelle, pinching my arm. "Thanks to this legend here, this ain't gonna be no normal night out."

Looking at Chantelle looking at me, I had this weird "all your life flashing before your eyes" moment—well, all your nights out flashing before your eyes.

Normal nights out happened however often Chantelle could fix the rota so we'd all get the same night off at once. We'd start at Chantelle's, slurping vodka through curly straws with titchy plastic versions of Peppa Pig clinging to them. If there was a friend of a cousin Chantelle wanted to chat up, we'd go to 'Spoon's. Sometimes the friend was there; usually he wasn't. When Nicole once got so pissed she ended up saying, "Hey, Chantelle, how come we always come here to see these guys but they're never here? Or if they are you don't even talk to them?" Chantelle chucked the bottom of someone else's beer all over her face, then gave her the evils for a whole week.

On the nights we were too pissed or pissed-o to stand up, or when she failed to guilt-trip her half-sister or her ex-stepsister to babysit, we'd stay on her balcony so long, laughing and chatting shit and laughing some more about the shit that we were chatting and placing bets on which celebrities were in the planes that occasionally slid across the sky, that eventually Jayden would poke his little head out of the balcony window and say, "Mum, your noise is all breaking into my dreams, please shut up," and we'd squeal and say how cute he was, and Chantelle would lift him up, and even though he'd be squirming, you could tell he loved it, and Chantelle, the look on her face, well, it was a look you didn't see the rest of the time; it was enough to make anyone want to be a mum; it was love so pure it could sober you up, however many vodkas in, no matter how loudly the sky screamed that it was already tomorrow.

On the nights we *did* make it out, oh boy. Oh boy, oh boy, oh boy. We'd get to the strip of grass outside her block, and the BMX boys might or might not whistle at us, and if they did, it would be up to Chantelle to either kiss her teeth and shake her chest and do her best *what-you-looking-at* face or—and the rest of us would hold our breath while waiting to see which *or* it would be—she'd wiggle her bum in their faces, yelling, "You want some of this?" And when they grinned, she'd say, "You must be kidding!" Then she'd grab their BMXs and refuse to give them back until they gave us some weed or some coke or whatever the Big Men had stuffed down their baggy boxers that night. We'd skin up, snort or swallow whatever they gave over, and unless Chantelle was off on one about that thing the boy's big brothers once did or didn't do under the table in science class in Year 8 or was it Year 9, we'd stumble towards Streatham High Road.

The thing about Streatham High Road is, all the things that make it bad when you're sober—it's long, it's straight, and no matter how far you walk down it, you never get away from the same mix of chicken shops, charity shops, pawn shops and shops without names that are forever closing down, broken up by the occasional Polish deli or Sainsbury's Local and, of course, the Odeon—make it the best place to be when you're fucked. You walk, you roll, you stumble, but you don't get lost, you don't get scared; you either know where you are or you think you know where you are. Either way, you keep going in the same direction until you get to wherever it is you're going, i.e. Wetherspoon's.

"So, what you gonna wear?" Chantelle jabbed me in the ribs.

"I don't know."

"What?" She shook her head at me. "Sometimes I don't get you. You got ass and everything now, besides—well, you got a bit. I've got something special but, it's, like, top secret."

"Ooh, what is it? Tell us!"

I didn't pretend to be interested in what Chantelle was going to wear; I couldn't. I was bricking it. Proper bricking it. I wanted to suggest we go to 'Spoon's instead. I wanted to tell them everything. I wanted Phil to tell me that he wanted me. He wanted me more than the life he was trying to escape from. But the moment I started to think about all this, I felt like I was going to throw up.

If there's something you want to forget, London—especially central London—is the best place to do it; wherever you are, whatever you're doing, you can bet whatever is or isn't in your bank account, you're never more than a metre away from someone or something a *hell* of a lot weirder. Like a pigeon munching an iPod headphone. Or a kid shouting at his mum about quantum physics while the mum is asking her pug with the designer waistcoat did the lady in the dog spa *really* give you a shampoo? A lanky boy in his Tippex-splattered school blazer spitting out the dirtiest most craziest rap you ever heard. An old man mumbling something about the Bible, or about

God, or the devil, or, what, what's *this*, is he talking now about *Primark*? Walking through central London, you breathe and—along with the taxi fumes and the skyscraper shadows and the ding-ting-ting of the tourist bike rickshaws and the gurning gargoyles that stare down from the tops of buildings—you inhale all these people and, with any luck, you forget you're you.

Unless, that is, you're with Chantelle: "Selfie-time!"

We took selfies outside Leicester Square tube station and selfies in the square itself. After three attempts, we got one with a sprayed-silver human statue behind us; he was scratching his nose, and Chantelle wanted to get another one, but I said to keep it. What I didn't say was that I needed this evidence that not everyone was the thing they were supposed to be.

Chantelle kept stopping in shop windows to check herself out. She was wearing this lime green jumpsuit that was too bright, too tight and—partly because her boobs looked likely to pop out of it at any moment, partly because, even though she was the last kind of woman you'd see in a magazine, she looked amazing—people kept stopping to check her out as she checked out herself. "Does it make my bum look massive in a good way or a bad way?" she'd ask. "Good way!" Lisa and Nicole would yell, and she'd grin. "Yeah. That's what I thought. Just checking, though." I laughed and nodded and said the things they expected me to say. But the butterflies and the bad thoughts and the constant checking and wanting to check my phone to see if your dad had called about the wedding ring, they clouded around me. I kept noticing the way other people stared at us—this group of German or French tourists in Converse and Eastpak backpacks strapped to their front, and a little blonde girl in a puffy dress, in particular. One of the Eastpak and Converse girls even took a photo of Chantelle looking at her arse, then ran off giggling. Chantelle didn't notice—she was too busy thinking about herself—but my hands twitched with anger. We only lived a few tube stops away, after all. Did we have less right to be here than anyone else?

"Häagen-Dazs café! Oh my days. Oh my days, I've been wanting to go here for TIME."

"So let's go."

Chantelle wrinkled her nose. "It costs like a tenner for a lick of ice cream though."

Your dad's ring was tucked up in my flat, under my pillow, but his money was right there in my purse. "It's on me," I said, waving the twenties in their faces. The only time I'd held that much cash was when I was counting it out for Dale. But I didn't have to hand it over this time; it was mine now, to spend how I wanted.

"Did your boyfriend give that to you?" said Nicole.

I nodded.

"You're SO lucky. I wish I'd get a boyfriend who was rich. My last one moaned when he had to buy me a drink in 'Spoon's.'"

"Come on, then." I marched towards the queue.

Lisa and Nicole started to follow, then they saw that Chantelle was still, arms crossed, eyebrows raised.

"What?" I said, staring into the window of Häagen-Dazs, as I knew without looking that her face said, *what is this BS?*

"We ain't your fucking charity project, that's all."

"Ah, Chantelle." Lisa gave her a little hug. "It's not charity. She doesn't even have a collection bucket or anything like that. Besides, we've eaten out your freezer enough times."

In the corner of my eye, I saw the beginning of a smile. "True."

After queuing so long Nicole almost wet herself— "Someone left an extra large Diet Coke in Screen Two: it's not my fault!"—we slid into our very own fake-leather booth. The fake-leather was lilac; it reminded me of grandmas.

"What should we choose?" Chantelle frowned over the menu like it was an exam.

"Anything you want," I said.

"I want the chocolate sundae deluxe. No. The banana split special. Nah. The Belgian chocolate surprise. Ah, I don't know!" Chantelle slammed the menu shut and crossed her arms.

"I'm sure," said Lisa delicately, "they'll all be good."

"Why don't we get all the ones you said and share?" I suggested.

Chantelle gave me a look like maybe I wasn't so bad after all. "All right."

At last, we ordered. For once, no one had anything to say; we just leaned our heads against the fake-leather and stared at each other and at all the people outside the window and at the people in the café eating ice cream with long spoons. Something weird was going on, and it wasn't until the waiter swooped two sundaes and two platters down on our table that I clocked what it was: we were nervous. We didn't know how to act so far from our normal places.

The ice cream changed all that. "Fuck me, that's good. That's better than my best fuck."

"Better than a Magnum."

"Fuck Magnums."

"Häagen-Dazs selfie. Come on."

We were squeezing into the frame when my phone buzzed. "Beth! You ruined it."

I ran out of the café, not caring if I'd ruined the selfie because things were already ruined and this call was going to make it a lot harder to pretend otherwise.

"Where is it?" Your dad's voice was cold and hard, like the iron railings I leaned up against while we spoke.

"I'm great, thanks," I said. "And how about you?"

"Oh, for God's sake, Bethany, grow up." The coldness from

the railings was seeping through my skin. Seeping right through to my bones.

"*You* can talk," I said.

"What's that supposed to mean?"

"Nothing."

"Seriously, Bethany. Where are you? Just tell me and I'll get a cab over. We had . . . We had a really bad fight this afternoon."

"Oh?" Maybe he was going to leave her. Maybe he was going to drive over and stay with me for ever.

"We both had the day off, and we were having quite a nice time, we were about to . . . But anyway. The point is she noticed and then I noticed . . . And I need it back. I need it back right now. I've got a party to go to tonight and if I'm not wearing it, I . . . I don't know what will happen. She thinks I'm looking for it at work."

It had been raining; Leicester Square was a carpet of soggy flyers and leaflets and the *ShortList* and the *London Evening Standard* and some other free paper no one wanted to read. The spray-painted human "statues" kept peeking up at the sky, begging it not to betray them.

"Well, I can't give it to you now."

"Bethany. That's not an option."

"I'll give it back, but not tonight. Come round mine tomorrow."

"Tomorrow? I can't. Look, Bethany, this has got to—"

"You come to mine tomorrow at seven or you don't get it back."

"Beth—"

"Or I'll flush it down the loo right now."

I heard him punching something. "Fine. If that's how it's going to be. Fine. Text me your address." Then he hung up.

I had a plan and it was going to work; it had to.

"Where the fuck were you?" Chantelle asked when I sat back down.

"Oh, that was Phil," I said. At least they knew his real name. "He's running a bit late. He said we should get predrinks, first."

"Ain't you even gonna eat no ice cream?" Chantelle nodded at a soupy brown mess in the sundae glass. A few specks of nut were floating on the surface; they made me want to throw up. "We saved some for you but you took so long to come back, it's gone mank."

"Thanks," I said, "but I'm not hungry. Let's start on the drink."

I slapped two twenties on the table and walked out. I felt Chantelle's eyes on me but I didn't look up. When we got outside, she grabbed my shoulder, held me back. "You've gone see-through," she said. "What's up?"

"Nothing."

"Come off it, Beth. You can tell me."

But I couldn't. Couldn't couldn't wouldn't. Things had gone too far. "I'm just cold. A drink will sort me out, I'm sure."

"Where we going then?" Lisa and Nicole hugged their own goose-pimpled arms.

"Where do you lot wanna go?" I asked.

"You decide," said Chantelle. "Take us to one of these great places you've been with Phil."

"Sure," I said. "There's a great place just down here." And I swaggered down the next side street like I 100% knew where I was going.

"People say Central is all that," said Lisa, as we stopped by a display of huge rubbery pizza slices so Nicole could fiddle with the strap of her used-to-be-metallic-coated Primark wedges. "But the thing is," she went on, "it's not. It's exactly the same as Streatham or Walworth or anywhere normal, except the people didn't just end up here—they're here on purpose."

Me and Chantelle shared a look, like, did Lisa just say

something clever? I was about to link my arm in hers when, turning away to check herself out in a lingerie shop window, she said, "But are we here on purpose, though? Or is Beth just making it up as she goes along?"

Her words hit me hard. They rubbed up against all the other things I knew but was trying my best to pretend I didn't know, and I had to stop walking. On one side of us was what looked like an old man pub, same as anywhere else. On the other, one of those shops so expensive they only display about four hangers per rail; the lights were still on and right at the back of the shop stood a woman with her arms crossed. She looked lonely and small and bored. No way could we go to either of these places.

"I need a piss," said Nicole, again. "Does ice cream make you piss?"

At the end of the street, I spied a neon blue glow. Looping letters. I walk-ran towards it and it spelled out Billy's Blues Bar. "This is it!" There was a neon blue sign pointing down a narrow metal staircase. It looked like the entrance to a different world, which was exactly what I needed.

"A *Blues Bar*?" said Chantelle. "Sounds like a place to put old people."

"Blue's my second favourite colour," said Lisa. Nicole said she didn't care so long as there was a loo. And before Chantelle could say anything else, I walked down those stairs.

"Sure you're in the right place?" the bouncer asked, looking us up and down, his eyes settling on Chantelle's lime green arse.

"Yep," I said, ready for a fight.

But he just laughed. "Go on then."

The Blues Bar reminded me of black-and-white film clips from the cool kind of olden days; the Johnny Cash and Marilyn Monroe and whisky hip flask and cigarette holder kind of olden days; the kind of olden days that every other person in that bar besides us, with their suits and their flouncy dresses and their curled hair and their pencilled-on beauty spots, obviously reckoned they were part of.

The Chuckle Sisters were empty-faced as they waited to see what Chantelle said. Her face twisted from WTF to *ooh* to picking me up and spinning me around, declaring, "Fucking *amazing!*" Declare's an official word, the kind of word they use in courts; I used it here because Chantelle's like that; she says something, and it's 100% ™ certified true.

"Yeah," I said, "I've been a few times and it's pretty cool. Now, drinks on me."

"Whatever," said Chantelle, already pushing people aside so she could squeeze into the cave-like room where there was a live band. There were a lot of people crowded around the band, but they weren't dancing so much as shuffling from side to side and jiggling their arms. There was a big empty space behind them and Chantelle stepped right into it and began dancing. The band were playing this song about a girl called Lola, and how great she was. Behind me, people grumbled that this wasn't the Blues. But when Chantelle got going, they shut up. "She's got balls, that one." "She's got something, don't know if it's balls. Definitely something." She stretched out her arms, wiggled her arse, unafraid to take up that space. The band were grinning, angling their instruments towards her, as if she was the one they were singing about—she was Lola.

"Ain't you getting our drinks?" Lisa yanked my top and shouted into my ear.

I watched Chantelle for a few seconds, trying to work out how she did it, how she became this Lola. But I couldn't, and the Chuckle Sisters were panting for a drink, and so I set off towards the bar. Most of the time, I like being small; I like being able to squeeze myself into spaces where no one else can. But when you're in a crowded bar and you and your mates are starving for a drink, it sucks. You say excuse me but no one hears. You shout; still no one hears. Then you try jutting your shoulders into other people's backs the way tall people do; no one moves. Someone laughs and points at you, as if you're a mouse, or some other dumb cute thing. Which meant it took forever to get to the bar, even longer to get four double vodka and Cokes and some tequila shots, and so by the time the barmaid told me all this came to sixty quid, I didn't care that the last of your dad's money had gone to Mr. Häagen-Dazs; there was enough in my account if you included the overdraft. As for the things I needed it for—rent, Council tax, food, electric— they could wait. Right then, it was more important to get wasted. Anyway, how was I to know that I should have been saving for a whole new human, too?

Half of the vodka had slopped over my hands by the time I'd fought my way back to the dance cave, but the others didn't notice: Chantelle was twerking all over the place, and wannabe olden days people were pressing up around her, clapping and swaying.

"My girl!" When she saw me, she motioned for the Chuckle Sisters to take custody of the drinks (which they did). Then she pulled me into the middle of the floor. I'd only had a few slurps of vodka-Coke and that was no way near enough to stop me noticing that the people round the edge of the dance floor, they were half laughing with us, half *at* us. But then Chantelle spun me round so hard and so fast, I had no choice but to stop caring. The Lola song was playing again, only its beat was all broken up, which somehow made it easier to dance to, and for a moment, I thought, maybe I can be Lola, too. Maybe I can be the woman who's so special, she stars in songs.

As soon as the music stopped, all these big-bellied granddad types slimed out of the shadows, free drinks in hand. "For you two beautiful ladies." Thankfully, Chantelle just grabbed the drinks and whisked us away. She spoke right into my ear: "Try to look pale."

"My mate, she's got a heart condition—that's why she's proper titchy—you got to let us sit down." This is how she got us a table. It was in a side-cave just off the dance-cave; the ceiling was close enough for a tall person to bash their head on and every few minutes it dripped sweat on to my head.

After the shots and the free Coke-whatevers, before the vodka or the possibility of silence or questions or thoughts like where are we going next, I said, "Truth or dare." I tried to say it the way Chantelle said things: like they were already true.

"Yay!" the Chuckle Sisters yelled.

Then Lisa wrinkled her brow and shouted into my ear: "Not being rude but what did you say?"

This time, I shouted.

Chantelle made some kind of shape with her lips but seeing as the air was too crammed with music to carry words from one person's mouth to another, I decided it meant "Great idea."

"Cool," I said. "I'll go first. I'll do a truth and what you should know is—"

But Chantelle yanked my ear to her mouth and shouted: "WE ALREADY KNOW EVERYTHING ABOUT EACH OTHER."

"WE DO NOT."

"WE KNOW EVERYTHING WORTH KNOWING."

"I DON'T KNOW WHAT PROPER SCARES YOU."

"YOU DON'T WANNA KNOW THAT."

"I DO."

"YOU DON'T."

"I—"

"FINE. BUT SHOTS FIRST. THEN ONE PERSON. AT. ONE. TIME." We downed our shots, and then she pulled me to the place which has the highest percentage of truth of any club, anywhere in the world: the women's toilets.

The door flaps closed behind you, muting the music, filling

your ears with sniffles and cries and laughs and words like *what a fucking knob why don't you leave him/oh but he's good in bed, well, he's not that good but he does change the duvet every week which is more than I can say for my ex oh and do my knees look O.K. in this I always feel self-conscious about my knees in this dress have we done all the coke?*

The air was puke mixed with the slightly gone-off lollipops and bubble gum you could, if you were pissed/desperate/pitying enough, buy from the toilet attendant for £1.

Chantelle had a piss, then I squeezed against the cubicle wall so she could get up and I could sit down. Then we squeezed past each other again, and I was about to unlock the door, when she flipped down the toilet seat, sat on it, then pulled me down on to her lap. "Let's chill here for a bit," she said, squeezing my waist. "You're so light. You're lucky."

"So? It's not like it makes me happy."

She twisted me around until we could see each other's faces. "You're not happy?"

"No. Yeah. I don't know. I was. For a while. It's just, I'm small, yeah, but I feel like there are all these bricks inside me. Weighing me down. Some days I forget about them, other days they melt down into this, I don't know, this muddy river. It spills out everywhere and makes a mess of everything and I spend all my time mopping it up. And then other times I feel like I'm not here at all. Like I'm not really here. I just want to feel normal." These weren't the kinds of truths you were meant to share in "Truth or Dare" but what did I care? The booze had smudged out that part of me that normally wagged its finger to stop. The booze plus something else. Some weird, wobbly thing.

Chantelle tightened her grip around my belly. Some girl outside the cubicle was asking some other girl if she thought Matt had been looking at her weird because she wasn't being paranoid or anything but he was definitely looking at her weird.

"My little weirdo," said Chantelle.

Instead of asking why I had to be hers, instead of asking why she liked me being little, I asked again what she was scared of.

"I'm scared," she pulled me back tight against her boobs, "this is, like, it. Me, the flat, the Odeon, the kids. I'm scared I'm never gonna do nothing else with my life. Never gonna be the person I was meant to be—just this woman what stuff happens to and I don't have no control over what that stuff is or when, it's just, oh look, you're pregnant, oh look, you need a job, oh look, there's a special offer on washing-up liquid oh why don't I try it . . . Know what I mean?"

"I—"

"Oh, but what am I on about? You got it going on with your big-shot boyfriend and stuff."

Outside the cubicle, some girl was crying. Another girl was saying she should really be feeling happy right now because she'd worked hard to fit into that dress and she looked really, really good. And also, if they didn't get back soon, the others would drink the rest of the whisky without them.

"It's not like that," I said. "He's not such a big shot. And anyway, he hardly takes me out of the Holiday Inn. He's got a wife and a kid and everything."

Chantelle loosened her grip. "What?"

"He moans about his wife and I kind of hate her even though I can tell she's not a bad person. She's just normal, you know? I think . . . I think I'm the one who's a bad person."

The cubicle was shaking but I couldn't tell if the shaking began with me or with Chantelle or whether it had nothing to do with either of us. I felt ten times more drunk than I had when I'd sat down, even though we didn't have any drink. I felt strange and wobbly and free.

"Sometimes I feel like he knows me better than anyone in

the world, other times, like he doesn't know me at all. At first, he made me so happy it hurt, but now . . . Now I often feel sick when I'm around him and I don't know why. I guess I just want us to get away from that Holiday Inn."

"Honey," said Chantelle. "Why didn't you tell me?"

"I thought, if I didn't tell you, if I didn't tell myself, it wouldn't be true."

She laughed. "You really can be a retard, even if you are a brainbox."

Every now and then some girl shouted through the cubicle at us.

"You gonna make him leave his wife? Don't let him make a slag out of you."

"She's already a slag! My sister's husband left her for some twenty-one-year-old. She's alone with the kids and everything."

"Yeah, but it's the guy's responsibility."

"Oh, don't give me that feminist bullshit."

"What's wrong with being a feminist?"

"Come on." Chantelle began to wriggle underneath me. "Let's get out of here. Get up."

Everything looked dark and blurry, like my eyes were grubby glass.

"I can't."

"Course you can." She stood up and I flopped against the door. Somehow, I moved one foot and then the other. I couldn't feel them, though. I couldn't feel my feet or see properly and I hadn't even drunk much; something was happening with my body and it wasn't good.

I remember Bella's. I remember the word, and how Chantelle kept saying it, we were out in the street and she was shouting it at people, and people were pointing, and the Chuckle Sisters were dragging me along because I couldn't feel my legs.

I remember the Chuckle Sisters, and how their faces were

one orange blur. I remember Chantelle's arse, always a few steps ahead of us like some wobbly, lime green beacon.

Jenny's face: I remember that, too. It was the same as the one I'd memorized off Facebook, except it wasn't smeared with chocolate or smiles; it was smeared with tears.

What I don't remember is what I said to her, or how. Or what she said back.

* * *

Because the next thing I remember is waking up to the too-bright hospital lights.

"SUP?" yelled Chantelle. Then she clapped her hand over her mouth. Bowed her head. "Sorry. I'm sorry."

I waited to see whether I'd only woken up to a dream.

"I shouldn't have let you have that drink."

But no. Here I was, in the real world. And Chantelle was saying sorry. And there were tubes coming in and out of my wrists. I didn't even feel too bad.

"What?"

She rubbed her forehead. "Those drinks. From those granddad sleazes. Yours must've been spiked. Spiked with some weird shit, that's for sure."

"My legs disappeared." Jenny's face swam into my vision; I pushed it away. "That's all I remember; my legs disappeared."

Chantelle groaned, still rubbing her head. Then she told me what happened; how all I would say was Bella's, I was obviously too wasted and she kind of knew I should just go home but I wouldn't shut up about it and neither would the Chuckle Sisters, they'd got it into their heads they'd see a celeb, or something, and then they asked a few people and it turned out it was just around the corner, and so . . . "What? What happened next?"

She let go of her head. "Sorry. Just, I've got a banging head.

Wasn't lucky enough to get a stomach pump and a drip, not like you . . . "

"Did I . . . DO something?"

For the first and last time, she made a face like she didn't know the answer. "It was weird. We were almost at Bella's, at least, I think we were, and there was this woman. She was all on her own, she didn't have any mates with her or anything. She was crying her eyes out. I felt kind of sorry for her, even though her dress was FUG-LY. Then you started grabbing at her, she jumped away, I tried to hold you back but even though your legs were buckling, you were going mental with your arms, and then . . . Then you said you just wanted to be mates with her and you collapsed."

"Some night out."

She sighed. "Yeah. Anyway, will you be all right now? Better get back to the kids or no one will ever look after them again."

I nodded and she turned to go but just before she reached the door, I called her name.

"What now?"

"Thanks. For, you know, staying. For making sure I was all right."

Another first: she hunched her shoulders like she was embarrassed. "No worries."

And then she was gone. And I remembered that it was Saturday and I was meant to be making dinner for your dad. There were no nurses about so I yanked the tubes out of my hand and left, almost believing that I was cured; that they'd pumped all the bad things out.

13.
A SOFT EAR IN HARD TIMES

Your dad texted me more in those twenty-four hours than ever before or since:

8 P.M.: What the hell are you playing at? We're at the party and neither of us are wearing our rings and Jenny is going round telling everyone this ridiculous story.

8:20 P.M.: She keeps laughing too loudly and people are looking at her like she's mad. If you'd just give me back the ring things could go back to normal.

8:45 P.M.: This isn't a game, Bethany. This is my life. Our life. And I need it back now, thank you very much.

9:40 P.M.: That things went so far between us, it was all one big accident.

7 A.M.: O.K., you're obviously not going to come to your senses so I suppose I'll have to come round tonight. I'll be there at 8 to collect the ring. The ring and nothing else.

He wasn't angry; he was just confused. He was confused because of Jenny. Because he was stuck with her even though he didn't love her. Because he loved me but he didn't know how to do it. This was because he'd only seen me in hotel rooms and bars and takeaways and that curry place in Tooting; he couldn't imagine me in a home. In his home. But that didn't matter because he was coming round that night and I was going to show him. Most of the stuff I'd bought with Marcia was broken, and what with spending so many nights at the Holiday Inn and so much time at Chantelle's, I'd more or less stopped cleaning. One whole bathroom wall was now black with mould. Crumbs and dust everywhere. But it didn't scare me. I'd go to Wilko's and buy some things to carry on making myself "at home" where me and Marcia left off. Then clean like a maniac.

I used to think, when I went to other people's houses, that every poster on every wall, every cushion, every doormat, was part of some big plan. Some life blueprint that everyone had except me. However, once I'd been to the Home sections of TK Maxx and Wilko's and Morley's, this started to look like a BS idea. Like the couple in Wilko's who spent half an hour arguing over which soap dish to buy. Half an hour. It went like this:

Her: Let's get this one.

Him: Why that one?

Her: It'll be easy to clean. And it's a nice colour.

Him: But it's well expensive.

Her: It's not the most expensive.

Him: It's ugly. It reminds me of my grandma.

Her: But you love your grandma.

Him: I love her. Not her flat. I don't want our mates thinking we live in a grandma flat.

Her: Since when did you judge your mates by their soap dish?

Him: You wanna go Subway?

Her: What?

Him: I'm starving.

Her: But we really need a soap dish.

Him: Fine. Let's just get this one then.

Another woman, red-faced and sweaty from the gym,

heaped tea towels and hand towels and towel-towels over her arm, not even checking their size or price or colour, and dumped them at the nearest checkout. Then a man marched up to the old woman stacking shelves and asked whether they were stocking the bread bins that were featured in the *Sunday Times* home magazine last weekend. The old woman stared at the guy like he was talking some other language. The guy sighed and unfolded a scrap of magazine from his pockets. "This one. With the wood-effect. I've looked all over Home but I can't see it anywhere." "Oh that," said the woman. "That's not in Home, it's in Special Promotions." And the man huffed off.

These people didn't have a plan. They didn't even have the paper or the laptop or whatever to write the plan *on*. They did things by hoping, by guessing, by holding their hands out in front of them and trying to feel what was just ahead. They'd buy stuff, and they'd fill their flats with it, and people would come round and think, so this is who you are, and they'd think it, too; they'd fool everyone and themselves it was all *meant*.

I already had a turquoise soap dish, so I bought a tea towel and a hand towel to match. I got some turquoise place mats and turquoise salt and pepper shakers. I got a framed poster of some turquoise flowers and a set of turquoise tins in different sizes which all fitted inside one another like Russian dolls. Did I remember why I'd chosen a turquoise soap dish in the first place? Was it even me who chose it, or was it Marcia? It didn't matter. Phil would come round and he'd think, *Bethany is a turquoise person. A bright and unusual person. I never knew.* It also didn't matter that I was scraping the bottom of my overdraft; as soon as Phil left Jenny, he wouldn't mind helping out with stuff like that.

That afternoon was one of the happiest of my life. I turquoised over my flat's damp and dirty places. I wiped and sprayed and scrubbed. In a few hours, me and your dad would be starting our new life together, which would start with food.

Proper grown-up food. With napkins and candles and wine. Plenty of wine. I'd never *cooked* for anyone before, not even myself; I only heated things up. (Actually, I often didn't bother to do that, I'd just cram something down my throat, standing up, cold, but never mind.)

5 P.M., and I ran down to Tesco, which was jammed with mums juggling trolleys with babies, with beanie-hatted students lugging beer crates and piles of frozen pizza to the checkouts, with couples who clearly couldn't wait to get back into bed with each other; I didn't mind. I didn't mind all these people and their lives because for once, I felt that I, too, was a person with a life. I bought a tablecloth, napkins, a set of wine glasses, two bottles of wine, salad, olives, tortellini, tomato sauce, crisps and Parmesan. All you had to do was heat it up but the pictures on the packets made it look like proper grown-up food. It was all Tesco Finest, almost every packet containing words like "artisan" and "rustic"—your dad would be impressed. Of course, they ID-ed me, but I didn't care; I just handed over my passport and smiled.

6:30 P.M. and I couldn't sit down because every time I did, I noticed a speck of dirt; the more I cleaned, the more dirt I saw. I'd never cleaned under the sofa, for example, or wiped the skirting boards or the windows or the bathroom mirror. I scrubbed the bathroom until my hands were red raw with bleach, and it still didn't look clean.

7 P.M. One missed call. Unknown number. Voicemail. I listened to it straight away, but it wasn't your dad; it was the hospital. They wanted to check I was all right. They'd done some tests and they needed to talk to me about the results so if I could call them back straight away please and thankyouverymuch. Well, I would not be calling them back. Not yet.

7:30 P.M. What if he got here early? What if I wasn't ready when he did? I was like those dumb-arses on *Come Dine With Me* who "forget" they're hosting a dinner party on TV and then make their meal in a massive rush. Except, I hadn't forgotten; it was just that I'd never done this before (microwaved beans on toast doesn't count). I opened the Tesco Finest artisan crisps. Tried one. It was good. Tangy. More like a potato than a Dorito. The problem was, I didn't have a big, beautiful bowl to put them in; I only had two bowls in my whole flat; they were small and white, different shapes, both chipped. And we needed them for the pasta. I ripped the packet down the seam and laid it flat on the table. It reminded me of a pub. Then I remembered the olives: surely they'd make it more grown-up? I didn't have a bowl for those, either. Or a dish. What was the difference between a bowl and a dish? Did it matter? Was it grown-up? It was silly. 100% silly. But not as silly as the olives looked, all oily and bored at the bottom of that plastic packet. Something—tears, anger, fear—prickled at my throat and I might've cried had I not unscrewed the bottle of wine and glugged it straight down. This wasn't exactly a grown-up thing to do, but no one was watching so what did it matter?

7:45 P.M. Tesco claimed the tortellini only took five to seven minutes to cook, so there was no point cooking it yet. But I laid out the pans and boiled the kettle so there'd be as little as possible to do when he got here. Then I had a few more glugs of wine.

7:55 P.M. The salad! I'd forgotten about the salad. Rocket and wild leaves. It tasted bitter. *Makes a delicious accompaniment to Italian pasta dishes. Balsamic dressing recommended.* Balsamic. What was that? I didn't know and I didn't have any and the wine made me not care so I glugged some more. I arranged the salad in two little mounds on two little plates. It looked a bit sad and lonely so I topped it off with some olives. I dribbled some of the olive juice on to the leaves, too. Yes, that was better. It was like what you'd see on *Come Dine With Me*. It was almost good.

8:00 P.M. No Phil. Yes, wine.

8:05 P.M. Wine. Wine, wine, wine.

8:10 P.M. A knock at the door. I opened it right up. And there was Phil, your dad, fingers on his coat zip, red-faced from rushing to see me. Just me.

"I missed you!" I flung my arms around him. He didn't hug back. He didn't even let go of his zip. "You must be cold," I said. "And tired and hungry. Come in." It was a strange-good feeling, being the one with the place to invite people into, not the other way round.

"Red or white?"

"Bethany—"

"I've tasted the white, I couldn't help it, and it's way better than at the Holiday Inn. Oh, and I've got crisps, too. Posh ones. *Artisan*." I shoved the packet under his chin and laughed and my laugh came out all loud and jagged but I couldn't help it, I couldn't hide it, there wasn't even any music for it to hide behind.

"Bethany."

"Just eat a fucking crisp." This was wrong. All wrong. No one swore on *Come Dine With Me*. Not this early on, at any rate.

"O.K." He munched one. A really small one. Then he raised his eyebrow like he was surprised. "Ooh, those are good." His hand disappeared into the foiled darkness; when it emerged, half of the packet was in his palm. I wouldn't have minded a few more crisps myself, but if they were making him happy and him being happy meant he'd stay, I didn't mind.

"You're hungry, aren't you?"

"Well, yes, but—"

"Take your coat off."

"Bethany."

"Take it off."

He opened his mouth and in that reddish darkness I saw a mush of crisps and words, none of which I wanted to see, so I grabbed his zip. I started to yank it but he grabbed my wrist and I said ouch, I said you're hurting me and he said, if you get off me, I'll get off you, but I didn't want to get off him and so I didn't and then he pushed me.

He pushed me really hard and I bashed into the table.

The olives fell on to my shoulder and I fell on to the floor. My hip hurt and my bum hurt and my heart, that hurt, too; and to top it all off, olive juice was dribbling down my neck and into my bra. This wasn't how it was meant to be.

I waited for him to say sorry. To squat down, ask if I was O.K., stroke me, help me, carry me to the sofa. Wipe the olive juice off with my new turquoise tea towel. But he didn't. He just crossed his arms and said I'd better give him the ring or the police would be getting involved.

"Why would they want to get involved?"

"The money."

"What money?"

"Bethany. Come on now. Just give me the ring and then I'll go." He took a deep breath, in and out. "And we can both get on with our lives."

"But . . . " If he wasn't going to help me up, I'd have to get up on my own. So I did. And I walked over to the hob and put the kettle on and poured the tortellini into the pan, but already it didn't look grown-up; it looked shrivelled, like a person who was way too old, or a baby that had been born way too soon. "I'm making tortellini. It's Italian."

As he opened his mouth to say something, the kettle steamed and bubbled. Turning my back on him, I poured the water over the pasta; I was about to put the lid on, because that was the next instruction on the back of the packet, only I didn't get a chance to pick it up because your dad was suddenly right behind me. I thought he might lean forward and kiss the back of my neck, like he used to. Instead, he yanked my arms behind my back—which is why I always look away when the

154 · CLARE FISHER

officers do that to the women in here. "Listen to me. This has got. It's gone. Too far. I never meant . . . I was confused, O.K.? And it was a bit of fun. That's all. But it's not fun any more; it's over. It's over, Bethany. That's it."

"But I've made you dinner. I've bought loads of—"

His grip tightened; later, there'd be big red marks where his fingers had been, and tomorrow, finger-shaped bruises. I was glad. "I don't care. Give me the ring."

"No."

Then he let go. He breathed in deeply. Maybe he was going to break down and cry. Maybe he was going to kiss me. But no. No, he didn't do any of those things. I'm sorry to tell you that your dad slapped me. He slapped me hard across the left cheek and harder across the right. Everything was stinging, singing an ugly song. My legs went all wobbly again and I had to grab the work surface to keep up.

"It's in my bra."

"What?"

"It's in the padding of my bra." I'd hoped this would be sexy. That it would be a fun, if slightly weird, warm-up to a make-up fuck. "If you want it, get it out yourself."

Huffing, he yanked my top halfway over my head and stuck his fingers down my bra and when he couldn't get it, he spun me around and undid the straps with both hands. His finger-tips were rough and cold, but they didn't rest on me, they pushed the skinny circle of metal out of the pouch where my bra pads were, then let go. He held the ring in the palm of his hand, staring at it as if he wasn't quite sure whether it was real.

"Phil . . . "

But it was too late. He was going, he was going, he was gone.

Gone.

And later, much later, when I remembered about the pasta, I found it, floating in the water, bloated, dead.

I wanted to run. I wanted to run into *away* and out the other side. I couldn't, though. I couldn't clear the table or empty the pasta pan or put the wine glasses back in the cupboard; I couldn't even look at them. I flopped on to my bed, which was cold and clammy with old sweat. No one was going to warm it up. No one. This was it; just me. I didn't close my eyes because I couldn't, because things were already dark enough. It was as if every person who'd ever left me was pinning me to the mattress. No point trying to get up.

"I'm here, Beth," said Erika, when I'd been silent for way too long. "I'm going to be here for you, no matter what."

"But how do I know that? Everyone leaves me, eventually."

"I won't. Now is not the past. But you have to work to make it different."

"What if I can't? What if I'm not clever enough?"

"Beth." She rubbed her left earlobe. Her hands were still raw but her earlobe was soft. It was big, too. "It's not about being clever. It's about being here. Being you."

I gulped. Her words were so kind, they hurt.

"Now, go back to that bed. How you were feeling. Only, this time, imagine me lying there with you. This time, you won't be going through it alone. O.K.?"

"O.K."

And she was right. I guess that's why people tell stories to other people, even hard ones.

The next morning, the sun woke me up. I hadn't bothered to close the curtains—there wasn't even much point as they were too small for the window—and so it shone straight on to my face. People say that bad weather only makes you feel worse than you're already feeling but I reckon it's the opposite; at least then you know there are bad things outside of you, too. All that warmth on my skin made me feel worse. Dry mouth, tight head. A hangover. At least this was a pain with clear edges; one I'd travelled into and out of a million times before. I ran into the kitchen and dunked my head under the tap, slurping straight at it, like a dog; this hurt my neck like hell but I didn't care because at least it meant I didn't have to face last night's bloated pasta and limp salad. Yet. Then my phone started buzzing.

"Hello?"

Maybe it was your dad. Maybe he'd realized what an idiot he'd been. Maybe—

"Is that Bethany?"

I had to think for a moment before mumbling yes.

"It's St James's. You left yesterday without being properly discharged? We need you to come back in for some more tests."

"Why?" The thought of going anywhere seemed impossible.

"Following the tests of yesterday, we have some concerns."

"What concerns?"

"We can explain when you get to the hospital."

"Manipulative fucks." Whether I said this before or after I hung up, I don't remember. My mind kept scribbling this picture of the hospital, all bright lights and pastel colours, and a bunch of nurses, hanging about and drinking tea and saying, *I wonder where she is? Where's that Bethany? I hope she gets here soon.* It was actually quite a good thing to imagine. It was also good to have a reason to leave.

The distance between my flat and the bus stop felt twice as long as usual, and every person I passed seemed twice as happy as usual, but the bus was half-empty and I got a seat and there weren't any stinky people sitting next to me so I felt a bit closer to all right. Replaying the nurse's words, I even felt important. Maybe I had cancer. Or some disease so rare they didn't even have a name for it. Maybe they'd run loads of tests and there would be an article about me in the paper and I'd set up my own Instagram and die quickly but die popular. People would feel so sorry for me, they'd be nothing but nice; they might even stick around. By the time I got to the hospital, I was 100% certain that getting my drink spiked had been an accident of the good kind.

"Now, we're concerned," said the nurse. "Because your blood tests suggested you're pregnant. And surely you must know that your current level of alcohol consumption could be harming your baby."

"Pregnant?" The word felt strange in my mouth. "I can't be."

The nurse sighed and raised an eyebrow like she'd seen this episode way too many times before. "Are you sexually active?"

"Yeah."

"And do you use contraception?"

"Well . . . "

She shook her head. "Honestly, there's enough education these days. It's not like before. Here."

She pushed what looked like a test tube towards me. "Pee in that."

Apart from its warmth, I found it hard to imagine, as I handed the test tube of pee to the nurse, that it had anything to do with life. No way could I imagine another human deciding to grow inside me.

Except you were.

"You're pregnant. Six weeks in, so early days. I wouldn't go round telling everyone yet, or anything—that is, if you decide to keep it."

"I'm pregnant?"

She rolled her eyes. "Yes."

"You're sure?"

"Yes."

"Like, 100%?"

She almost laughed. "Yes. Yes, I am."

My face was all smile.

"So you were trying?"

I shook my head. "It was an accident. Total accident. But a good one."

She smiled back. "Good. But look, don't rush into anything. Talk to someone you trust. Read these leaflets. Then think about what's best for the baby—and for you."

"Thanks." I shoved the leaflets down into the bottom of my bag but I didn't look at them; I already knew I was going to keep you.

As soon as I got home, I swept the pasta and the sauce and the crisps and even the turquoise things—when I looked at them, they screamed *him*, not me—straight in the bin. I chucked the wine glasses on top, listened to them smash, then tied the liner up extra-tight and dragged it all the way to the huge metal bins outside. Chucking it in, I waited to hear it smush against everyone else's rubbish. It did. Then I walked back to my flat and I wasn't even sad because I wasn't alone any more; you were inside me and you weren't going anywhere because you couldn't, not unless I said so; you were 100% mine.

14.
How cats can find sun to lie in, even on a cloudy day

Most women in here get letters every week. Happy letters, sad letters, angry letters. Letters about that new Chinese that opened up around the corner, they do a chilli-teriyaki chicken that will literally blow your head off—you should try it when you get out. That's if I still have my head! Letters to say their daughter has been caught swiping tuna mayo sandwiches from the canteen yet again. "They must've made a mistake; she don't even like tuna mayo." Letters about their divorce. "I never wanna see that bastard and his bastard moustache again." Letters about how they bloody changed all the bus routes so now you've got to walk the long way round to the shops. Letters about the letters their mum's sent to the Council about the bins but they don't bloody reply. Bet they put the bloody letter straight in the bin!!

I'm now an expert at making myself invisible when the letters are handed out: I do sit-ups or read in my cell, or I go to the library. But the women read their letters so many times that the words of the people who've written them—people who, often, love them too—jump out of their mouths in the line for dinner or the shower or exercise. When you're in line, the only way to make yourself invisible is to step out of it, which will only make you more visible, which means I've no choice but to breathe in deep through my nose and say something normal like, "Oh, really?" I'll say it as loud as I can in the hope of blocking out that mean little voice, the one only I can hear, that hisses: *See? You're so bad, no one ever writes to you.*

But the other day, I got a letter, too.

"Are you sure?" I said, when the screw chucked it into my cell.

He walked back, looked me up and down, and smiled like I was a bad joke he'd just found on the internet. "Can't you read? It's your own chavvy name on it."

I pressed my lips together. Counted to 1, 2, 3, 4, 5. If he'd still been there on 5, I'd have said something stupid; luckily, he was already at the next cell, tormenting someone else.

I lay down on my bed and looked again at the envelope:

Bethany Mitchell, HM Women's Prison, Leesthorpe, 112 Leesthorpe Way, Sussex. The handwriting. It was tall and loopy and I knew exactly who it belonged to and you're not going to guess who. Can you? Can you guess?

My mum.

My mum was the person at the end of the hand that wrote the letter. My letter.

The woman who'd carried me in her belly for nine months and then pushed me out into this world—just like I did for you.

I dropped it. Then I lay down on my mattress and shut my eyes and tried to rewind everything that had just happened. Too late. My heart was banging around my chest. My belly churned. Worst was this voice—a mix of mine and hers—that spiralled around my head, each word louder than the last: *So I heard what you done. I'm disgusted. Makes me certain I was right to leave you. I knew, even when you were a kid, that you were destined to do seriously bad things. I don't know how long your sentence is but I sincerely hope you don't get out for a long, long time.*

No matter if the envelope was still lying under my bed, unopened, hugging up dust, I was 100% convinced that when I'd open it, I'd find these words. They followed me around, making it hard to sleep or eat or focus on what I was supposed to be doing, like watching the tutor explain how to divide two fractions on the board, or standing in line or pretending to listen to Jeannie's story about how that scary new woman with the purple hair stole her toothbrush.

Erika told me to open it. "The reality can't be as bad as what you imagine."

"Oh," I said, "it's probably worse."

"Why assume that?"

"Because. We don't have a good history, me and letters."

Growing up, my foster parents were constantly getting them from school: Bethany is bunking off/naughty/stupid/mad/driving us mad/just not good enough. When I moved into my own flat, the doormat was always thick with special offers and newsletters and bills for "The Occupier." I'd never occupied any place before, so at first, I'd rip them open as soon as I got in from work, only to find a discount voucher for protein powder or an electricity bill from April to June three years in the past. Sometimes, the bills were headed up with fat red letters threatening debt collection agencies if the outstanding sum wasn't paid by blah blah blah. This didn't scare me because if they came, I'd tell them that two years ago I was living in Yeovil, which was where they should go to find this protein-loving person, because the social had set up a Council flat swap. They'd be so grateful, they might even give me a bonus, or something. Except, no one ever came. And as my life filled up, I stopped opening the letters; I'd just step right over them.

By the time you started growing inside me, the pile was so high that one evening I rushed in, bursting for a pee, and tripped right over it. Stuffing the letters into the bin, I noticed that the ones on the top didn't just say "The Occupier": they were addressed to me. The bank, the water company, the Council. I owed them all money, apparently. The bad thing was, I couldn't pay them. What with all the turquoise stuff I'd bought then chucked out, and then, seeing as I wasn't spending half the week at the Holiday Inn any more, having to spend more on electric and on food, I was constantly balancing on the edge of my overdraft. Have you ever balanced on the edge of anything? Like tried to stand up straight on a tall, skinny wall? You've got to hold out your arms, focus on one still point, concentrate. For a minute or two it's O.K., but eventually, your brain gets tired and your body gets bored, and you fall off. That's how it was with my overdraft.

"Chantelle, can you give me any more shifts?" It took me weeks to get around to asking this, but I did it.

"Why? You broke?"

"Nah, it's just . . . I want to save up."

"Save for what?"

"Just. Stuff."

"You been acting weird recently. I mean, weirder than usual. You got some new foundation or something? You're a weird colour."

For the past month, I'd been either throwing up or looking for a toilet or a bowl or a sink or a bin where I could do it without pissing people off. It wasn't like normal throwing up, where you do it and then you feel better; it was bright yellow and it made me feel worse. Chantelle was right: my face *had* gone a weird colour, too.

"Can't really give you any more shifts than you've already got, but if any of those stoners wimp out at the last minute, I'll let you know."

"What do you do when your money runs out?"

Chantelle frowned. "The best thing," she said, "is to borrow from a friend. Them payday loans—DON'T ever go to them. They're evil. Like, proper evil."

"Why?" I said. "What do they do?"

She shook her head. "You don't wanna know. What I'm saying is, ask someone but not just anyone—someone who has money and who owes you something."

The answer was simple: your dad. He was the only person I knew with money, the only one who owed me something. And he'd pay up, of course he would; he wasn't a bad person, he was just confused, and he'd do the right thing when he found out about you, of course he would. So there was really no reason to watch my spending.

When I wasn't too sick or tired to think, I'd think up things to say to your dad:

There's something I need to tell you.

You remember all those bits of you that you left inside me? They're growing into another person.

In six months' time a brand new human is going to pop out of my body and into the world. And it's yours. And I'm going to need money for a pushchair and nappies and Babygros and baby socks and all the other things that a brand new human needs.

You should see what this baby is doing to my boobs! I've gone from a 32A to a 34B. They would look good in your hands. :)

We'll teach it philosophy! We'll read it tons of books. It's going to be a proper brainbox. So best start thinking up clever names to call it! Although promise me you won't buy it one of those slogan T-shirts. There's nothing worse than a baby in a slogan T-shirt. Except maybe, being away from you and your laugh and the things I'd say just so I could hear it.

Aside from being sick, I was exhausted. 100% exhausted, 100% of the time. Keeping my eyes open and managing to say basic things like, would you like a Large, Extra Large, or Jumbo popcorn, and, that'll be £11.60 please, used all the energy I had; even *thinking* about getting in touch with your dad wiped me out.

"Hey, it's my birthday next Friday," Chantelle said, in the middle of all this. "You coming, yeah?"

"Not sure. I've got . . . plans."

"*You?* Plans?"

"Yeah. Why can't I have plans?"

She shrugged. "You get back with Phil or something?"

"No."

"Then what you up to?"

"Just . . . stuff." I couldn't explain that I'd be busy lying in bed, praying I wouldn't throw up, because that would lead to her asking why. I didn't have the energy to make another excuse up. Instead, I walked into Screen Three even though she hadn't told me to. The Orange Wednesday advert was on. I sat on an empty chair at the back and closed my eyes. The adverts were stupidly loud but I'd heard them so many times, they were easy to block out; I could just about hear that good inside voice, the one that's always one step ahead of the rest of me, and what it said was: *There will come a point when it will be obvious, you know. So you might as well just tell Chantelle and Phil and everyone else right now.* The voice was right, and I knew it was right. But my eyes were already shutting, and the other thing I knew was that by the time I woke up from my nap, the voice and all its knowing would be gone.

The letters kept coming and you kept growing—you'd been growing in me for three and a half months, the doctor said, so it was likely you'd stick around for the full nine—and if I didn't tell your dad soon, it would be a payday loan or . . . But there was no *or.* No choice.

On the night of Chantelle's birthday bash, the letters turned into phone calls: "Is this Ms. Mitchell? Have you not been receiving our letters? You're five months behind on Council tax. Your discount expired three months ago and you hadn't set up a direct debit, so . . . " Apparently, they'd given me a whole six months to "get myself on my feet"; now I was expected to pay every month, the same as everyone else. I didn't tell the woman that I wasn't on my feet just then; I was lying flat on my back, wondering when I was going to start feeling normal. I hung up and tried my best to erase the conversation from my mind. I couldn't, though; even snuggling under Marcia's fleece blanket didn't help. I rang Chantelle.

"Your birthday thing still on?"

She was silent for an unusually long time. Then she breathed in sharply and said: "I thought you had *plans*."

Her voice was muffled by the boom-boom-shout of lots of people having lots of fun in a space that wasn't meant to have much of either. It didn't make me feel good.

"Chantelle . . . "

I wanted to tell her I was sorry. I wanted to tell her about the letters and about your dad and about this voice, new yet old, strange yet familiar, which told me everything would be O.K. if I stayed away from other people.

"Yeah, whatever. Come if you wanna come. Just bring something good to drink." Then she hung up.

Getting out of bed and of my flat and of the estate and down the road and into the offie and out of the offie and up the stairs to Chantelle's flat was about ten times harder than it used to be. By the time I reached her front door, my eyes were fluttering shut. Yet I couldn't help feeling proud of myself. Proud for ignoring the voices. Maybe acting like everything was O.K. would mean it would be.

Some girl in a bright pink catsuit opened the door and batted her fake eyelashes at me like she was the opposite of impressed. "CHANTELLE! SOME GIRL'S HERE." Then she pushed her way into the crowded hall and was gone.

There were so many people in the flat, I couldn't see the sofa or the table or the fireplace which was crammed with weird cardboard things the kids had made at school; I couldn't see Chantelle or her kids; even the Chuckle Brothers weren't around; the ground shook with music and with footsteps and with words, and I couldn't move without brushing someone's elbow or hair extension or bum or boob; yet I didn't know any of them and they didn't know me; my heart was beating too fast, my thoughts moving too slow; this place had nothing to do with the places I'd been before and I needed to leave.

"Excuse me."

But I was trapped behind a wall of sweaty backs and none of them heard.

"*Excuse me.*"

The Lambrini was still cold, so I pressed it to my head. I reminded my heart that I wasn't running; there was no need to beat that fast, no need. I closed my eyes and tried to remember how to breathe.

"You all right, sweetheart?" One of the sweaty backs had turned into a smile topped off with bright blue eyes and hair that was either wet with sweat or with gel.

He must've seen the *nooo* stretched across my face, because the next thing was, he put his arm around my shoulder and with a magic power no one has ever shared with me, got people to move out of his way, so we could go into the kids' bedroom. The room was crammed with shoes, bags, scarves and coats. No people. I flopped on to the bottom bunk. It smelt of Sharina. I closed my eyes and tried to imagine her lying next to me, me reading her a story; I tried, but I couldn't see it: that part of my life felt far away and before I knew it, tears were bulging behind my eyeballs.

"Ain't seen you before."

The mattress sank as he sat down beside me.

"How you know Chanters?"

I opened my eyes. "Chanters?" I'd never heard anyone call her that.

"Yeah, that's what we called her, back in the day."

"Where are the kids?"

"The kids?" He wrinkled his nose as if I'd said, "Where's the bin?" "Dunno." He wriggled closer. "You're the one I wanna know about. You're cute."

He was the kind of guy the Chuckle Sisters would say was

fiiiittt. The kind of guy who'd get to the semi-finals of *X Factor* whether or not he could sing. But I didn't care. I closed my eyes. "Only thing there is to know about me is, I'm bare tired."

"Oh," he lay down next to me, "I'm sure there's more than that."

I adopted the same survival tactic as with the bills: if I pretended he wasn't there, sooner or later, he wouldn't be.

Except it didn't work; not with him, not with the bills, not with anything.

He rubbed his body right up against mine. Then his hand crept under my top and all the way up my stomach, to my boob, which was super-sensitive, and I shouted out, "Fuck."

"Ssh." He jammed his other hand under the waistband of my jeans. "You like this?"

"Get off!"

The more I shouted, the harder he pressed on top of me; eventually, I gave up. *It's not happening it's not happening it's not happening it's always happening what's the big deal?*

"What the fuck?" Chantelle's voice. It was definitely Chantelle's voice.

The guy climbed off me and rolled on to the floor. There was Chantelle, wine bottle in hand, the door wide open behind her, and other women already crowding around, sticking their necks in, making faces like, *What's going on? And, how am I gonna tell this story later?*

"Beth? Dan? What's going on?"

"He—"

"Little Beth here," he said, turning away from me, "she needed a lie down. So I said I'd help her. Didn't I? And didn't she like that?"

"OUT! Get out. Now."

Watching him scurry away from her, I wondered how she did it; how she could turn him from this big, scary creature into a pathetic small one. Except I never got a chance to ask because, the moment she'd slammed the door on those gossip-hungry faces, she went off on one: "Of all the guys here, you had to choose Dan? I mean, seriously? You knew we were getting back together. You knew and still . . . "

But I didn't know. I didn't know Dan was Sharina's dad. I didn't know they were starting to get back together. I swore she never told me, swore she never showed me a photo of him, but she kissed her teeth and then she said all this stuff about how she'd sort of thought I was a slut to begin with but she'd given me a chance because I was smarter than everyone else at the Odeon and I made her laugh. "For a while, I even thought I could count on you. I thought . . . Oh, but it don't matter because it's obvious now that I can't. No way. You're as bad as I first thought . . . You just care about getting what you want and that's it."

I laughed. "Like you don't."

"What's that supposed to mean?"

"It means, how come you can say whatever the hell *you* want about other people but no one can ever say what they want about you? Like how come you can say how I got no arse and how Lisa's spot looks like a second nose but we can't say that you're a fat bitch?"

The look on her face yelled STOP. It yelled that if I went home right now, we'd give each other the evils for a couple of days, but after that we'd get bored, then we'd start to miss each other, and then finally we'd forget about it. But the bad voice was back again, snarling at me that I'd already fucked everything up anyway so why not fuck it up a bit more? I didn't stop.

"Everyone thinks that, you know. And that you're dumb. You talk shit about doing shit that you're never going to do. And, and, you're a bad mum. Your kids are gonna grow up like—"

"Enough." She pushed me on to the kids' rocket-shaped rug. "Get your slutty arse away from my daughter's bed. It's no wonder your real mum walked away. Jesus Christ." I clung to the rocket, hoping it would shoot me to some other, better place. She jabbed me with her heel. "You deaf? Get the fuck out."

See? said the voice, over and over, as I dragged myself back to the flat that no longer felt like home. *You deserve to be alone.*

My stomach churned. I squatted down on the pavement and waited to be sick, but I wasn't, and then the other voice, the wise one, it whispered: *But you're not alone. You've got a human growing inside of you, remember?*

I rolled up my top and looked at myself in the mirror. There was no baby belly, not yet, but there was definitely more of me than there had been before. Despite everything, I smiled.

"The thing about history," said Erika, when I'd finished, "is, it changes."

"Not with me, it doesn't. It's just the same thing, over and over."

She raised her eyebrows. "Beth. Do you remember how you were when you started this list?"

"Yeah. It was only a few months ago."

"Do you feel the difference?"

The Beth at the beginning of this list was scared. Scared of the world inside of her and of the world outside. Scared to look. Scared to connect, ask, feel. Remembering her made me want to cry, so I just nodded.

"Good. Because I see the difference, I really do. But that doesn't make it easy. It's hard. Very, very hard. And you should feel proud of yourself."

I did feel proud. But I also knew that little things—a nasty look from a screw in the corridor or a comment from someone at dinner—could knock the pride right out of me for whole hours or days at a time. I pushed the letter into the middle of the table. "Mind if I open this now?"

Erika half-smiled. "Of course not."

My heart was banging and my hands were shaking and the bad voice was screaming but I still ripped the envelope open. I unfolded the paper and I read it.

Dear Beth

I've been meaning to write this letter for a long time. Too long. Since I read what happened in the papers. There are all sorts of excuses I could come up with but the real reason is fear. Fear of what to say and how; I was waiting for the perfect moment, the moment when I knew exactly how to tell you what I've been feeling all these years, what I felt when I read about your case, etc., etc. But then various things happened and they showed me that that moment would never come. I just have to go with the bits I can say now, which is: I'm here, if you want to write. Or talk. Or for me to visit—even if it's just so you can shout at me/tell me how angry you are, which is your right.

I'm writing this from a desk at the window of my flat and through that window I can see next door's cat rolling in a patch of sun. Its eyes are closed and its paws are curled and its belly is tufty and fat. It's almost always lying in a patch of sun, even on those days when the sky seems to forget the sun ever existed at all.

Love, Joanna, your Mum

"How do you feel?" asked Erika.

"I feel . . . Everything. Everything at once."

"Deep breaths. Let it in."

We shared some silence, but then it was the end of the session and I had to follow the screw back to my wing, and I couldn't help eyeballing every person I passed. Could they tell? Could they see I was different? That I was now a person with another person outside of this place who was thinking of them?

As soon as I was back in my cell, I wrote to Mum:

Dear Mum

Thanks for your letter. I liked the bit about the cat. It's the things like that I miss most. Things you don't think you'll miss when you're on the outside. Everyday things.

It's actually not as bad in here as you might think. I guess I just try to be like that cat: rolling in the sun whenever it's out, if you catch my drift. I've been reading and writing a lot in here (I'm redoing my GCSEs but I take books out of the library and read them whenever I can, too) and it's making me think and feel a lot. It's good but hard. Right now I'm thinking about being pregnant, and I guess what I want to know is, how did you feel when you were pregnant? How did you imagine our life would be?

Beth

15.
BABY BELLIES

It's been three days since I posted that letter but I'm not freaking out. When the bad voice creeps close—*she's got so many bad things to write about you, it'll take her MONTHS to get through them*—I chase it away by doing whatever the voice is telling me *not* to do, like eating one of the chocolate bars Linda keeps giving me to say thank you, or jumping up and down on the spot, or running as fast as I can on the treadmill, or starting a conversation with Linda or the Lee or Jeannie, even if I don't have anything to say. At first, your mouth or your legs or your heart or whatever it is you're trying to move, it will moan and groan and creak. But you put one foot in front of the other. You chomp down and you chew. You say some ready-made sentence like, "Do you reckon this chicken curry is worse than last week's?" And the ground pushes back, the sugar sparks you awake, or someone says, "What? This week's is way better, no contest. Although do you remember how the curries were when Sabrina was in the kitchen? She was magic, was Sabrina. Shame she got ghosted to Sandwood, she was on Enhanced and everything, but they didn't even give her any warning. I guess that's why they call it ghosting . . . " By the time you notice that you're out of breath or answering back—"Which Sabrina was this? Sabrina the teenage witch?"—it's too late: life is happening to you and you're happening to it and there's nothing either of you can do about it.

While my mum is probably staring at that sunbathing cat, wondering how to begin her letter about being pregnant with me, I'm sitting in the library, watching the librarian read her own book under the desk, writing about being pregnant with you. And you know what? Once I'd stumbled through the exhaustion and the sickness and the constant cloudiness, it was great.

Chantelle wasn't speaking to me, and Chantelle not-speaking to me meant that the Chuckle Sisters weren't speaking to me and that I got the worst shifts, but I didn't care; I'd either just been for an appointment or was planning my bus route to the next one. The feeling I'd had in the first few months, like other people were dangerous, it had turned inside out; now, I couldn't stop talking to strangers. I say strangers; mostly, they were women. Women who had kids snoozing on their laps or a tired-yet-satisfied look in their eyes that made me sure they were mums. Women who looked kind.

"Mind if I sit down?" I asked this granny-like woman on the bus. The seat beside her was free so I didn't need to ask, but I was on my way to my twenty-week scan, and the words just rushed out of my mouth.

"Oh, a nice polite one!" the woman said. "A slim one, too." She shuffled about in her seat, trying and failing to make her bum fit into the space meant for one person. "Wish I could say the same for me."

"I won't be for much longer," I said.

The way she looked at me, you could tell she wasn't used to strangers talking to her on the bus; not just that, but she was glad. "And why's that?"

"I'm pregnant."

She stared at my belly and shook her head. "You can't be far gone."

"Twenty weeks. I'm on my way to the scan."

"Oh! Lovely. That's the exciting bit. When you see the little blob on the screen. A blob that can be anyone, anything. With my first, I was thinking, nuclear physicist. Engineer. By the time the third came along, I'd already learned that they were just going to be whoever they were, no arguing. Which is for the best, I think." The bus lurched around corners and over speed bumps but I didn't mind; looking straight into her round, creased face, her brown eyes shining with years and years of happyish life, I felt like I was somewhere much cosier. Like her living room, or something. "Take my sister. Years and years, she wasted, trying to make her son into a genius. Private tutors, extra classes and what have you. Turned him off it completely. He flunked his O-levels, or what is it now, his GCSEs. But he ended up a very successful builder. Got a big house down Mitcham way with two garages, a garden, and everything. What I mean is, whatever you want for them won't be half what they can build for themselves, if you let them."

"I know what you mean," I said. "The other day, I was in the park and I saw this mum and her daughter running. The mum kept yelling at the daughter to hurry up. The daughter kept stomping and sticking out her bottom lip. But as soon as the mum stopped to chat to some other woman who was walking one of those annoying little yappy dogs, as soon as the daughter knew she wasn't looking, she started to run really fast."

"Oh, running! I wish I could run. Definitely missed that boat."

"I love it. At least, I did. But I'm not going to force my kid to run if they don't want to. I'm not going to force them to do anything. I'll show them the things I like, like running and reading and walking around and looking at things. But I want them to learn all sorts of other things—things I don't know about, like, like . . . Well, I don't even know what—that's how little I know. Point is, I want them to be able to choose."

She tilted her head and looked at me like I was surprising her in a good way. "You'll be a brilliant mum."

"Thanks."

Her words stayed with me all the way into the hospital and up in the lift and along the corridor and down another lift and through two sets of heavy swinging doors, to where my appointment was. When they called my name and the nurse asked whether anyone was coming with me, I had to look all around me before I was sure that the right answer was no.

The woman who was going to scan me—her official name was something like a *snoreographer* but I was so excited to see you pop up on the big screen, I didn't really listen—told me to lift up my top and pull down my trousers.

"Lie down on this couch," she said. Recently, I'd only been told to pay, hurry up, clean the toilets, and other bad things, so to be told to lie down, it was nice.

"Comfortable?"

"I could fall asleep."

"Bless you! Feel free to close your eyes. I'm just going to rub some gel over your bump."

The gel was all cold and gooey; it made me laugh. She laughed with me, then wrapped me in some sort of tissue paper. "I feel like someone's Christmas present!" I said, which was true. Me being able to say exactly what was going on inside of me was another new, strange thing that had started happening. I guess it was because I'd gone for so long without talking that when I finally did, the words just spilled out, like they knew this was their one chance. "I'm well excited. You know, it kicked for the first time last week. At first, I thought it was because of a dodgy panini, so I stopped with those paninis, but it carried on. Then I, like, really listened to it, and I realized, it felt different. More like fluttering. Like butterflies but, you know, real ones."

"That's lovely. Sounds like your baby is a gentle one—they don't all feel like butterflies, that's for sure! Now," she waved what looked like a remote control in the air. "Are you ready?"

I nodded.

She rubbed the remote over my belly, back and forth, back and forth. It tickled, but I didn't laugh, I didn't yell; my eyes were fixed on the big screen.

"And here it is!"

Water wobbled all over the screen, and in the middle was what looked to me like a question mark; your head was the balloon-like body of the question, your body the squashed-up bottom. Here was a human, wrapped in wobbles, in a hollow that was inside me.

"Here we are. It looks a healthy size. Would you like to know the sex?"

"Yes."

"It's a girl."

And it wasn't until the smile pushed and pulled at my lips that I realized how much I'd been hoping for this. You being a girl made it even more likely that you weren't just one flukey good thing to happen in a bad story; it was the start of a whole new one, a better version of me.

Women in newspapers and women in magazines, women in TV shows that are supposed to be funny and TV shows that aren't supposed to be funny and even real-life women—they're always on about their baby bellies like they're a bad thing: "People are still asking me when it's due, and Bella's *seven*!" and, "You'd never guess she'd given birth two weeks ago— apparently she had this live-in paleo PT who'd wrestle her to the ground every time she went at the fridge. Lucky for some!" And on the fronts of the magazines I read while waiting for my scans and my doctor's appointments: "How I Lost My Baby Weight in Just Two Weeks!"

Well, I loved it. I loved watching my body grow into something bigger and better and stranger than it already was. By thirty weeks, my bras, my pants, my tops, everything had got tight; my belly was starting to push a gap between my tops and my trousers, but I didn't mind; I wore the tightest things on purpose. I wanted everyone to know that the person I was then wasn't the only one I was ever going to be.

The doctor said that, given my low weight and my bad eating habits, I was lucky to conceive. Lucky that you were growing as fast as you were. "But you've got to make every effort," he said, "to look after yourself." He paused, licked his lips and added: "That includes eating and sleeping as well as you can." I took all the vitamins he told me to take. I read all the leaflets he gave me and I checked out as many of the library's pregnancy books as I could carry. Some of these books were jammed with sentences which began "You must . . . " "Never . . . " "Always . . . " "Whatever you do, don't . . . " Others had long sections about the dangers of eating non-organic vegetables and of breathing in too many car fumes. I didn't get far with these books: they just made me angry and scared.

I focused on the books with more words like "You could . . . " and "How about . . . " The books with clear instructions, like: "Eat regular meals and plenty of whole grains, protein and fresh vegetables." This was a challenge enough: before you, I didn't pay attention to what went into my mouth or, more often, what didn't. I'd not bother to eat until my head was about to float away from my body and, if I stood up too quickly, everything would go black. When I did eat, I'd eat whatever was nearest and cheapest: popcorn, a pack of Maltesers, chips, paninis, etc., etc. At home I mainly ate Weetabix, spaghetti hoops and beans on toast. These were the things you could buy anywhere—and which I'd eaten and enjoyed eating in every single house I'd lived in growing up.

I took the doctor's words seriously: for the first time in my life, I bought onions, garlic and cooking oil. I made pasta and tomato and vegetable sauce with grated cheese on top. It came out a bit burnt, but I didn't mind; I was proud of myself for making it. Plus, the sickness had been replaced with hunger: I was eating, or thinking about eating, almost all of the time. I'd eat and I'd eat, often reading pregnancy books at the same time, or just staring at the books and imagining you in a few years, kicking your legs under the table, telling me you couldn't eat spaghetti because it came from monsters, why couldn't you have pasta twists? And I'd have to think up some story to convince you otherwise. One of the books suggested taking a Tupperware of finger sandwiches on "outings" so that your kid wouldn't pester you for sweets. I didn't have any Tupperware so I bought them and made cheese and Marmite sandwiches and cut them into finger shapes. I'd go to the kind of place I could take the future-you—the park, the shops, and maybe, once you were big enough to walk and talk and scoot on a little plastic scooter, somewhere in Central, like London Zoo— and, as soon as I'd found a good seat, I'd eat the sandwiches and talk to the future-you. Mummy, why's that missile so big? Mum, why are those women just standing in the tennis court chatting but not actually playing tennis? Mum, what do you think it's like to be a tree? Mum, do you think that man over there with the weird glasses might be a spy?

The bigger my belly, the more people noticed me. They'd offer me their seats on the bus. They'd ask, in a soft, whispering voice, when it was due. But other people didn't notice. Or if they did, they'd stare until I stared back, and in the split second before they looked the other way, their eyes would flash with what they thought of me, i.e. that I was an embarrassing and wrong thing.

"Right."

"It's a girl."

"Congratulations."

Whenever I saw another pregnant woman, I'd stare at her as hard as I could and with any luck she'd stare back.

Sometimes, when I was waiting for appointments, the woman sitting next to me would sigh, and I'd say, "Tell me about it," and she'd look at me like she was surprised and relieved, and then she'd tell me how much her back hurt from carrying heavy folders up and down two flights of stairs at work, and how her "so called colleagues" would gawp at her huffing and puffing but wouldn't in a million years shave a few seconds off their lunch break to help. "I'm counting the days until maternity leave, I tell you. Are you on maternity leave yet?" I didn't know how to tell them there was no maternity leave on a zero-hours contract. Or about how it now took me twice as long to go up and down the steps and ramps between the road and my flat. Instead, I'd tell them something I'd read in a library book about how to relieve backache in pregnancy, only, I wouldn't say I'd read it in a book; I'd say that I got it off my aunt or my mum. "Oh, I've tried that," the woman might say, "but it didn't work. Your body must be a lot better at handling this, at your age." Then she'd smile at me and I'd smile back and in those few seconds, it didn't matter that she was in a business suit and I was in a tracksuit; we were two women with two new people growing inside us and we were trying to grow them the best we could.

The other good thing about a baby belly is, you're never alone. Not only are you not alone; you're with someone you love. Someone you're not afraid of because they're already as deep inside of you as it's possible to be. It's not just your belly that grows; it's your whole world. You notice new things, like how there are four different types of tree in the patch of grass outside your flat; you don't know their names but you know that one has a smooth skinny trunk, the other a fat knobbly one, the other strange silver streaks, the last finger-like leaves. You promise yourself you'll look all this up in a book, that you'll be 100% cleverer by the time your baby's born, except you never do because five minutes later there's a group of old ladies on the grass doing t'ai chi, at least, you think it's t'ai chi, you want to ask what they're up to, but you don't because now you're looking at the street-sweeper, wondering where he comes from, if he misses where he comes from, what he's thinking about as he pushes his sweeper along the path. You wonder how you've lived so close to so many things for so long without seeing them. You can't wait for time to skip forward, for the world to be even bigger—even more yours.

I went to your dad's house maybe ten or fifteen times before he knew it; I went on Google Maps in the computer room in the library. The man next to me kept asking the girl on the desk to help with his visa application, but the girl on the desk didn't know about visas, and anyway, there were other people who needed her help, like a man whose YouTube Bollywood show kept getting blocked by the library filter—"is not fair; is not dirty"—and a woman who really, really needed to print off her dissertation and no, she couldn't wait until tomorrow, the deadline was today, wouldn't anyone swap with her for ten minutes, oh please? Some people tutted when these people's problems poked holes in the silence, but me, I just smiled inside; any problem was good so long as it wasn't mine.

On Google Maps, your dad's house looked exactly the same as every other house on its street: grey pebble-dash walls and a red-brown roof, a neatly trimmed hedge and a freshly painted garden gate. The day the Google Maps van snuck down his street, the sun was out and everyone was away at the park. It was easy to imagine myself into the neat yellow body of the Google Maps man, carefully unhooking the clasp on the gate, walking up the garden path. I'd go there on a Sunday after-noon—Jenny hated going anywhere on a Sunday and so they never did—and when he saw me, he'd realize how sad and bored he was, and he'd leave. Small. Neat. Simple.

The Wednesday before going there for real, I finally obeyed

the doctor's orders to go to antenatal classes. The class was in a community centre near Brixton. When I left my flat, I was excited; at last, I'd be able to talk about the strange, new things happening to my body. I'd learn all kinds of things that would make me look and feel like a proper grown-up, and when your dad finally saw me in the flesh, he'd know. Also, I might make a new friend, or something.

But when I turned off the High Road into a quiet house-lined street and saw the squat little scout hut with grills over the windows and a noticeboard in its yard so grimy you couldn't read any of its notices, my heart began to beat its get-me-out-of-here beat.

All I could see was Paul dropping six-year-old Beth off at Brownies, her refusing to get out of the car, him saying she had to, she had to try, her kicking the seat and the glove compartment because she didn't know how to explain to him, or even herself, why things kept going wrong; why, no matter how hard she tried to make friends, other kids ended up hating her, and because she hated that they hated her, she'd do bad things to them, which of course, would only make things worse.

I can't go in.

Course you can.

Can't.

Get a grip; that was then; now is now.

I went in. This community centre/scout hut was a lot brighter than the one where—until I got banned—I went to Brownies. And there were no kids, just women. The problem was, they all knew each other already, and were standing in little clumps, looking at and, in a few cases, pressing their hands against, each other's bellies. Some had guys with them, and it was the guys I stared at as I found a corner to hide in; they looked as scared as I was.

There was one pregnant woman with her mum; you could tell it was her mum because she was basically a fatter, wrinklier version of the pregnant woman. Plus, the pregnant woman was saying something to the older-her through gritted teeth in the way that is 100% acceptable so long as you share the same blood. They argued, back and forth, back and forth, and then the mum pointed at something in the leaflet she was holding, and they both burst out laughing.

"Hello! I don't think we've seen you before, have we? What's your name?" The only non-pregnant woman in the room marched over to me and gave me a little pat on the shoulder. I didn't know her and I didn't particularly like her but watching that mum and daughter had emptied the air around me, and so I didn't mind the weight of her hand.

"Beth," I mumbled.

"A lovely name," she said. "I'm Gloria. And this . . . " she beamed at my bump, "is?"

"We're not sure yet."

"Of course not. There's no rush. You wouldn't believe the number of women who have a sort of brainwave just before the birth. Will the father be joining us or . . . ?"

When I'd said *we*, I'd meant me and you. I was hoping that I'd work out from the way you kicked and wriggled when I shouted different words, what you wanted to be called. But she'd obviously thought something else. "He's at work."

A few minutes later, Gloria clapped her hands together and told the "mums-to-be" to sit down. Everyone looked around, but there weren't any chairs. "Sorry about that!" laughed Gloria. "I was so busy chatting to some lovely ladies, I didn't even notice. Those bloody cadets." She clapped her hand over her mouth. "Apologies for the language. But your babies won't understand . . . yet!"

As we wobbled and squatted towards the brown carpet, the woman next to me muttered, "Bloody NHS. I'll stick with the NCT after this."

Then Gloria opened her mouth. She didn't close it for a

long time. She spoke as if she was reading off a screen, but when I turned around, there was no screen, only a few notice-boards covered with some kids' drawings of dragons and some photos of old people eating cakes. She spoke as if she'd swallowed three or four Wikipedia pages and was spitting them out. She spoke about what to pack in your hospital bag and when to pack it—"as soon as possible"—and what pain relief to go for in the hospital—"you're never going to be offered this many drugs at once, so don't waste the opportunity!"— and what to expect after the birth—"a lot of tears and nowhere near enough sleep." She spoke about all the things that could go wrong: how your baby could stop moving or could move in the wrong way or could just die right there inside of you and you'd have to give birth to it blue. Blue! Or some other thing to do with the placenta I can't remember the name of. Or yet another thing. There were so many things, so many of them bad, and from what she said, it seemed like all the good ones needed money and planning and a lot of kind, helpful people around, none of which I had, and I didn't want to think about not having them, and I didn't want to talk to the other women, who were all making notes or muttering that they knew all this already, and my heart was being weird again, so I slipped out before the end.

By the time I got home, there was an idea in my head, a new and exciting one: what about my real mum? Sure, she'd walked out on me. Sure, she'd probably forgotten I even existed. But what if she hadn't? What if all the time between now and then had made her forget how bad I was? What if she was forever checking her phone, hoping I'd call? What if she could imagine no better thing to be than a grandma?

The other thing I noticed at the class was that all the other women were wearing proper pregnancy clothes. They all had the "Baby On Board!" badges pinned to their coats. They argued passionately about different brands of buggy: "Oh, the new PramWin is so good, but I think £500 is a bit much . . . Then the MumuLife is only £345 . . . " When they met me, their eyes would linger on the stripe of skin between my jeans and my T-shirt. If I saw them looking before they saw me looking, I'd see the thought that I was doing it wrong smear across their eyes. *They can all fuck off*, I thought. Except they didn't; their words followed me around for days, eventually pushing me into Mothercare. Wandering round the rows and shelves and rows and rows of Babygros, baby mats, baby socks and hats and bibs and coats and car seats and pillows and toys and chews and nappies and wipes and creams and dummies and rattles and mobiles and monitors, it hit me: you weren't going to stay inside me forever. Soon, very soon, you'd be a real person. A person who needed stuff. So much stuff! There was no way I could afford it, no way. The time had come to tell your dad.

As I left my flat to see your dad for real, I felt 100% sure things would work out. Freshly washed clothes stretched over a freshly grown baby belly: I looked good. But by the time I got off the tube at Harrow and Wealdstone, I felt more like 77%. By the time I'd walked down four identical cul-de-sacs before finding his, it was more like 45%. After that, I stopped counting. The houses weren't much bigger than on Google Maps but they *were* complicated; some had "Vote Conservative!" posters Blu-tacked to their windows, others had Labour or Green. Some had cut grass, others wild rushes, others cracked up concrete and plant pots with no plants inside of them, just earth.

Then there was your dad's house. Someone—probably him—had been chipping away at the pebble-dash since the visit from the Google Maps van; the left half of the house was brick, the right side pebble-and-concrete puke. The line between the two sides was jagged. Had your dad spent weekend after weekend chipping away then giving up? He'd never mentioned it. Maybe there were other things he hadn't mentioned, too.

There were no net curtains, so through the window I spied a sofa, a TV, a huge table piled with exercise books and an empty fruit bowl, two huge plastic boxes of toys in the corner, and, snaking between all these things, a train set. The lights were on and I was wondering whether they really were home, whether this was the one Sunday afternoon they'd gone out, when I heard a squeal. It came from the alley that ran down the left side of the house. Then a kid ran up it, all blond curls and dungarees and wellies shaped like frogs. He was holding one of those blow-up beach balls. His cheeks were bright red and he looked mighty pleased with himself.

"You must be Hamish." I walked up to the garden wall. He frowned. "Who are you?"

"I'm a friend of your dad's."

"Dad's not happy today. Mummy wants him to make a table in the back garden but he doesn't want to."

"Oh, that's not fun!" I said.

Hamish's curls jiggled about as he shook his head. He had your dad's nose. I liked him. "It's not fun no no. I wanted dad to play ball but he wouldn't do that either."

"I'll play with you."

Hamish licked his lips, obviously confused. "Most of dad's friends don't want to play with me."

"I'm different."

He still looked worried so I held out my hands and smiled. "Throw to me!"

Squatting down, he hurled the ball into the air. It rose high above his head, then plopped into a flowerbed. Some dainty pink flowers lay squashed beneath it. Bending over wasn't the best thing to do with you inside of me, but I did it. I threw it accidentally-on-purpose away from the house.

"Nooo!" yelled Hamish. "That's my best ball. It's going to get run over."

"Silly me!" I said. Then I held the gate open. "There are no cars yet, so why don't you come and help me rescue it?"

Hamish stepped towards the gate, then stopped. "I'm not supposed to."

"It's fine. I'm your daddy's friend, remember? And this," I rubbed my belly, "this is going to be a friend for you, too."

"A baby!" He reached out to touch you but I backed away, and so he stepped into the road, and I stepped back, and he stepped some more, and pretty soon there were a few houses between us and your dad's house, and part of me thought, oh no, this isn't what's meant to happen, but the big bad wolf part assured me it was awesome. I sat on a low brick wall, rolled up my top, grabbed Hamish's hand, and—smiling all the time so he knew not to be scared—I pressed it on to my belly. I pressed it right up against you.

"Oh," he said. "That's lovely and warm!"

And that was it. That was as much as you were ever going to know your brother.

"Would you like a little sister?" I asked. He nodded. Then he shook his head. Then he nodded again.

"Well, that's lucky for you," I said, ignoring the shake, "because that's what's in here."

He stuck out his bottom lip and pulled his hand away. "But you're not my mummy."

"No. But your daddy is my baby's daddy."

"But . . . " And then he began to cry. I sshhed him. I tried to distract him with the ball. He cried louder. I shouted at him; still, he wouldn't stop. He wouldn't stop and I could feel curtains twitching and people watching and so I grabbed him. I grabbed his wrist and then I grabbed his curls and then I was grabbing him everywhere.

"GET AWAY FROM MY SON!"

There must've been a time between me grabbing him and Jenny yelling in my face. There must've been a time when the neighbours came out of their houses and their gardens and their cars and gathered to watch. Well, there were only three or four of them, but when I first saw them, they looked like a lot. Like too much. Everything was happening wrong and too fast and I didn't know why or how to slow it back down.

Jenny was a red-eyed, greasy-haired mess, dressed in one of your dad's old jumpers and a pair of leggings with a hole in the left knee. I tried to reassure myself with the fact that I was younger and better dressed, that I'd washed my hair. But she was holding Hamish over her shoulder, his cries had shrunk to cute whimpers, his head was floppy, and from the way the neighbours' eyes flipped from her to me to her to me, it was 100% obvious whose side they were on.

"Who are you?" she said. Her voice was low and shaky, like it was coming from some place buried deep. "PHIL!" She yelled back at the house. "Philip! Have you got through to the police?" Then she turned to the neighbours and, laying on a surprisingly pretty smile, she asked them to please go and "fetch" her "husband."

"Don't you want one of us to stay and . . . support?" asked a grey-haired woman in a bobbly lilac fleece.

"I'll be fine, Nell. But thank you. It's great to know I've got neighbours I can rely on."

Nell nodded, swallowing her disappointment, and hurried towards the house.

When we were alone, Jenny tightened her grip on Hamish, leant towards me and said: "Oh, I know about you all right. Phil told me everything. And can I just say thank you. Thank you because, you know what? Things are so much better between us now. *So* much better. After the hell he went through with you, he's worked out what he doesn't want—and what he does. Now, if you'll excuse me, I'm going back to my family."

My hands were shaking. Tears were busting out of my eyes. "I'm sorry," I mumbled.

Jenny laughed. "It's a bit late for that."

"I never meant . . . to hurt you. I think, I think . . . you're great." My hands stuck to my belly, which is a thing they'd started to do without me telling them to, especially when I got scared.

She was already walking away. "Jenny." I hurried to catch up with her. "He was the one who came after me." She was almost at the gate. "This baby is his." At this, she stopped. She didn't turn round but her shoulders heaved, as if all the air around her wasn't enough.

Your dad rushed out of the front door, phone pressed to one ear; when he saw me, the I've-got-it-sorted expression fell right off his face. "In fact, don't worry, officer. It's . . . fine now. Yes, sorry for the bother."

"What are you doing?" Jenny snapped at him.

"It's not . . . "

"It's yours." I thrust my belly in the air. "It's a girl. And it's yours."

Phil shook his head, very quickly, from side to side. "It is," I said. "We never used protection, remember? Twenty-eight weeks now. And look, I'm not expecting—"

"Phil, *do* something. God's sake."

Phil did nothing.

"You don't have to get back with me," I said, my voice creaky and faraway, like it belonged to someone else, "but maybe Hamish could see his little half-sister sometimes? Maybe you could tell him she was a cousin or something?" I could see it already; me and them at Christmas, a strange but happy family. "Or a long-lost sister. He could just call me aunty."

"Beth." Your dad marched towards me. "Get real. It's over between us. OVER."

"But she's here," I said. "She's in me."

"So what? She can't be mine."

"I haven't slept with anyone else."

They both laughed. "That," said Jenny, "I find hard to believe." She narrowed her eyes. "Like I said, he told me everything. *Everything.*"

She meant Dale. She meant the things I did when I was with Dale. And before. "That's not fair," I said. "I was fifteen."

"Beth," said your dad, putting an arm around Jenny, "if you don't leave in the next three minutes, I'm calling the police." Then he steered her into the house and they slammed the door. A few seconds later, they closed the curtains.

"You can't just do this!" I shouted. "She's your kid. She deserves a family. And I can't afford it. I need . . . " But there were so many things I needed, I didn't know where to begin.

"I think," the woman in the bobbly fleece and her friends emerged from who knows where, surrounding me with crossed arms and cross faces, "you'd better leave our street."

And I did. On the tube south, a woman jumped out of her seat and motioned for me to sit down. I rubbed my belly and tried to smile but I can't have managed it because the next thing she asked was whether I was tired, and I said I was, and she said of course, she said she couldn't believe how tired she got with her first. "The second one came out twice the size but I didn't get so tired. I suppose it was partly emotional, with the first; a part of you is constantly thinking, how will I do it? How will I become a mum?"

When she saw the way I was looking at her, she laughed. "Oh, don't be frightened. You'll surprise yourself. You'll be great, I'm sure."

At Maida Vale, the woman hopped off, but I thought about her all the way back to my flat. Her face, her hands, her words. She wasn't my mum—I couldn't remember my mum's face, but I knew that I'd recognize it when I saw it and this wasn't hers—but she could be. And someone, somewhere, could be looking at my mum, thinking she could be theirs. My mum was out there, living, breathing, sighing, picking food out of her teeth, just as real as anyone else. Maybe she was even thinking about me. Every other mum I'd ever seen flashed through my head: Cal's mum, the woman at the antenatal class, the women who shielded their kids from the Odeon pick 'n' mix and the ones who didn't, the woman I'd just seen at a bus stop, leaning on her pram and ssshing her baby while texting. Soon, I'd join these women; I'd be a mum. This had to be a good thing . . . Didn't it? And having my own mum around would help. It would help a lot. By the time I got home I'd mostly forgotten about Phil; I dug through the letters from Social Services until I found my new adviser's number. I wasn't going to stop until I found her.

We've been locked up for twenty hours now. We haven't done any new wrong things; they just do this to us sometimes. It makes some of the girls so angry, that the moment they're unlocked, they kick off at each other or at the walls or the screws or one of the dumb laminated signs that are stuck to the mouth-coloured walls; before they know it, they're locked right back up. I could have been one of those girls, but I'm not. I've got Erika and I've got this list and, with every word that I write, I'm getting closer to you.

The other person I'm getting closer to is my mum: she read my letter and then she walked down the street and went to Tesco and did lots of other normal things while thinking about me; then, she wrote back. Luckily, I got the letter before lock-up. I curled up on my bed and I read it and I read it until I fell asleep. I woke up with the paper crumpled against my cheek; then I rolled over and read it again. I munched the cheesy crackers and drank the juice I'd saved from the last canteen. I read until her words and her guts were a part of me. My heart is pumping them to every part of my body, making me strong. Strong enough to face the part of my story that's been locked up inside me for way, way too long.

Dear Beth

I can't tell you how much I smiled when I read your letter. In fact, I can: I read it on the bus. I was sitting beside a
rather nosy woman (I always end up next to a nosy woman.
Perhaps the universe is trying to tell me something?). "A
real love letter!" she exclaimed. "You don't see many of
those any more." "Oh," I said. "It's not a . . . " I was about
to say that it wasn't a love letter, but then I realized that it
was. It was a love letter, if not of a romantic kind.

I suppose I should tell you how I came to read your letter on the bus. It's not the sunniest of reasons but it's part
of my everyday life whether I want it to be or not. I saw it
on the doormat as I was rushing out for an appointment.
Seeing my name spelled out in those round, firmly-pressed
letters, it tugged on my heart. I knew even before I ripped
open the envelope that it was from you.

The appointment was at the hospital. You know—or
maybe you don't? I never knew how much they told you—
I've spent a lot of time there. Too much.

I hate having to go back.

The hour with my psychologist is invaluable; sometimes
it's hard, other times, exhilarating, but I've been working
with this particular psych for three years now and he's saved
me again and again. (Although I can already hear him
telling me off for saying that: "You saved yourself! We're
doing this work together, remember?") It saddens me to
imagine how different things could have been if I'd found
him, or someone like him, sooner. (I never hit it off with any
of the others.)

No, it's the getting from my flat to his room that I hate.
The squat Victorian building separated from the outside
world by high iron railings. The way all eyes stick to you as
you press the bell for that particular bus stop (which is too
far from any shops or bars or any other useful place for

anyone to doubt where you're going). I hate, too, the corridors. The reception. The distinct smell: a freshly deodorized armpit writ large. Not that it's gloomy; first-time visitors are quick to praise its cheerfully bright surfaces. What they don't realize (not yet, at least) is there's a reason they make the physical space as cheery as possible. That reason is the kind of darkness that resists even the brightest light. You may or may not know what I mean (I really, really hope you don't). I was trapped in it for many years, and although I'm not there any more and almost completely believe I will never return there, it takes a tremendous strength to stop the memories crowding in.

Sometimes, the hour with the psych is so good, I come out smiling. Other times, it's almost impossible to pull on the kind of face that won't make people flinch at you on the bus. Or I'll be jumpy for days afterwards, snapping at people at work, dropping cups, saucers, papers left, right and centre, bursting into tears at the slightest provocation. I'm incredibly lucky in that my boss's sister has had similar struggles to me; it's the first place where I've been open with my issues and where people have understood. "It's O.K.," she'll whisper, handing me a dustpan and brush, "I'm not going to sack you for breaking my second favourite mug!" Somehow—and I don't know if it's the new prescription or the fortnightly sessions—I manage to push through the motions until they keep moving of their own accord. Yes, I'll think, I have a job. I have a flat. I even have a few friends. No one's out to take them from me; the only person who's in danger of doing that is myself, or at least, my old self: I hope and mostly, mostly, I believe, that I'm beyond that. Beyond, I think, is a better word than cured.

Oh dear.

Two days have gone by and, reading over the above

paragraph, I'm afraid it's a little gloomy. I was tempted, very tempted, to scribble it out. Then I looked up and saw the two big words I've written in big felt-tip capitals and Blu-tacked to my bedroom wall: BE KIND. Destroying myself has only made things worse, and you can fall into a spiral of destruction at any time; it's easy to slip on as small a thing as a scribble. Besides, if we're to be honest with each other—and I hope we can be—you need to know these things.

Now, for some sun: the cat, since you ask, hasn't done much lying about recently. He's been too busy chasing birds in trees. He hasn't had any luck (at least, as far as I can tell) but he climbs the conifer's narrow branches and waits for hours at the top—a big black-and-white blob among the green; it's quite something!—eventually pawing at the air so clumsily that every bird within a half-mile radius flaps off. But that doesn't put him off. The next day he'll make the same journey all over again. The eternal optimist!

Talking of optimism, I was, in the words of the midwife, "one of the most ludicrously optimistic mums-to-be" she'd ever seen. I had all the books. All the answers. When I spoke to the other women at antenatal classes, they'd ask if I was on my second or third child. When people made that face at me when, after much poking and prodding, I revealed I wasn't in touch with the father, I quoted my col-league, who referred to her husband as her "biggest, most demanding and immature child of all." I quoted feminist child-rearing books. "There's no shame in feeling scared," the midwife said. But I wasn't; there wasn't a future human so much as a future knot of unending possibilities growing inside of me; I was invincible.

My psych would have a thing or two to say about this "optimism," and he'd be right. Nevertheless, the important thing is that I was excited. I felt, for the first time in my

twenty-four years, genuinely, completely, unutterably pur-
poseful. I papered the walls of my little flat with lists. Lists
of things to feed/say to/do with/sing to/check for in your
baby at 0, 3, 6 months. Things to do on rainy days, lists and
lists of free things to do with kids in London. (I was WAY
ahead of BuzzFeed, etc., was I not?!)

When I was pregnant I'd already been working for
Spark Arts for a few years. I initially got taken on as a temporary receptionist, but when they saw how I panicked and
chased away visitors with my fumbling and mumbling, they
moved me into the back office. I was quiet to start off with,
very quiet. But slowly, slowly, I stuck my head out from
under my shell, and was speedily declared a "creative soul."
This meant I was able to help out with pottery and poetry
classes from time to time. (They even started a class that
combined the two at my suggestion, which resulted in some
very unfortunate vases but was a lot of fun.) I was still working there until they lost their funding and I was made
redundant and, well, you know the rest. The point is, that
dusty old building was my home. The older women all
inundated me with bags of old baby clothes and books and
toys. They weren't up to the standards of my lists—no reality ever could be—but just seeing them stacked in the corner of my living room made me feel full. Yes, my life was
full, my body was full, and it was about to get fuller. Despite
everything, I can still circle back to that moment and bask,
once again, in its light. I hope you understand.

Joanna

"Do you want to get unlocked, or what?" the screw said. I
did want to get unlocked; of course I did. It just took my brain
a few moments to clock that the door was finally open. I hurried out of it before she could give me a negative. On my way
from the wing to the education block, I looked up at the sky.

It was just an ordinary grey one but it made me smile. It made me smile because I knew that however many roads and bus stops and barbed-wire crusted walls there were between us, my mum was living under the exact same one.

16

When your mum wraps a scarf around your neck

Your dad used to complain he felt weighed down by his history; one wife, one set of parents, one school, one set of streets. "Sometimes I just want to be someone else, just for a bit," he'd say. But I was tired of being someone else. Tired of floating about. The first thing I did when I got my case files was hug them. They smelt of dust and glue. They were heavy. Best of all, they were real, which meant I must be real, too.

I read them in bits, taking a few pages to read while I waited for a hospital appointment or a benefits appointment or any of the other appointments that took up a bigger and bigger part of my life. I even took some to the Odeon. I didn't take them out of my bag, but knowing they were with me made it easier not to notice the way Chantelle stared at my belly; it was a stare that said, "I'm sorry but I ain't gonna admit I'm sorry and I miss you unless you admit it first." Easier to believe that I didn't need her or anyone outside of my story.

Looked After Child Summary for transfer from Lambeth Council to Somerset Council effective 01.05.09

Name: Bethany Mitchell

Sex: F

D.O.B: 02.07.94

Place of birth: St James's Hospital, London

Birth Mother: Joanna Mitchell. Contact arrangements: see below

Birth Father: Unknown

Under Care of Lambeth Council since 18/08/97

Ethnic Origin: White British (and unknown)

Contact arrangements: contact with mother lapsed c. 2006 (see report A658)

Special Concerns: No physical health problems; Behavioural, Emotional & Social Difficulties (BESD); history of physical and emotional neglect (see EPR & Permanent Care Order 2000)

Criminal Record: None

School Record: 2 Managed Moves, 9 Temporary Exclusions

Reason for move: Vulnerability to older males—meets criteria for Fresh Start Pilot Project (see Report of the Social Work Working Group 2008 appendix 2.1)

Report A658—Contact Arrangements: Bethany Mitchell and Joanna Mitchell

Effective from 01.04.06

Contact between Looked After Child and birth mother to be terminated until further notice. Contact was intermittent for many years owing to birth mother's on-going mental health difficulties; after birth mother repeatedly failed to attend Contacts and was sectioned for a second time under the Mental Health Act, contact was reduced in the interest of the Looked After Child's emotional welfare. Birth mother is now more stable, however, the Looked After Child has clearly stated her wish to remain apart. Given her age and her existing behaviour issues, it has been decided by all parties that this is in her best interest. However, the situation is to be monitored and the Looked After Child to be given the choice to resume contact and make own arrangements should she wish to do so.

North Hatbridge High School—Principal's Report to the Local Authority 06.12.05

Despite the challenging personal circumstances of which the school is aware, it is felt that a Managed Move would be in the best interest of Bethany's educational and personal well-being. Bethany can at times exhibit imagination and enthusiasm for her studies, however, her predilection for creating drama of which she herself is the centre combined with her volatile disposition has made it impossible for her to build lasting relationships with her peers.

Her lack of regard for her peers' personal space and privacy has raised concerns among several staff members regarding Bethany's well-being outside of school. These concerns are significantly bolstered by rumours that Bethany offers sexual services to some of the older boys in return for money. Bethany has been known to boast about such transactions, as well as about her associations with certain "postcode" gangs outside of school. Whether or not there is substance in these claims, the school is not in a position to say. However, it is clear from the evidence of her subject teachers' reports, and from the fact that she has scored the highest number of negative behaviour points in one term—367—on record since our introduction of Simmons Behaviour Point Plus system, that her current environment is not conducive to her progress. If the Local Authority decides she should remain in her current environment, we will do everything within our means to support her education, however, this would be flouting Rule No. 3.14 in the parent-school contract which states we have the right to permanently exclude students when they have executed more than six exclusion-worthy offences (Bethany has managed 17 in her short time at the school).

Community Social Work Report 03.04.08 L. Myers
The Foster Parent (Miss Geraldine Wormold) is understandably at the end of her tether with Bethany. GW is a long-standing foster carer with this LA and says that of all the chil-

dren to have passed through her doors, none have been as hard to crack as Bethany. Bethany was difficult to begin with, GW said, and so she was deliberately gentle with her, knowing she must be in mourning for her previous foster carer who died. However, as time wore on, Bethany grew increasingly difficult (GW said). GW was reluctant to provide details but when I pressed her, she said smashing dinner plates of freshly-cooked food on to the floor was an average example. GW then broke down—tears, shaking, etc., etc.—saying she was beginning to doubt her ability to keep these children safe, for she had woken up in the night on several occasions to hear Bethany stumbling through the door "off her face" and, in one case, sobbing into her tights, which she had balled up in her hand. GW then began to fear that she as the carer would be prosecuted for allowing this to happen. I reassured her that this wasn't the case but she waved her hands in the air and said, "What do you expect me to do? Lock her up?" NB I was unable to consult Bethany on any of this as she remained locked in the bathroom. I recommend a transfer as soon as possible—preferably to a new and contrasting location.

"I'm happy to tell you that your baby is of ideal size at this stage. Your uterus is the picture of health." These words came at the end of a doctor's appointment in the middle of reading my notes.

When I thanked the doctor, he frowned and said I had nothing to thank him for: "On the contrary, you should thank yourself for taking such good care of your child. I assume you've been taking all the supplements? Staying active and so on?"

I nodded. It was true that even if I'd not eaten all the pricey food recommended by his leaflet, I *had* swallowed the vitamins. I hadn't thought of this as a thing to be proud of, but I was glad he thought it was.

"I have to say, Bethany, I'm impressed. Compared to your first appointment, you've really . . . *bloomed*."

"For real?"

I wanted him to tell me more. Point to the scan and tell me where. How. Why. If I knew all this, I could make sure I didn't flop back to my old ways, or if I did, that I could bloom again.

But he just typed something into his computer, then opened the door. In real time, the appointment lasted twenty minutes. In Beth time, however, it went on for hours. Days. I replayed his words, over and over, to remind myself that I was more than the things that had once happened to me.

Community Social Work Report 01.02.99 F. Philipson

Miss Mitchell was referred to me by her GP due to concerns over the impact of her sustained anxiety and depression on her ability to care for her four-year-old daughter, Bethany (see report MED MM 5.2). However, Miss Joanna Mitchell (JM) appeared in infectiously high spirits, welcoming me with a pot of fresh tea and a smile. I was immediately struck by the depth of connection between Miss Mitchell and the young Bethany; they joked and laughed with each other, and when Bethany interrupted her mother to ask whether she could show me the picture book she was "writing," Miss Mitchell encouraged her to fetch the book, then said: "She's so imaginative. So bright. I never thought I'd have a kid like that. Or any kid!" After reading me what was an imaginative—if not terribly comprehensible—picture story, Bethany insisted she give me a tour of the flat. Miss Mitchell was noticeably nervous as we followed her daughter around the house, and it's true, the rooms were rather cluttered, but not beyond the bounds of normality, I don't think.

There was some friction when I brought up the father: "I've no idea where he is and I hope I never find out." She was aggressively resistant to the idea that we might help trace him through the Child Support Agency. "Things have been hard," she said, "but I'm doing well. I take my medication and every-thing. A few years ago, I could never have imagined having someone like Beth in my life." When I questioned her as to the nature of her difficulties, she was somewhat terse. Her parents were dead, she said, but she didn't care; it was years since they'd been in touch anyway. She studied English at UCL for two years before dropping out. "Uni wasn't for me," was her only explanation. She has supported herself since then by working as an administrator for a small arts organization and lives in a housing association property. "We don't have much money but we have everything we need. She's gone through all the kids' books in the library, practically. I take her to all the free museums and stuff."

My other observation was that Bethany was noticeably less animated when separated from her mother. When I knocked on her bedroom door—as instructed by JM—she let me in but was reluctant to engage in conversation owing to her game. The bedroom floor was carpeted with what appeared to be a crayoned jungle, drawn on to the inside of old cereal boxes. A medley of different plastic and wooden animals balanced on top of this jungle, along with the occasional toy truck or train, and in the middle of it all, a stuffed frog, of which she didn't let go the whole time I was there. What's happening in the game? "Everything," she said. "Can you tell me a bit more?" "It's complicated." "Does your Mum understand?" For the first time, she looked up from the game. Slowly, she shook her head.

Considering the state of resources and the evidence at hand, I therefore recommend that no further action be taken.

I even went back to the scout hut. "At thirty weeks, it's time to start bonding with your baby. Of course, this will have been happening since conception, but now is the time to start doing so consciously." Gloria rubbed her baby-less belly. When none of us pregnant mums moved, she told us to hurry up and get bonding. The woman nearest to me on the carpet—Gloria still hadn't found the Community Centre's chairs; there were now beanbags instead—closed her eyes and began to whisper. She must've felt everyone staring but she didn't care.

"Maybe some music will help."

All around me, a mooing. Not cow mooing; mooing with guitars. It was silly but also quite good. I was so happy to be away from the things in my flat, especially the letters from the payday loan people reminding me that my next payday would really be their payday.

"I didn't go looking for you; you came for me. You stayed. You grew yourself into a space I didn't know was there. You grew exactly as the doctors hoped you would. When I look down at my belly, I still can't believe it. Some days, I'm scared. I'm scared because there are so many things outside of you and me—things I can't change. Bad things. But our life will be a good one. We'll have adventures. We'll do fun things, like waking up with the sun and running to the park and scaring all the birds. We'll do dumb things, like messing our faces with icing sugar and talking in silly voices. We'll bake. We'll host parties. Yeah, parties. Not grown-up parties; kid parties, with matching paper plates and cups and napkins, all branded with some film you'll 100% love but which hasn't even been imagined yet. And you—you'll tell me things I don't know. Could never imagine. You'll make me laugh. Sometimes you'll mean to and other times you won't, and you'll stamp your foot and get grumpy if I laugh when you didn't mean it, and this will make me laugh more, and I won't be able to explain that I'm only laughing because I love you. You haven't even been born yet and already I love you more than anyone else."

What we did for the rest of that class, I don't remember;

having started talking to you, I couldn't stop. Between the words of those reports, I'd glimpsed the life my mum had imagined for me—imagined but not quite made. Things would be different for you and me, though; they'd be good, and not just imagined-good, but real.

Beechdale Primary Safeguarding Query 15.06.99, Ms. Isabelle Massfield (Year 2 class teacher)

I realize this is meant to go through our school safeguarding officer but when I tried, I was reassured that "all issues had been dealt with." However, I see Bethany on a daily basis and I don't believe this to be the case. She really has undergone an alarming transformation over the past year; in September, she was one of the brightest members of the class, if prone to veering between reticence and a dominating confidence, but she bonded strongly with a few classmates and I was at first confident that she would bloom over the year. Sadly, the opposite has happened; she's slowly lost interest in her school work and responds to all offers of help or encouragement with outbursts of anger—she threw her maths book across the room after one of the teaching assistants tried to help her, for example—that I found quite out of character. Her friendships, too, have crumbled; almost every lunchtime one of the other children comes crying to the lunchtime supervisors about her behaviour, and when asked to discuss or apologize, she either has a tantrum or withdraws. Having what I thought was a strong relationship with her, I've tried to talk to her about this after class. But she refused to open up or even make eye contact.

The only clue I've found is in her weekend diary. Firstly, I should say that many of the children concoct the most ridiculous things that are patently made up; trips to Disneyland Paris on a Tuesday night, meeting the *X Factor* cast, etc., etc. Bethany's entries were notable for their profusion of real-life detail; she'd write long, if slightly rambling accounts of visits from Granny

Nina, progress on her Jungle Book game and some sort of elaborate chasing game she'd play with her mum. A few months ago, however, she stopped writing in her diary at all. When I encouraged her to continue, she kicked off and grew even more stubborn in her refusal. Since then, the only way I can stop her disrupting the class during diary-writing hour is by allowing her to read books. When I eventually managed to ask her why she was prepared to read books but not write her diary, she said: "Because I don't have any good things to write in my diary any more. The stories in the books are much better." I asked her whether there was anything she wanted to tell me. She shook her head and said, "My mum said not to tell anyone or they'd get me." Who would get her? "She never says," said Beth, "but I think it's spies. Can I go out to play now?"

As for Bethany's mother, Joanna, I've now lost track of the number of appointments she's missed. She did, however, come to parents' evening. I'll say now that things were a little awkward between us, owing to the fact that she'd missed so many appointments and so seemed scared to meet my eye, but also because we are, I'd guess, a similar age (around thirty). When I expressed concerns over Bethany's behaviour, she asked if I had children and when I said no, she raised her eyebrows as if this settled it. She was also noticeably thinner than when we met at the beginning of the year, with the bones horribly prominent in her face. She was by no means the most difficult or alarming parent I've had to deal with, but in light of the changes I've witnessed in Bethany this year, I did come away feeling that all was not well.

I sincerely hope my more senior colleagues are right in telling me I'm jumping to conclusions and that Joanna and Bethany are the least of our worries. However, on the chance that I'm right, I demand that you investigate the situation before it deteriorates any further.

"Beth . . . " It was my last day at the Odeon and the first day Chantelle had spoken to me since I "slutted up" (as she'd loudly put it to the Chuckle Brothers whenever I was nearby) with her "boyfriend."

In front of me, the High Road, with its 99p! Everything 99p! Store and its Wimpy stuffed with granddads and its Save Streatham Cats charity shop. Behind me, the Snack Station. Kilograms and kilograms of slightly stale popcorn. The red Slush Puppie and the blue Slush Puppie. And Chantelle.

I turned back. "What?"

She opened her mouth. Her eyes hovered on my bump. "I . . . Are you sure you're gonna be O.K.?"

She reckons you're weak and pathetic. No way can you be a mum. Hey, maybe she's right. Maybe—

"Course I am. I'm not an idiot."

She stepped away from the Slush Puppies. "It ain't about being an idiot. It's about—"

"Whatever," I cut her off. "It's too late. I've got it sorted. Laters."

Then I heaved us out of the doors and across the road to the bus stop. When I say "us" I mean you and me; it was impossible to eat or walk or sleep or breathe or sit down or stand up without remembering there was another human in my body with me.

When I say "us" I also meant me, you and my mum. All these years, I'd convinced myself she hated me. She hated me and that's why she missed all those Contacts. That thought loomed like some thick, high fuck-off wall between me and my memories of her; without it, I could see so far.

But now I could see the life we'd had together, me and my mum. I was surprised by how much of it was good, which is why, even if it came to me as I was supposed to be answering the Job Centre assistant's question or topping up my Oyster, I didn't push it away.

"Miss Mitchell? Miss Mitchell? Are you listening to me, Miss Mitchell?"

No, I wasn't, and I didn't care. At last, my mum was back with me; no way was I going to lose her again. Here she was, wrapping a scarf around my neck. No, no, I said, it's too hot, it's itchy. But that's because we're inside now, she said back, her voice softer than the scarf.

Outside, it's cold. The cold will get into you if you're not careful. Once it gets in, it'll never get out! And I'd say, oh no! And then she'd hustle me outdoors. Race you to the end of the street, she'd say, and then we would, and I'd win, she must've let me but I didn't know it, my feet were like rockets, they were boosting me to some place better and more fun.

She was reading me a story. I was telling her she was reading it wrong but she was saying no, no, these are the words, see? I don't care about the words, I told her. They're not as good as the ones inside me. Oh, she said, tickling my tummy, there are all sorts of stories on your insides, all sorts!

She was showing me how to mould clay. How to draw a really good animal. We were adventuring through the mud in the park. We were on a treasure hunt around a museum which ended by the toes of a humungous dinosaur skeleton. Where's the treasure? I'd ask. She'd point to the bones high above us. There. It's right there. Oh. I'd try not to look disappointed. She didn't like it when I was disappointed. But there's some treasure in here, too, she'd whisper. Then she'd open her bag and sneak me a squashed biscuit bar. Present from the dinosaur! she'd hiss. But don't let the guard see. I knew the bar was from her bag; they were the same bars we had at home. But her excitement was catching. And giggling and trying to eat behind her back so the guards didn't see, it felt like the best treasure in the world.

She was chasing me around the dining table with a fork. "Come on, it's only broccoli, it's not going to kill you, I promise!" Her voice twanged in and out of my head as she read me to sleep. Her fingers would brush across my forehead to see whether I had a temperature.

Most of all, I could feel her love weaving in and out of these scenes; it throbbed all over my body. Throbbed from my head to my heart to my belly to my toes, from me to you. The way it made me feel . . . Well, it was like drinking a cold glass of water when you're really, really thirsty. It was better than enough. I thought it was the only thing we'd ever need.

Call Report: Miss Nina Swainston to Lambeth Social Services 01.08.99

[NB Nina is an ex-colleague of Miss Mitchell.]

We always knew Jo was . . . Fragile. You never knew what mood she was going to be in from one moment to the next. One moment, she'd be showering you in hugs, the next she'd break down in tears and declare herself a terrible human being if you asked why she hadn't processed such-and-such an invoice. Having worked with her for over a decade, I suppose I took something of a motherly role with her; I regularly babysat for little Beth and helped her out in all sorts of other ways. Despite all that, I wouldn't say that I knew her. Not really. Whenever she seemed on the brink of opening up, she'd hurry away. But she had a certain spark about her—a liveliness and creativity which is hard to find these days (or, indeed, any days). When she wasn't bouncing off the walls or slumped in her chair, she was an excellent worker; very speedy and productive. That's why I persevered with her even as she was alienating other staff members left, right and centre; "Give her a chance," I'd say, but they'd tell me I was soft. She was a crazy bitch. She was taking me for a ride, etc., etc.

The loss of funding was a blow to all of us, of course it was, but with Jo . . . I suppose it made me realize just how close she was to the edge. I'm lucky enough to be able to retire, and the others have plenty of cushions, financial and otherwise, but the thing about Joanna is, she has no cushions. I've tried my best to be one for her but there are limits.

For weeks after we shut down, I heard nothing from her. I called, left messages on her answer machine, but she never picked up, never called back. Eventually I went round. I was . . . Shocked doesn't begin to cover it. The house had degenerated from a cosy chaos to an absolute pigsty. More worrying was her reaction to my visit: "What are you doing here? Why have you been calling? What do you want?" etc., etc. I tried to calm her down by making a cup of tea but there was no fresh milk in the fridge; no fresh anything. When I asked if she was feeling O.K., she said, "Oh, Nina, there are some things a cup of tea will never bloody solve." I said that was no way to talk to an old friend who was worried about her, who wanted to help. She then went off on one about how no one wanted to help, they just wanted to "get" her. When I tried to reason with her, she grew so aggressive I had to leave. The other girls from work say she's been this way for years; it's me who's refused to see. I don't think so. Until now, she was close to the edge, but she was on the right side of it. Now, she's fallen off. She's fallen right off. I tried a few more times to go round but she wouldn't let me in. I know getting social services involved doesn't always make things better, but I can't think what else to do. I hope you can help this woman in need.

Nina came back to me, too: all floating skirts, warm freckled arms and bangles. I remembered the time she fell asleep, and I drew a dot-to-dot between her freckles. My mum wrenched me off her and started to tell me off. "Nina won't love you any more if you do that!" she yelled. But Nina put her hand on my mum's hand. "Don't worry," she said, "it's the best use anyone's ever found for those freckles." Then she told my mum not to worry, she loved me like the granddaughter she didn't yet have.

"Nina's a good person," my mum would say, when she'd gone, "but that doesn't mean you can do whatever you want when you're with her. You've got to be careful." I couldn't read the face she made when she said the word "careful." It scared me.

"Will you promise? Will you promise me to be careful?" I said I would, even though I didn't know how. When I asked her what it was I needed to be careful of, she got angry. She'd shout about the bad people and then the shouts would melt into sobs and I wouldn't know what she was sobbing about. When the sobs finally dried up, I'd be glad. The problem was, she'd go quiet for so long, it seemed like she was dead. I'd push open her bedroom door and crawl across the floor and on to her bed. Sometimes, she'd be shuddering with tears. Other times, she'd just lie there. Gradually I clocked that when she was like this, she wasn't alive in the way people were meant to be alive, but she wasn't dead, either.

Whenever I asked why we didn't have other family the way my friends had other family, she'd say that no one was like anyone else. Other people's families were good; ours was bad. "I only want you to be surrounded by people who are good."

Some of my friends' mums would be "good" for a while; every now and then another "good" person would come to the flat or we'd go to theirs. But—*be careful, be careful*—they never stayed good for long. If I asked to go round to my friend's house, Mum would get angry. "I'm not letting you near that woman! Not after what she did to me!" Only I never knew what these people had done. "Your mum's really scary," my friends would say to me. Part of me would be thinking, yes, you're right. But the other part, the louder part, it got angry. *My mum's the best mum in the world! Shut up. It's your mum who's bad.* The truth was, I didn't know what turned good people to bad; all I knew was that it could happen any time, and it was scary. It was better to keep my distance, just in case.

Nina was the only person I didn't feel scared around. The only person I thought would stay good for good.

But when we didn't see her for ages, and I asked why, and my mum got angry and said she'd turned Bad, that was when I knew it wasn't just Nina who'd gone bad, it was our whole life. Mum not going to work had turned into Mum not getting out of bed for days then staying out of bed for days, scribbling and drawing and talking all day and all night, only to collapse back into bed.

Community Social Work Report 11.09.99 S. Miles

This was my fifth attempt to visit Miss Joanna Mitchell (JM). Upon entering her residence it became obvious why she has been avoiding contact: the place is a health hazard. Entry to the sitting room was blocked by a detritus of old magazines, boxes, broken toys, gadgets, etc., etc. that teetered above our heads. Given CSWR S.P 95, this deterioration appears to have occurred rapidly and is a clear sign of psychological instability.

JM became agitated when I brought up the state of the house. Having lost her job, she has now been unemployed for six months, yet claims not to have time for housework because "I waste most of my time on the bus to or from the Job Centre or queuing to speak to some idiot at the Job Centre or going to some idiot interview for some idiot job I'm never in a million years going to get." When I reminded her of the school's concerns (see SGR 96—pt2) and that this visit was a good opportunity to get the help she desperately needed, she raised her voice. How dare I call her desperate, she was managing very well thank you very much, and if I really wanted to help I could leave right now so she could get on with Bethany's dinner. Bethany I only glimpsed as JM hustled me to the door; she was lying prostrate in front of what looked to be a quite unsuitable American soap opera.

Recommendation: a minimum of five hours' home help for JM to ensure the house reaches a habitable standard. I would also recommend an increased frequency of visits due to her obviously volatile emotional state.

When I wasn't at the doctor or the hospital or the scout hut, I was at the Job Centre. I was queuing up so some woman could hand me a form, then filling out the form, then queuing up so I could give it back to some other woman. All this so that I'd have enough money to keep us both alive.

At my benefits appointment, I asked how long would it take for the benefits to come through?

"As soon as possible."

"What does that mean?"

"As soon as possible."

"But she's going to come any minute. I can't work."

"And why not?"

I patted my belly. "Because of this. And . . . and plus, I owe some money. A lot of money."

The woman made a face like she'd heard this story too many times before. "Did you take out one of those ridiculous loans? That's your business."

"But when the social . . . " The blood rushed to my cheeks. I hated telling people. Hated them feeling sorry for me. Or scared of me. Or something. "They said there'd be help. Because I'd been in care and that."

"When did you come out of care?"

"Ummm . . . "

She flicked through my file. "Ah, I see, fourteen months ago. Well, it's too late. There are benefits you can apply for in the first nine months."

"No one told me."

"You'll have been told. And it's in the leaflets. I'm sorry but your appointment is now running over so if you'll excuse me."

"What about school?"

Her eyes flickered behind me—a reminder of how many people were waiting. Then she opened a drawer and handed me a booklet. *Further Education Opportunities in South London.*

"Take this. Then, when you've had the child, when you're ready, make a careers adviser appointment—this will have to be separate from your benefit ones—and we'll see what we can do. But I'll warn you—that booklet is a bit out of date. Some of those courses have stopped now."

I can guarantee that I was the only person to leave that Job Centre with a smile. The money thing—that would work out. I didn't know how, but it would. The further education booklet was brick-like—a brick I'd build a house with. Our house. Our life. I'd work in the morning, study in the afternoon, look after you in the evening. It would be hard and we wouldn't be rich, we wouldn't even be able to afford Nando's or anything like that, but we'd have fun, and when I got my A-levels or my Foundation Degree or whatever, I'd get a good job, a job with hours and pay and holiday and sick leave you could count on, and everything would be good. My mum was out there, living, breathing, somehow knowing—and proud. She was 100% proud.

Memo for S. Miles 21/10/99
Received tearful call from Home Assist employee Angelina B saying JM "much angry" and "do scary acts" (Angelina's own words).

Memo for S. Miles 10/11/99
Received angry call from Home Assist employee Monicka S saying JM was "a mental stuck-up bitch what didn't deserve no help, she just had a go whenever I tried to clear up her crap."

"Everything's as it should be, Miss Mitchell. Now, the question is, have you packed your hospital bag?"

Everyone went on about the hospital bag: the doctor, Gloria, the other almost-mums at the antenatal class, everyone. It wasn't until I got to the worst part of the case files, until I was so big that even walking to the shops tired me out, until the days since my last shift at the Odeon turned into weeks— weeks in which I saw no one but doctors, benefits advisers, nurses, library assistants, strangers—and it was 100% clear that Chantelle wasn't going to get back in touch, that I got why.

Dressing gown. Slippers. Flannels. Eye mask. Water bottle. Book. Nightie. Face wipes. Just writing a list of the things you'd need, the things you'd need so you could turn from an almost-mum to an actual mum and still be O.K., it made things feel better. Smaller, calmer, neater. Even if you couldn't afford these things. Even if you woke up a few hours later and scribbled half of it out and started again.

The list made it easier to nod and smile yes, you were O.K., yes you felt 100% positive, no you didn't need extra support. True, you weren't in touch with the father, but you had plenty of other support, you had your finances and everything else in hand. You had your list. Your dressing gown. Your slippers. Your eye mask.

Urgent message for CYPMH Head Social Worker 18/11/99

Call from Beechdale Primary concerning Bethany Mitchell (see file YS23705). Teacher Miss Isabelle Massfield (? line fuzzy) concerned that social worker S. Miles not returning calls. Appears to have been miscommunication re. S. Miles's sick leave (on-going). Teacher indulged in anti-bureaucratic rant; I explained lack of resources, increasing incidence of severe social problems, etc., etc. She then admitted to new and alarming concerns vis. Bethany's physical and mental state, vis.

loss of weight, aggressive behaviour towards other children, falling asleep in class. Although finding teacher Isabelle Massfield's self-righteous attitude distasteful, I am inclined to think she is right. I hereby recommend an emergency visit ASAP.

EMERGENCY POLICE REPORT 27/11/99, DC Ahmed

Miss Joanna Mitchell found wandering streets c. 2 A.M. in agitated state (poss. psychotic). Physical appearance v. bad: scratches on face, inadequately dressed given the time of year, shivering and a bit blue. When PC James and PC Khan asked her what she was doing, she swore and "lunged for a brick like she was going to chuck it at us" (PC Khan) meaning that "we had no choice but to restrain her" (PC James). She claimed we had been sent by "Them." When PC Khan asked if she had anyone waiting for her at home, she began to hyperventilate and said, over and over: "They're going to take Bethany. I knew it, I always knew it. I knew They'd never let me keep her!" Paramedics agreed with PC Khan and PC James's assessment that Miss Joanna Mitchell was suffering from severe psychotic symptoms and should be detained under the MH Act as she was clearly a danger to both herself and others. Paramedics sedated Miss Joanna Mitchell soon after and PCs were then able to extract her personal documents from her clothing, which is how her home address was discovered.

I read the hard bits in the library, in a big squashy seat at the end of the Art and Crafts aisle. I tried to balance the papers on my belly but they fell off so I wedged them between me and the seat. The seat smelt of old people but I didn't mind; I wanted to be as close to as many different stories as possible. I wanted us both to believe that the one we were about to finish reading was only the start of a new and better one.

EMERGENCY ON-CALL SOCIAL WORKER REPORT 28/11/99

House door open. Unpleasant stench of damp, refuse, etc. I didn't believe the house was still inhabited, but after clambering over bin liners, old toys, etc., I found the child curled up inside a nest—composed of scarves, towels, etc.—on the floor. She awoke at the sound of my footsteps. When she saw my face, she asked what I'd done with her mum. I said I was here to help. She moved aside her towels and ran her finger over what I saw was a thick covering of paper and card, on which she'd drawn . . . Well, it was hard to tell what it was, but it evidently meant a lot to her. I asked where her mum was and she said that she wasn't supposed to tell anyone. I reassured her that telling me might help her get back her mum. At this point she sat up, faced me and said that her "inside mum" went away a long time ago but that it wasn't until recently that "her body" disappeared, too. "She tells me to go to sleep and that she'll be back before I wake up but sometimes she isn't and anyway I get scared in the house by myself." Where did her mum go? "To where the baddies are." Had she ever seen these baddies? Slowly, the child shook her head. "Sometimes, I think they don't exist. But when I asked Mum if they were real, she got angry. And when she gets angry, I get scared. I don't like being scared."

London Borough of Lambeth vs. Miss Joanna Mitchell 04.05.00

Miss Joanna Mitchell—STATEMENT

I can't believe this is happening. I didn't mean for any of it to happen. I know I've been bad but that's only because you took Beth away from me. She was . . . O.K. Let's go back a bit. Before Beth, I wasn't. I didn't feel. Like a real person. I . . . [Judge asks about her history of mental illness.]

I knew I shouldn't have started on this! Yes. Yes, I've had

episodes. But they're just episodes. There have been long stretches between when things have been fine. And it only started because . . . because of what happened.

[Judge asks JM again to elucidate.]

This isn't the sort of thing it's easy to say. Not to a person you trust. Definitely not to a room full of people you barely know. People who are here to judge you. It's . . .

[Judge tells her she can take her time. She sobs for a period then continues.]

It started at Uni. I had a lot of time to myself and things started to get . . . weird. Everywhere I looked there was a pattern. If I stared at the pattern long enough, I'd find out this big secret—one no one else knew. I'd read and read and write and write, convinced I was nearing the secret, but when I handed it in the tutors said it made no sense and then, then, I'd fall into this . . . It was like a hole. I'd just feel dead. I'd stay in bed waiting for the magic feeling, the feeling like everything was in a pattern, to come back. Sometimes it did, sometimes it didn't. Other times it was replaced by this other feeling . . . I guess it was the opposite of a pattern. Like nothing made sense. I wasn't handing in essays or going to tutorials but I didn't care. It didn't matter. Nothing mattered. I pretty much stopped eating, sleeping, studying, everything. Eventually I figured out that if I sunk low enough, the patterns would creep back, and I'd feel like doing things again. When I went home for the holidays, my step-mum was shocked. What was I playing at, taking dieting so far? I explained it wasn't a diet. The problem was, I couldn't explain what it was. They kept trying to make me eat doughnuts. I wouldn't; they weren't part of the pattern. Soon after that, Dad got diagnosed with cancer. Of course, I got blamed for that. Never mind he'd chain-smoked for decades. After he died, I was glad not to have to keep seeing my step-mum.

[Judge asks Miss Mitchell to return to the issue in hand.]

So much for, "take your time Miss Mitchell!" God, there's really no point, is there? You've already decided. Already got me marked as a crazy. Beyond hope. Never mind that I managed perfectly well for years. I mean, look at me now. I'm not hearing voices, am I? No, of course you'd have no way to know that. But I'll assure you, I'm not. Things . . . Well, that job, it may seem like a silly little thing to you, but to me it was—well, getting that job for Spark Arts, it was the first time I realized I might have a hope of life. Of being something other than this girl who'd gone a bit mad, dropped out of Uni, then used what little bit of money she'd got from her Dad's death to set up some attempt at life in London. I belonged there, you know? I know I burned my bridges in many ways. I thought . . . Well, it's just, things, they got the better of me. It felt like the world was against me, blah blah. I pushed away anyone who suggested I had a problem because I didn't WANT to have one. But I recognize now that I do. But you know what'll get me better? It's getting Bethany back. I'll look after her, I'll do it right this time, I promise, I promise . . .

[JM breaks down in sobs and is excused and declines to continue her statement at next session.]

Case Worker's Statement—Mr. B. Johnson 17.03.00

Bethany was found in a state of physical and mental neglect when removed from her mother's care under an emergency care order. After spending some months in temporary foster care, she is now in a long-term placement with Paul and Susannah Jones. Since settling with the Joneses, she has flourished both physically and mentally; school teachers report a huge improvement in her behaviour and attitude. Although claiming a wish to return to her mother at every available opportunity, she also exhibits strong affection for the Joneses and for her new friends at school. The Joneses report that she at first used to hide food under her bed in case "things went bad and it ran out." Given this evidence and in light of the doctor's report concerning her physical state and Miss Mitchell's on-going in-patient treatment for a diagnosis of Bipolar Disorder and Borderline Personality Disorder with Pyschotic Tendencies, I strongly recommend she be placed under a permanent care order and that the local authority put her up for adoption as soon as possible. She is still young and her chances of being placed with a family are high.

Permanent Care Order 04.05.00
Bethany Mitchell to be placed under the care of the Permanent Authority with a view to long-term foster placement (with Mr. and Mrs. Jones in the first instance) and adoption. Contact with mother every 12 weeks (to be reviewed quarterly).

Please stop, I told the memories. Please just stop for now. "How can I help you?" asked the Customer Care Adviser. I was at the Council help desk. Something to do with Council tax. Only I couldn't remember what it was I needed help with because all I could see was my mum, sitting in a pile of old newspapers, and when I asked her was she going to make dinner, she yelled that she had more important things to do than make dinner, this was a crucial moment, she almost had it, everything was lining up, it was all making sense now, it was going to be perfect.

"I don't know."

I bumped into people. I would've left my handbag on the bus if a kind woman hadn't run after me. I'd get off the bus at the wrong stop or even if I got off at the right one it would take me a minute to remember which way to go. Because everything was new; every inch of now was littered with the past and it was hard to work out who or what or where I was.

It had been the same at school, after my mum got bad. My

mum said she didn't need food and when I asked her for it she would start to cry and so I stopped. I ate all the biscuits. I ate all the crisps. Then I noticed that if I drew or wrote, I didn't feel so hungry. I didn't feel so angry or scared. My scribbles would turn into a toucan, a parrot, a lion, a tiger, a jungle. If I made a drawing that was big enough, beautiful enough, interesting enough, I'd remind my mum how to be properly alive; she'd see what I'd made and she'd remember that the things we used to do, like doing impressions of people while eating our dinner at the table, or watching silly films, or playing cards, or talking to Nina, or drawing, or reading stories, or running around, or going to the park, were really, really good.

"My mum says your mum's weird."

"Your mum looks like Skeletor."

"Why do you smell like that?"

"How come you're stealing Jason's lunch?"

"Why are you always doing those weird scary drawings when you should be doing your work?"

If I kept drawing, my mum—the real one, not the strange, bony ghost she'd become—would return. I shouted or spat at or kicked whoever questioned this, or, worse, said or did things to make me question it; no way could I consider that she might not come back. Or that by the time she did, it would be too late. Far too late.

All this rattled around my head while, with another loan—the benefits were taking forever to come through and somehow I still believed that as soon as you were born, your dad would change his mind when he saw how cute you were and how much you looked like him, he'd pay up—I bought Babygros and baby bibs and bottles and nappies and a sling and a crib and one of those prams that look like 4x4s. I bought things for me, too, things for my hospital bag: a dressing gown and slippers and an eye mask and a new towel. And, of course, the bag itself.

The more time I spent in Mothercare, the more I missed her. Missed how, if she were here, we'd laugh at baby rugs shaped like octopuses and buggies shaped like spaceships and Babygros that said things like "I'm with stupid" and "I'm THE DUDE."

Missed the good and the bad and the in-between times. Missed her kissing my forehead before I went to sleep every night, her breath soupy with wine and toothpaste. Missed the way her eyes would widen when she was having the most *amazing* idea. Missed the way she'd smile when I started to tell her a story. Missed seeing her at the school gates. Missed the way she cried. The way she laughed. Missed our little house, its big mess. I even missed the way she disappeared.

For the first time in a really, really long time, I cried. I cried for her. Cried for me. Cried for the help we didn't get, and the life we could've led if she had. Sure, it wouldn't have been a "normal" life; it wouldn't have been spiky in the middle and rough round the edges. She'd have had down-times and up-times and I, as I grew older and wiser to the truths and lies of the way she was, would have got angry. When friends came round and she was "off on one," I'd have got embarrassed. Maybe I'd have stopped inviting them round altogether; maybe she'd notice and maybe she wouldn't; maybe we'd have a massive argument, or maybe it would be one more thing we wouldn't talk about. But we'd have held on, the both of us, just about. And now, I'd be coming home from Uni with a bagful of dirty washing and a mouthful of dirty stories which we could share like the friends/sisters/mum-and-daughter we'd become.

When I was done with crying, I saw that things wouldn't change on their own; you had to change them. You had to rise up out of that lazy part of yourself that did what it had done before just because it was easier, and do the new thing, the strange thing, the thing you were scared of. If I wanted things between me and you to end different, I had to do something different now. So I did: I rang Chantelle.

May not seem like a big deal, ringing someone. But you have to understand, that with a baby in my belly, with a ton of memories in my limbs and that mean old voice telling me not to trust anyone, what was the point, to ring any person, let alone one who for months and months had been angry with you, it was. It was a pretty fucking big deal.

"What is it?" she answered after two rings. Peppa Pig in the background.

"Chantelle, it's Beth."

"I know who it is, my phone tells me, you retard."

"I know, I . . . I just wanted to say . . . I'm sorry. Sorry for everything I said at your party."

She said nothing for a while and then she said, "Whatever. Is the baby coming out or something?"

"No, not yet—"

"Thank fuck. When I last saw you, I thought, *man*, that girl is about to *burst*!"

"Chantelle."

"What?"

"I'm scared." There. I'd done it. I'd put myself out there. I'd always imagined the world would laugh at or spit on this self once it saw it for what it was. But you can't spit at people over the phone.

"Oh, honey."

Don't ask why someone naming you after a sweet, sticky thing makes you feel better—it just does.

"I don't know if I can do this," I blurted. "Like how am I going to get the baby out? Or what if it decides it can't be arsed, what then?"

"Honey—"

"And what if she *does* come out? What am I going to *do*

with her? How can I tell her what to do, when, let's face it, I don't have a clue what I'm doing myself?"

Chantelle laughed a kind laugh. "Honey—put it DOWN. DOWN!" Screams in the background, followed by a long wail.

"Sorry," she said. "It's World War Three over here. Maybe I should—"

"Can you come round?"

"Aw, yeah sure. But I'll have to bring the little monsters if you don't mind."

"Course not. And Chantelle?"

"What now?"

"Thanks."

"Calm yourself, I'm only coming to sit on your sofa—it ain't like I'm saving your life or nothing."

Then she hung up and I breathed out two lungs' worth of relief. Because I'd never dared ask anyone for help before. If only I'd remembered this in the weeks and months to come, things might've turned out different for us—and by *different* I mean *better*. But maybe that's how it is. Maybe life is an endless cycle of learning and forgetting and then learning what we've forgotten we've learned, all over again.

Here are some more of the things I'm only just remembering that I learned that night with Chantelle:

Hugs shut out your fears for longer than they last.

Squashing on to the sofa with three other humans and laughing at nothing is like stepping on to some kind of hovercraft which glides you up, up and away from your troubles—not forever, but for a short and wonderful time.

Drinking tea and eating Cadbury's mini-rolls even when you're not thirsty or hungry will fill you from head to toe.

Every time a person who knows as much of the real you as anyone is ever going to know smiles at you, it sends a message to the snarky you're-less-than-human part of you, and the message is this: "Fuck you, I'm GOOD."

Getting kicked off the sofa so two kids can defend the spaceship from the death-resistant space monsters makes you laugh. When you've stopped laughing, it makes you worry less about the way things are because you've just been reminded that things can also be something else.

"Give me a call, anytime?" said Chantelle, when it was time for her to leave.

"Sure," I said. "I will." And if only I had. If only.

17.
Doing the things that scare you most

Dear Mum
Thanks for your letter. I read it over and over and I do understand. I'm angry and upset and confused but I do understand.

I started reading our case files right before I gave birth. Most people would find them depressing but not me; before then, I had no story to shove between me and that dark little voice that says, "You're evil, this is your fault, everyone hates you, stay away from them." Now, I had a history.

I was ready to contact you. Wrote out your number and took it with me whenever I went outside and everything. Then my waters broke as I was waiting for some benefits appointment, I was sitting in my own puddle until the receptionist looked up and rolled her eyes and said, how could you have got this far without noticing? And I cried, not because it hurt, but because I was scared, I didn't know what was going to happen, and I wished that I had someone to sit through it with me.

I had a friend, Chantelle. We were really, really close, then around the time I got pregnant, we had a fight. I said some bad things. I did ring her and apologize, but not until it was way too late. It was like I was wrapped in some stiff scratchy wool; no way could I make any decisions, no way could anyone get in, not even if they tried. Did that happen to you, did it? Just getting from one breath to the next was hard enough; I couldn't imagine anything else. Couldn't imagine After.

I gave birth in a room overlooking the Thames; from the window, I could see Big Ben, the Houses of Parliament, everything. They gave me gas, air, I don't remember what else, but it had a long scientific name and it made me feel even further from what was happening in my body.

My midwife was on another emergency call or something and the baby was taking its time and so they left me alone for hours and hours. I stared at the window and the water and at the Houses of Parliament and at the seagulls and at Big Ben. I imagined I was talking to Big Ben at one point: Will this ever end? I asked him. Will this baby ever get out of my body or what? Tick, tock, he said. Tick, tock. Which I knew meant: of course. But the baby won't come out on its own. You've got to help it along. You've got to push.

When the contractions got down to business so did I. And so did the baby. Some nurse held my hand and told me I was doing good, squeeze as hard as you need, she said, and so I did, and everything inside of me, all the small things and the big things, the slimy things and the hard things, all the things outside of me; they were ripping, tearing, popping, twisting, squeezing, pushing, huffing us into some world which would be as strange and new and unknown and terrifying as a blank page—only with blood. Lots and lots of blood.

People go on about how awful birth is and it's true that it hurt like hell but you know what? It was brilliant. It was bloody brilliant. (Literally and not.) And I would do it again if I could, honest.

It was after that things got. They got. Well, you know.

There's a lot more I want to tell and ask you but not here. Not on the page. I want to watch how you move your face as we talk. See what you do with your hands. Would you come and visit me? Dates are below. Don't worry if you can't but it would be good. It's hard for me to admit this, but it's what I need.

Beth x

18

RUNNING AS FAST AS THE THAMES FLOWS

The bad thing which got me in here, the thing I spend 99% of my energy at any given moment trying to push away, it happened in my flat.

Our flat.

Straight after it happened—at least, I *think* it was straight after, but who really knows because the thing about such bad things is, they mess time right up—I showered and put on the first pair of cleanish clothes to touch my body since the bum-flashing gown I was wearing as you got born. I stuffed the last of my last loan into my bag. Then I turned my back on the life I'd tried and failed to make for us and then I guess you could say that was when the running got serious.

I ran north. I ran right across the Elephant and Castle roundabout; the air was all horns and other voices, human voices, telling me to watch myself and that I was a crazy bitch. I knocked over a plastic bowl of tomatoes, and when the man behind the stall shouted that I owed him a pound, I ran even faster, because the plastic bowl man, the horn-beepers at the Elephant roundabout, they knew what I'd done. It was written all over my face and my hands and my neck and even my grubby ankles.

I ignored the ache of so recently pushing you into the world. I ignored the voice reminding me that the further I ran from the thing I'd done, the more it would hurt when I stopped. I didn't believe I would have to stop; my mum had been right; things did match up; if I could just keep running as fast as the water was flowing, as fast as the pigeons and the seagulls and the planes were flying, everything would reset; the next time someone asked me if I was O.K., I could honestly reply *yes*.

The north side of the river was different, at least, that's what I told myself, what I had to, as I sweated all over and under the Trafalgar Square tourists who had nothing and no one to run from. One or two people stared at me like they knew what I'd done, but mostly they were tilting their iPhones up at lonely old Nelson, and for a few seconds, I watched them, wishing that I, like Nelson, could hide so high above the ground. Then the tourists set off in search of fish and chips and, realizing that Nelson's column was not the place to escape to, I carried on. How many people I slammed into, I can't be sure, and just when I was thinking, does this city have an edge and if so how do you get to it, I saw the ugly grey tower of Euston.

An hour later, my train was pulling into Milton Keynes. I didn't know what Milton Keynes was, only that, according to the moustached guy in the ticket office, it wasn't London. As soon as I got through the barriers, I relaxed; the old man was right: this was definitely not London. Everything was flat, straight, grey. There were a lot of people in suits, too busy staring at their phones to stare at me. I started running, but who knows where or for how long, for every street looked the same, and so did every house and every gap between every house and every tree and even every gap between every tree, and every roundabout.

Eventually, I reached a shopping centre, which was just a bigger version of every other shopping centre I'd ever been to: same shops, same receipt-scarred tiles between the shops, same signs reminding you these were the Final Days of the sale. I followed this one mum and daughter around Primark; the daughter's chubby little body was stuffed into a One Direction hoody, they were shopping for her first bra, she was half-embarrassed, half-excited, but her mum was so nice, she suggested this one then that one and oh, what about this one, it's purple, don't you love purple? Which would she choose? I was so desperate to find out, to make their life into mine, that the daughter said, "Mum, can't we try a different shop? That woman's been following us around and she's scary." It wasn't until the mum grabbed her daughter's hand, glared at me, and pulled her in the opposite direction, that I clocked she was talking about me.

The only thing I knew was that the only time I felt O.K., the only time I could almost believe that the bad things had nothing to do with me, was when I was running. So I went into the Adidas shop. There was a DJ spinning discs between the rucksacks and the sports bras. As I pulled on the brightest, funnest leggings—the Nike ones with stars on—I tried to dance around. Tried to kid myself I was getting ready for some epic night out. That any second now, Chantelle would whip back the cubicle curtain, bright pink Lycra stretched across her boobs, and tell me I looked hot, even if I was a skinny bitch. But I couldn't. My legs looked sad under my Nike stars. My boobs had disappeared back into my chest. And my face—there was nothing anyone could do about my face: ghost-white cheeks, and a darkness under the eyes and in the eyes and in the corners of the mouth that no one should have to see. But stars were better than no stars and I couldn't think what else to do, so I bought the leggings anyway.

Next, I went to Toni & Guy. This would be the last of my money, but who cared? It was going to run out anyway. And wasn't that why people spent their whole lives trying to make more of it—so they could fool themselves they weren't so bad?

"Chop it all off," I said to the smiley blonde stylist. "Make it as different as possible."

She laughed. "You changing your identity or something?"

Laugh back, I told myself. *You're meant to laugh back*. But I couldn't. Instead I just said, "No."

"O.K., so how about . . . " I *heard* but I didn't *understand*; I just nodded and said that's great, and later, when she started cutting, asking me questions like, what did I do, had I taken the day off work, was I from round here, I said nothing because I knew that if I opened my mouth no words would come out, only some terrible, animal sound which didn't belong in any shopping centre.

The haircut cost a whole £60. I only had £40. The receptionist said not to worry: "The cash point's just around the corner. You can nip out. Just give it in one go when you get back."

Of course, I nipped out, but instead of nipping back, I nipped to the station and then—via the slowest, cheapest train—to Leicester.

As for what happened in Leicester—you already know about that.

After Leicester, I was tired; tired of running; tired of guessing who this person was I was supposed to be. Nothing felt real. Nothing felt right. How going back to London would change any of this, I had no idea, but it was the only answer I could find to the question of what to do next, so I climbed on to the train. As soon as my bum sank into the seat, I fell asleep. I fell into the black hole kind of sleep you can normally only fall into when pissed. When I woke up there was an oldish man waving what looked like a huge calculator in my face and shouting something about a ticket. A ticket? Did I have one?

"No," I said. The part of me I lied with had run out. "No, I don't have a ticket. I've never had one."

"But you have to," he said. "You have to get one before you board."

"I tried," I said. "I've been asking for one. My whole fucking life I've been asking. But they wouldn't give one to me."

The inspector raised his eyebrows and I wondered, was I meant to know him? Was he some uncle I didn't remember?

"*That*," he said, "I find very hard to believe. Leicester is well served for ticket offices."

"You don't get it," I said, and at this point, I felt other people looking at me. I peered around the old man and yep, sure enough, the strangers in the next seat were looking up from their phones and their Kindles. "None of you do. You never will."

All eyes shot back to the nearest screen and the old man sighed and said I'd have to pay the penalty fare, which was £90.

"I don't have £90."

The inspector snorted. "No," he said. "Of course you don't." He ran his eyes over my Lycra-ed legs. "You never do, you people. Spending all your dosh on designer sports clothes and what have you. Bet you don't even do any sports."

This train terminates at London at approximately 15.53, announced the loudspeaker, but I couldn't believe it. I couldn't believe this journey would end any place I'd been before. "You don't know a thing about me."

"You'll end up with the British Transport Police if you carry on like this, young lady." *Young lady*. Just two words, two tiny words, but they were big enough to push me over the edge.

"Oooh! The British Transport Police! I'm so scared," I said, but it didn't feel like me saying it.

"This is your final chance. £90 or—"

"I don't. Have. Ninety. Quid."

The inspector's face was filled with blood and hate. I didn't want to look at it any more so I closed my eyes and leant back in my chair. I didn't hear anything else for a while, I thought maybe he was just a bad dream, when the train stopped for a really long time and then there were footsteps and clinking and "madam."

"Fine. I admit it. It was me that—"

"Madam?"

"I'm sorry."

My face was wet. My hands were shaking. When I looked up at the uncle who wasn't my uncle, and at the police who weren't police and who hadn't been there before, and at the advert for a family season ticket behind their shoulders, it seemed like all these people were shaking, too. "It was me."

"Madam, I think—"

"There were loads of bills and stuff I forgot to pay. Loads of things I forgot to do. But I don't care about any of that. I only cared . . . "

Of course, all the British Transport Police cared about was the ticket, so I said it again, again and again I said it until they handed me to the actual police, who rang up Lambeth police, who drove all the way up to get me in what apparently was Bedford.

"We've been looking for you for some time," they said.

They were worried, they said, about my mental condition. "I'm fine," I told them. "I'm not my mum. I did a bad thing. But I'm not my mum. I'm not mental."

"Miss Mitchell, you can't have been . . . "

"I knew what I was doing and I did it anyway. I did it. I did it. It was me."

"So why did you run? Why did you keep running?"

What I could never tell them or any other human who wasn't you, is that I wanted to run until my body broken and the world broke and time broke, in the same way they'd broke in the seventeen hours in which I panted, paced, lay, sat, cried, screamed, stood, swore, grunted and pushed and breathed and pushed and breathed and breathed to get you out of my body and into this world; maybe I could run right back into the beginning, and start again. Start better.

I didn't see a thing for a while after they caught me; then, all I saw was the end.

The end means nothing matters; nothing can get any better or worse than it already is. Which is why I said whatever they wanted me to say: *Yes,* I meant to do it. *Yes,* I meant to run away. Yes, I'd been in a firm mental state. No, I had nothing to add. *No, yes yes yes, no.* You can be honest, said my lawyer, about your mental health issues. But I didn't want any "extenuating circumstances', or any other circumstances. I was bad. 100% ™ certified bad. I needed to be punished. It's only now, two years and all these words later, that I see: having a diffcult story is not necessarily bad.

19.
KNOWING THAT WHATEVER ELSE CHANGES,
YOU WILL GET UP AT THE SAME TIME EVERY DAY

When Erika told me she was going away for three weeks, I was silent for ages. Then I said: "I can't do it. I thought I could but I can't. It's too big. Too heavy. No one wants me."

"I'm only going on holiday," she said. "And it's to see my sister. In Canada. I warned you about this a long time ago, remember?"

I didn't want to remember because remembering that she had a sister and a husband and three children and a house and maybe even a dog or a guinea pig or a goldfish meant remembering that she was only listening to me because it was her job. She cared but she was still paid to be here and there was a difference.

"No."

"Oh, come on now, Beth."

"And Linda's gone." I'd thought that not speaking or writing about this would make it less real. I thought that if it was less real, it would hurt less. But as soon as the words dropped out of my mouth, I knew this was wrong. Some things hurt, and pretending they don't is only going to make them hurt more.

"They ghosted her to DeerView. I waited for her in library hour. Waited and waited. She didn't turn up and at first I was pissed off, especially since I was about to read her the ending, the part when the big mistakes are made and everything fucks up; I wanted to see how she'd react. Later, I asked the Lee what had happened to Linda, was she in solitary or what, and she laughed and said, 'Oh, you really do live in your own world, don't you?! She's been ghosted. DeerView. And she won't be the last one, you mark my words.'"

Sadness swamped my throat. "Story of my life. I'm just getting settled when, bam, it ends. The ending has nothing to do with me; it's never when I choose. Didn't even get a chance to say goodbye. That's it. Gone. And I can't write to her because she won't be able to read it and I bet there won't be anyone to read it to her, either."

I didn't tell her that part of me saw her disappearance, and the fact it had come just before the end of the book, as a Sign: a Sign that no one wanted to hear the next part of *my* story. No one would stick by me if they did.

"How did you feel when you read to Linda?" asked Erika.

"When I was reading to her, I didn't worry about anyone or anything. I felt . . . *needed*. Special. Good. Now I just feel . . . And my mum hasn't replied to my last letter, she's probably changed her mind about contacting me, and now you're fucking off . . . "

I was losing my appetite, too. Almost like it had been ghosted away with Linda; I like to imagine her in the dining room in DeerView, scoffing every last crumb with an appetite for two. Telling Erika this would have been a good idea but something stopped me.

"Beth. How long has it been since you wrote to your mum?"

"Umm . . . Six days." Saying this out loud made me feel a bit silly. It felt like ages. It felt like about a year.

"Right. And how long am I going away for?"

"Three weeks."

"And you know I'm coming back, right?"

I shrugged. The new, grown-up part of me, the part that's getting bigger and stronger as I write this, it knew she was right. But the other part, the part that told me not to tell her about the ghosted-away appetite thing, or the believing in Signs thing, it kicked up a fuss. *Oi!* it yelled. *She's not coming back. This is just a repeat of the bad things that happened before. You thought you could escape but you couldn't; you never will . . .*

"There are other things you like about being in here. Other things besides me. And Linda."

"Yeah."

"Why don't you write them down. Add them to your list."

"O.K."

* * *

Besides Erika and Linda, here are some other things I like:

College. Five hours a day. English, Maths, ICT, Science. Some of the lessons are boring. Others are stupid. But a lot of them are interesting. I put my hand up and I answer questions and often, I get them right. If I get them wrong, no one looks at me like I'm a bad thing. No one laughs. For those five hours, I'm not a prisoner; there's a "no crime talk" rule, so I'm not a person who's done a bad thing, either; I'm just a person who's trying to learn things. Best of all, I *can* learn them; I think and I read and I think and I try and if I make a mistake I just shrug and carry on and eventually, I find the answers. They say I'm on track to get As and A*s. After that, I'll train to become a library orderly.

Getting up and eating and sleeping and going to college and getting letters and not getting visits and exercising and having association at the same time every day, every week. On the mornings when I wake up with my heart thumping up my throat because I've forgotten then remembered then freaked out about where I am, knowing that breakfast will be at this time, Maths at that time—it's a comfort.

Reading books which make me laugh and books which make me cry and books which make me feel a bit more O.K. about who and where and what I am.

Having people who, even if there's a lot you can't say to them, even if a lot of what they say you don't understand, you can laugh and sit side by side and eat with.

Looking up at the sky in the exercise yard just as a bird is swooping over our heads; wondering what it would feel like to stroke its feathery belly.

Running on the treadmill so fast that the other women on the weights and the cross-trainer stop and say rah, look at that, she can *run* you know; running until I can't see the mould on the gym ceiling or the tiny barred windows or the other machines; closing my eyes and pretending, for a second or two or however long my heart can stand it, that I'm climbing to the top of the world's tallest hill; everything is spread out before me; I'm free.

20.
WHEN A BABY BITES YOUR NIPPLE LIKE IT WILL NEVER LET GO

It was ages before I could walk instead of waddle, ages before my body stopped dripping blood and milk. The nurses and the health visitors kept giving me leaflets with titles like *Managing Pain After Birth: Top Tips!* I didn't read them. Unlike the pains that lurk in the places no doctor will ever scan, body-pain has a beginning and an end and who would want to forget what was the beginning not just of pain, but of a whole new human being?

All we did for the first weeks of your life was stay in bed. Every now and then, the sun would shine through the window, and I'd think that maybe I should take you out and show you what kind of world you'd been born into, but waddling to the bathroom was as tiring as running ten miles. Holding you against my chest, feeling your warmth and your unbelievable softness and your dribble seep into me—all this was so good, there didn't seem much point in anything else.

Days, nights, probably lifetimes went by, and all I did was stroke your cheek. Kiss your toes. Sniff your flaking scalp.

The wind would smash shouts against our window, and I'd pull the duvet up over our heads, pressing you tight against me, not wanting anyone or anything to come between us.

The first time you bit my breast, I yelled, it hurt so much, but I didn't mind. You sucked and sucked; my boobs swelled and oozed and ached and so I didn't even have to look at them to remind myself that my body was making another human being grow.

Even now I have nights when your cries wake me up; your hands struggle out of the dark, all tiny and smooth, as if they're made of something way better than skin, and I reach out but they're gone. I'd do anything to go back to when it was just you and me, me and you, me figuring out how to make your pain go away, because as long as I could do that—as long as the crying eventually stopped—there was no way you'd leave me because how could you leave when I was the only one who could give you what you needed?

Health visitors came and health visitors went. They plopped you into a bowl-sized silver weight which dangled off a spring. They smiled. I smiled back. They asked questions like, was I happy? Did I have people looking out for me?

"Oh yes," I said. "Yes, lots and lots. Yes, I'm really happy."

They smiled some more—where they got their unlimited supply of smiles from, I don't know—and told me I was a natural. They'd never seen anyone take to breastfeeding so easily. I thought they might give me some gold star stickers like other kids got in school, but they didn't; they just left me some vouchers for nappies, reminded me to go on regular walks to the park, said keep up the good work, and left. With their words, I tucked us even tighter into bed: a *natural*. Not naturally bad or mad or weird; a natural *mother*. A person who was made to make other people—not just babies, but big, healthy grown-up people. I didn't know what was going to happen but what I did know was that even if some voodoo occurred and I ended up discovering the cure for cancer or some other cleverclogs thing, this was the one I'd be most proud of.

The bad thing wasn't me and it definitely wasn't you; it wasn't your spookily long eyelashes or the tiny mole on your left shoulder or the way your face wrinkled up like an old man when you yawned.

It wasn't the way you'd blow spit bubbles when you were

having a five-star dream. It wasn't the way you'd bite my nipple like you never wanted to let it go.

It wasn't your little round belly, your pinprick nipples or your wide blue 100% ™ certified human eyes.

No, the bad things were outside of us.

It was not having anyone to hold you while I peed or showered or just stood on the balcony for a few seconds trying to remember who I was.

It was dropping my phone down the loo while trying to stop you crying and pull my trackie bottoms up at once, then not really caring because who was going to ring me besides robots telling me I'd won loads of money or people in call centres who sounded like robots telling me I owed loads of money and if I didn't pay it they'd do who knew what because I always hung up?

The bad things were these sticky clouds of . . . Well, I don't know what to call them but they were the opposite of pain and the thing they made me feel was the opposite of alive. Every time I tried to do some supposedly-normal thing, like get washed or dressed or eat or speak, the clouds would crowd around me, so I held you as close as I could but my body was so numb that sometimes I had to squeeze you until you cried to make sure you were still there.

The harder I fought the clouds, the thicker they grew; some days they grew so thick that even when I managed to get us both to the park and the sun was out and every other face said, *life is good*, I'd wheel my pram into people without realizing it. I'd open my mouth to apologize but my mouth was full of clouds and on their faces would be scribbled those same old words: *bad person. bad mother. bad . . .*

The bad things were the memories which lay behind the clouds. Mum leaving and Cal leaving and Phil leaving and

O.K. so maybe Chantelle didn't leave, maybe if I managed to get outside and fix my phone, I'd find a ton of messages from her, but I didn't really believe that and even if it turned out to be true, there was no point seeing her because she wouldn't be able to see me through the clouds and sooner or later she'd realize I wasn't worth it, and she'd leave.

The bad thing was the payday loan. How, before you were born, they'd called and asked if I wanted to "roll over" what I owed; this would mean I'd pay them back next month instead of this month, and I'd said yes. You do realize this will mean you pay more interest overall? they asked. I said yes. I didn't hear when they said *more*; all I heard was *later*. Later was good. Except I never thought your dad would keep refusing to admit he was your dad. I never thought later would turn into now and good to bad.

The bad thing was spending forever trying to stuff you into a Babygro and then an all-in-one baby coat which said "Easy On!" and was a very bad joke if you ask me. Then strapping you into the pram and pushing it to the door, only to realize that I wasn't wearing any shoes. Then getting out of the flat and finding the lift was broken and having to bump-bump-bump you down too many steps to count, by which point you'd be screaming, you weren't having any of it and I didn't blame you, I shushed you and kissed you and stroked my favourite soft spot in the middle of your forehead, I promised that one day we'd move somewhere with a lift that worked, or, better still, I'd fix it myself, I'd learn how to be a handyman and we'd have this 100% brilliant life together where everything worked. The bad thing was that you hadn't been in the world long enough to understand words, and so you kept crying, and so I shouted or cried or, if the clouds were really thick that day, I just let go of the pram and stared.

And in other people's eyes, even friendly people who tried to start conversations in the park, I saw nothing but *bad*. And so by the time I made it to whichever appointment I was meant to be going to, I'd be so late and so angry and so far inside the cloud that I'd either spew out a lot of words that were as bad as the things those people's eyes said about me or nod and shrug and say the nothing that the cloud was making me believe I was.

The bad thing was that even when people smiled, even when they said things like "what a cutie" and "good job," the cloud stopped them from reaching my heart. When I made it to the high street, when there was enough cash in my purse and enough *me* in my brain to remember to buy things like nappies and wipes and paper towels and food, I didn't always remember to use these things. You ate from my boob but even though the doctor and the nurses and the health visitors kept reminding me to eat more than usual, eating was a thing I couldn't bring myself to do. I got as far as moving a few spoonfuls of beans from the can to my mouth, but they tasted wrong and then they hung around in my belly, yet another weight that I didn't need. If I stood up very quickly or rushed across the room to pick you up, the room would wobble. If I'd known that in hurting myself I was hurting you, I'd have marched to the fridge and stuffed my face with whatever was in it straight away. But the clouds made the emptiness in my belly feel like the only one that was right.

The cloud didn't protect me from fear. Fear of the letters I hadn't opened and the calls I hadn't answered, fear that, now my phone was dead, they'd come, heavy-booted and heavy-armed, to take everything I had which really wasn't anything but you. Every time I heard footsteps, I'd freeze, clamp my hand over your mouth. I'd keep the lights off just in case.

More than the loans, I was scared of the cloud. Scared of

the world. Scared I was turning into my mum or that she wasn't my real mum or I wasn't a real human.

It's hard to say how long this went on for because the thing about the cloud is, it pisses all over time, but according to the calendar, it was two months. Two months.

Then there was a knock at the door. Not an imaginary knock; a real one. I hugged you to my chest. Another knock—a bigger one. You scrunched up your eyes and opened your mouth and cried.

"Shut up," I hissed. "There's no one there."

But there was. And you knew it. And so I had no choice but to go to the door.

"Miss Mitchell?"

I clamped my hand over your mouth but that only changed your cry into a scream.

"We can hear your baby crying, you know. Look, we ain't going to hurt you. Just open up."

With the chain still on, I opened the door wide enough to see a slice of bald head, bloodshot blue eye and stubbly chin.

"You know why we're here, don't you?"

"No."

"Come on, Miss Mitchell, even you can't be that thick."

A thump at the door. "Let us in."

I leaned on the door but they kicked it towards me and I staggered back and then a big hairy hand slid around the edge of the door and undid the chain.

You're welcome," they said, as they stomped down the hall.

I closed my eyes and hugged you tight and whispered to the both of us that everything was going to be all right. I couldn't see the bailiffs but I could hear them; they were flinging things around, laughing and yelling what a dirty chav I was, how the flat stank.

"She ain't even got a telly!"

"Or a phone!"

"What about this? These are pricey, you know. My Michelle—"

"Shut it. Let's go."

I opened my eyes to find them squished into the hall, your 4x4-style pram in the hairy one's hands. "This don't count towards your payment," he said, breathing cheeseburger breath all over my face. "But it does buy you time. Three days. Three days and you'll pay up or . . . "

"Or you don't want to know," said the one without the pram. "Now, if you'll excuse us."

Then they were gone, but the memory of them was everywhere: in the big black footprints up and down the hall, in the bag of rubbish they'd emptied all over the sofa, in the upturned mattress and the tin of beans they'd tipped on to the kitchen surface just because. Even when you'd stopped crying, when I got us huddled under the covers, when I closed my eyes, I could feel them. They were pacing up and down on the grass outside my flat, messing up the Africans' football game, working out how to fuck me over next.

* * *

The next afternoon, there was another knock. "Please, you said three days. It's not even been two." I tried to shout this but it came out more like a whisper. Then I put my head under the duvet and tried not to notice the knocks getting louder and faster, until I heard a voice: "Oi, Bethany, earth to Bethany! You in there? Skinny bitch?"

It was Chantelle. Somehow, I got us out of bed and opened the door.

As she walked in, she put her hand over her nose and made a face like she was going to puke and said, "Oh my God, why haven't you answered my texts? Can't believe you didn't even put no pictures on Facebook. And why haven't you chucked out any of her nappies?"

"I lost my phone."

"I don't know what that's got to do with putting the bins out. Jesus Christ." Chantelle stomped around my flat, sweeping up the nappies and bottles and towels and bibs that even the bailiffs hadn't bothered to pinch.

"Stop," I mumbled.

Her I'm-here-ness was poking holes in the cloud and if those holes got any bigger, I'd be in trouble. Big trouble. Because the feelings the cloud was hiding me from, they were bigger than big—too big to deal with when you had no person to hold you or hug you or remind you you were still you.

"STOP."

Chantelle turned. "How'd you make such a mess every-where?"

"Please, just go. *You're* the one messing things up."

Chantelle shook her head. "Girl, you need help. Get in the shower, I'll watch the little one. When you're done, this place will be back to normal."

But it was too late for normal. The bailiffs would be back in two days and, even if I told her about them and about the cloud and about my mum and everything else, there was no way she could change that.

"No. Please get out."

"Beth . . . " Chantelle walked towards me. Each step widened the hole in the cloud; by the time she reached for my arm, I had no choice but to push her away as fast as possible, i.e. to bite her.

Yes, I bit the arm of the only person who cared about us.

"Fuck."

"Just go."

"Fine. I was just trying to help, but whatever."

"I don't need your help," I shouted. "My boyfriend will be round soon anyway."

Chantelle shook her head at me. "It's your life." And then

she was gone. But the holes were still here, they were flooding
with pain, and then

Then

You screamed.

You screamed and you screamed and you wouldn't stop

And your screams made the walls and the floor and the ceiling and the mould on the ceiling scream.

Your screams made the soap dish and the shower and
your bibs and your nappies
my pants and my socks and
the windows the sky trees concrete
                                    people
on the other side
of the windows
scream, too.

And I don't know why
But your screams
scraped
the good
right out of me.

They scraped and they scraped and they wouldn't

"*Stop*," I begged. "You can scream later, but not now. Not
now."

In reply, you screamed some more, and so did all the other
things inside and outside of me.

"Shut up," I said. "It's not that bad."

But your screaming said that it *was*. It was that bad. It was
worse.

"You don't even know what it's about," I told you.

Your eyes said that you knew all right—even if you didn't
have the words or the thoughts, you knew in your bones and
your blood how much it hurt. Your eyes said there was a reason

for everything in this world, all the big things and all the little ones, including your scream-scream-scrape: you'd clocked this world for what it was, and already, you'd had enough.

"Just stop. STOP."

You didn't listen because you couldn't and so I picked you up and jiggled you because this had worked in the recent yet gone-forever past of yesterday and the day before and all the times you screamed before that, but you weren't falling for it this time. And so

So

I jiggled you harder.

"STOP."

You carried on.

"STOP STOP STOP STOP."

And so I jiggled you some more

and somehow

the jiggling of you closed up the holes

and so I kept on jiggling

and jiggling

jiggling jiggling

because jiggling

is what all the bad things

the things that weren't me and weren't you

were telling me to do.

You did stop screaming and so I laid you back down in your crib and lay down on the carpet next to your crib and closed my eyes and fell into a hole that was way deeper and darker and further away than the one where you go to sleep. How long I was down there, I've no idea; all I know is that when I woke up, you were still not crying. Maybe I was a good mum after all; maybe you'd decided the world was all right.

But then I picked you up and when my skin touched yours, it was cold.

Too cold.

I picked you up and jiggled you and kissed you and told you it was not your fault, not one hole was your fault and neither was the cloud, and soon I'd get better, I'd get help, it was, after all, days and maybe even weeks since I'd had a proper sleep, this was a strange time, a hard time, our life wouldn't be this way for ever, it was worth hanging on for, it was it was it is it is

But you wouldn't listen

Because you couldn't

Not even with your bones

Because crying wasn't the only thing you'd stopped doing;

You'd also stopped breathing.

And peeing and pooing and blowing spit bubbles and gurgling and sucking and dribbling and wriggling and sleeping and waking up and blinking and wrinkling your already wrinkly nose and fingers and toes and stretching out your arms and kicking your legs and—

And living. You'd stopped doing that too.

The cloud had burst, and the pain was flooding into me, and I knew that if I didn't run as fast and as far as I could, it would *become* me.

I've been running from that pain ever since; even this book is a kind of running because all this time I've been kidding myself you're out there living some other life when the truth is you're not because the only life you lived was for eight weeks and six days and it was with me and it ended and the reason for that ending, whatever anyone says or thinks, is me.

Yes, me.

My hand is shaking as I write this.

Pretty soon, my heart will be shaking, and my eyes and my toes and probably also the ground. But I'm not going to run because I can't. Because this pain is all I have and I'm going to feel it until it's 100% mine.

21

I killed my baby. I'm a 100% ™ certified bad thing.

Clocks ticked, the nights filled with days, the days dulled into nights, and still these words blocked the smiles and the "swap your bread for my chips?" and the winks and the "Beth, what do you think this chapter is about?" and the sun and the birds and the kind little voice that told me it wasn't all my fault, I'd done a bad thing but I wasn't a bad person, I deserved to be here, I deserved to do the things that made me feel good.

The bad voice worked out. It grew teeth and hair and bulging muscles: As if Erika's really coming back. As if your mum will write back. You're alone and that's how you're going to stay because that's what you deserve. The only way to shut it up was to obey.

"You not eating that?"

"Got a bad stomach."

"Yeah, they never clean out the toilets properly."

At first, the Lee and Jeannie and the others fought over the beans and the peas and the pies I wouldn't eat.

Then they got worried: "You got to eat something, girl."

"You're already bare skinny."

"I'm not hungry," I said.

My belly didn't even bother to grumble. Every mouthful sat in my belly, weighing me down, making me feel huge and heavy and 100% wrong. The emptier I got, the easier it was to float; float away from everything I was and wasn't, everything I'd done, everything I'd lost; being empty was the good thing.

One night the Lee pulled me aside in the corridor and grabbed my hand and said I needed to stop.

"But I'm not doing anything. I'm not hurting anyone."

"Yes, you are," she said. She shook her head and if there had been a window right there, she'd have stared out at it; instead, she just stared at the wall. "You're hurting yourself."

"It's what I deserve. For what I did. I—"

"Kid, we *know*. We were hard on you to begin with, but hey, it was pretty obvious you'd already been through hell. You—"

"I killed my own kid." There. I'd said it. I'd said it out loud.

"There's more to it than that and you know it. Listen." She shook her head again. "I've seen women. I've seen them come. Go. Get ghosted. Get out. Seen them top themselves, cut up, starve themselves. There was one woman used to bite herself so bad she got infected. But there's no point to it. No point. If you don't look after yourself, no one will. And you know how to, I know it." Then she pressed a Twix into my palm and left. I stared at the Twix. I knew I should eat it. I went into my cell and I did pushups and sit-ups and stretches and lunges but it was too late; the part of me that knew the Lee was right, knew I should forgive myself, it was just out of reach.

I don't know how I kept running on the treadmill, but I did. At first, it was easy; the emptiness filled my legs with a strange, zingy energy. After the first week, it got hard. But I kept on. And on. And on. Until, one day, my heart began to judder. The room began to blur. My legs were wobbling, my head floating, and while somewhere, deep inside of me, a small voice whispered that maybe stopping would be a good idea, I kept going; I had to;

Because for a second

Or maybe

Two

All the things inside of me

All the good and the bad
All the outside-things
They were calm
Safe
Still.

"Beth."

There was a voice outside my head but it wasn't yours; it was the screw's. It got closer and louder but I couldn't work out what it was saying because my eyes had stopped seeing but I didn't mind because I was sure that any moment now, I'd be back with you.

22.
THE PROMISE OF A BLANK PAGE

B ut I didn't get to you: my heart messed up and so did my lungs and my head; I blacked out; my body crumpled and my head crashed against the treadmill.

When I woke up in the hospital bed, my arms ached and my legs ached and my head ached and my heart ached and my back ached and my belly ached.

"That's quite a fall you had there," said the doctor. "You're going to hurt for a while."

I nodded, even though I knew the aching wasn't just because of the fall. The aching was my body's way of telling me how much it missed you. How you were gone and I was here and nothing and no one could change that. It was time to let the rest of me miss you, too. I missed the way your toes curled tight when you sucked my nipple. Missed the soft skin at the back of your head and the way you frowned when you were about to shit. Missed the fluff on the top of your head and your ears and your earlobes and your soft, soft hands.

"We have to run some tests on your heart. You've put it under a lot of strain with eating so little."

For the first time since I lost you, I cried.

I cried and I cried.

Everything ached. Everything missed you. Even the dirty white walls of the hospital ward seemed to miss you.

I missed the life we were meant to live together. I missed watching your first steps, your second steps, your first words, second words, first questions, first insults, first opinions. I missed teaching you to brush your own teeth and tie your own shoelaces. I missed shouting at you for crawling on to my bed and pulling my eyelids apart to wake me up at 6 A.M. I missed wiping your nose until you got old enough to shout at me not to. I missed thinking up ways to entertain you at the bus stop. I missed you telling me crazy, funny weird things which 100% changed how I saw the world. I missed shouting at you to eat your greens and do your homework; I missed you stomping into your room and slamming the door and cranking your music up way too loud. I missed knocking on your door with a hot chocolate, you biting on your bottom lip to stop yourself admitting that you'd forgiven me, that in a few moments we'd be made up. I missed you telling me all about your day at school, your friends and your lessons and your teachers, and how lovely and irritating and stupid and clever they all were. I missed you growing bigger and taller and stronger than me; missed coming home from work to find you'd cooked me a meal, all on your own, for the first time; missed you sneaking in after midnight, your first proper boyfriend clasped to your hand. Missed you learning more, learning better about the world. Missed telling you the story of your name, missed you hating it, then accepting it, then loving it, then, finally, grow-ing into it. Missed getting old while you marched off into the world, bright and new, young and strong, to make so much more of it than I ever could. Missed you ringing me in tears from your new, grown-up life: "Mum. Can I come round?" And me: "Of course!" Missed opening the door, my hand wrinkled, most of my life behind me, and knowing, because you're my daughter and I'm your mum and there are things you don't need words for, that a new life was sprouting inside you. "It's fine. I'm here. You'll be a great mum. You'll be won-derful."

I missed you because, for the first time since losing you,

this was a feeling I was allowed to feel. I missed you because I was beginning to wonder whether your death wasn't 100% my fault.

"I feel awful," said Erika. Her holiday was painted all over her face, in freckles and brown skin and a peeling patch of red raw skin at the very end of her nose. "I should've seen this coming. But. Well. I. I didn't think. You were making such good progress . . . "

She leant her elbows on her knees and leant her head in her hands. I didn't need to see her face to know how bad she felt. How harshly she'd be blaming herself.

"Erika, it's not your fault. I . . . " My cheeks were twitching. So was my mouth. Then I clocked what was happening: a smile, that's what. "I'm glad this happened, in a way."

She sat up. There was water in her eyes. "But you were already fragile. I put in requests for you to be monitored but I didn't, I've never, I should've—"

I scooted down the bed and laid my hand in hers. If a screw came in, I'd get in trouble. I didn't care. I squeezed her hand. She looked up at me and squeezed back.

"I needed to do it. I needed to push myself like that."

"No, Beth. No, that's not right."

"I did. I needed to be sure."

She scratched the red patch on her nose. "Sure of what?"

"That I wanted to be here. That there was a way I could be here. That I'd find it."

Slowly, slowly, she smiled. "But you should've—"

"Whatever," I said. "I thought you said no *what ifs*?"

She threw her hands up in the air; they were soft and brown. The holiday had given her a break from the washing up; of this I was glad. I was glad that good things were happening to her as well as me. "You got me."

"It's done now. And you know what, now I'm sure. I'm sure I want to be here."

"Really?" She glanced at the pot of yoghurt which squatted, unopened, on my bedside table.

"Those yoghurts are kind of disgusting."

"Actually . . . I bought you something. A present. From Canada." She handed me a bright green packet. I popped it open. It was full of tiny chocolate balls.

"Chocolate-covered beans," she said. "And I remembered you saying they were a thing you liked eating, so." Her cheeks were almost as red as her nose.

"Thanks." I wasn't hungry but I popped one in my mouth and I chewed. "That doesn't taste anything like chocolate or beans but it's good. Really good." My hand popped another in my mouth. And another and another.

"They're from this cute little deli right round the corner from my sister's house. Spent a fortune there, buying all sorts of treats for the kids. When I saw these, I thought of you. I just had to get them."

Halfway through the packet, my belly began to rumble. "How come I only get hungry *after* I eat, not before?"

"I don't know. Why do you think it is?"

I shrugged.

"I think you know."

I closed my eyes. I listened out for my aches; they were getting quieter all the time but I could still hear them. "I reckon, well, my body can't be arsed with being hungry because it doesn't believe it will ever get full. Like *proper* full. *Good* full. Happy. Satisfied."

She smiled. "So would it find that hope, if it didn't eat?"

I shook my head. She left soon after that but I've eaten and I've eaten since then. I've eaten right into the hunger and out of the other side. My heart is O.K., they tell me, but I had a close one: I'll need to make a "concerted effort" to eat properly from now on. They're going to send someone to sit with me at every meal until they can trust me to make this "concerted effort." It's a bit embarrassing, I'm not going to lie, but I don't care; mostly what I care about is that I've got the energy to stand up straight and ask questions and answer questions and listen and look and touch and feel. Especially, to feel. I'm not scared to feel hunger or fullness or sadness or happiness or anger or any of the other feelings that whoosh through you at any moment, whether you want them to or not. I'm not even scared to feel proud of myself for doing well in here; I'm not scared to try.

Do you know where I am now? I'm in my cell. I'm writing what I know will be my last note to you. Because you're gone. And I'm here. And it's time to look forward. I'll leave a pen and paper on my pillow so that when I'm back in my cell this evening, I'll remember to write to Chantelle.

Any minute now, I'll get unlocked; then I'll walk over to the Visitors' Centre. I'll sit at a table and I'll wait for the woman who is probably right now as I write getting her passport scanned or her armpits patted down to make 100% sure she's safe to let in.

I don't know what she'll be wearing or whether she'll have her hair short or long.

What I do know is that she'll sit down opposite me and her heart will be beating too hard and her palms will be sweating and part of her will just want to run away and another part will be telling her she's a bad thing, but somehow—

Because what is it? What really is it that keeps us going?

She'll fight it off. She'll look me in the eye. She might just smile.

"Hello," she'll say.

"Hi."

And then we'll talk. We'll talk about everything that happened and everything that didn't happen. We'll sigh. We'll laugh. We'll breathe the same words and the same silence. We'll let our stories grow.

Now, I hear footsteps. The scrape of the key in the lock. So I'm saying goodbye. I'll sleep with this notebook under my pillow, right next to my new one. I don't know what I'll write in it yet; all I know is, it will be good. Not always easy, but definitely, 100%, no arguing, *good*.

"Mitchell!"

Now I really am letting go of this pen.

It's time.

ACKNOWLEDGEMENTS

Books aren't finished without readers, so thank you so much for being one of them.

Thanks to my agent, Zoe Waldie, for your on-going wisdom, faith and honesty, both on and off the page. Thanks, Venetia Butterfield, for believing in Beth from the beginning and for your editorial brilliance. Thanks to everyone else at RCW and Viking for providing a warm and nourishing home for both me and my work.

Thanks to everyone who helped me research women in prison, in particular Lucy Baldwin and everyone at HMP New Hall education department.

Thank you to my writer-friends for sharing your time, shoulders, brains and words: thank you, Rosa, Rachel, Raquel, Sophie and Alice; thank you, Drusilla; thanks to Anna and David for becoming readers when called; thanks to everyone at WordLab and to the Failed Novelists.

Thank you, Laura and everyone at Spread the Word for giving me all sorts of opportunities to develop as a writer. Thanks to my MA tutor, Francis Spufford, for taking me seriously before I took myself seriously as either a writer or a person.

Thank you to all my friends and family for showing me, in your own strange and wonderful ways, how to get better at being here.

Thank you to my runner-friends and in particular the veggie runners. Thank you, Dea and thank you, Nicola.

Thanks to my parents, Anna and Jethro.

Thank you, David, for everything.